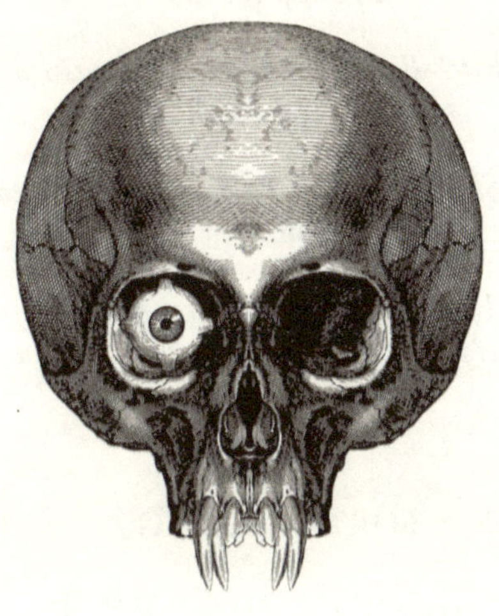

OTHER TITLES FROM JACKANAPES PRESS

Really, Really, Really, Really Weird Stories:
A New Edition with Four New Stories
by John Shirley

The Ettinfell of Beacon Hill: Gothic Tales of Boston
By Adam Bolivar

The Miskatonic University Spiritualism Club
by Peter Rawlik

The Eldritch Equations and Other Investigations
by Peter Rawlik

Book of Shadows: Grim Tales and Gothic Fancies
by Manuel Arenas

Not a Princess but (Yes) There was a Pea and
other Fairy Tales to Foment Revolution
by Rebecca Buchanan

FORTHCOMING

Darkest Days and Haunted Ways
by Ashley Dioses

A Wheel of Ravens
by Adam Bolivar

The Exile and Other Tales of Carcosa
by Galad Elflandsson

The Black Wolf
by Galad Elflandsson

www.JackanapesPress.com
www.facebook.com/Jackanapes-Press

PRAISE FOR JOHN R. FULTZ

"John R. Fultz is a powerful and creative writer
very much in the *Weird Tales* tradition.
He is well worth your attention."
—**Darrell Schweitzer**, former editor of *Weird Tales*

"...a master of his craft."
—**Don Webb**, Author of *Building Strange Temples*

"Fultz delivers the goods."
—**Howard Andrew Jones**, Author of
The Ring-Sworn Trilogy

"...an author with an exceptional talent for
characterization and world building."
—*The Library Journal*

"Fultz has rapidly matured into a major fantasist."
—**Laird Barron**, Author of *Occultation*
and *Black Mountain*

"His world-building is in a class by itself."
—**RT Book Reviews**

"This is fantasy of the Dunsany, Smith and
Vance school, where breathless wonders spill off
the page in spendthrift profusion."
—**John Hocking**, Author of *Conan
and the Emerald Lotus*

Also by John R. Fultz

Seven Princes (2012)

Seven Kings (2013)

Seven Sorcerers (2013)

The Revelations of Zang (2013)

The Testament of Tall Eagle (2015)

Son of Tall Eagle (2017)

Worlds Beyond Worlds (2021)

DARKER THAN WEIRD

DARKER THAN WEIRD

FOURTEEN TALES OF HORROR

JOHN R. FULTZ

ILLUSTRATIONS BY
DAN SAUER

JACKANAPES PRESS

Darker Than Weird: Fourteen Tales of Horror
Copyright © 2023 by Jackanapes Press. All rights reserved.
www.JackanapesPress.com

Publication history for individual stories can be found on page 176.

All stories copyright © 2023 by John R. Fultz
Foreword copyright © 2023 by Don Webb
Cover art and interior illustrations copyright © 2023 by Daniel V. Sauer

Cover and interior design by Dan Sauer
www.DanSauerDesign.com

First Paperback Edition

1 3 5 7 9 8 6 4 2

ISBN: 978-1-956702-11-8

For my lovely Aunt Deb,
who introduced me to horror with
Night Gallery, *Chiller Theatre*, and
tales of Ol' Bloody Bones...

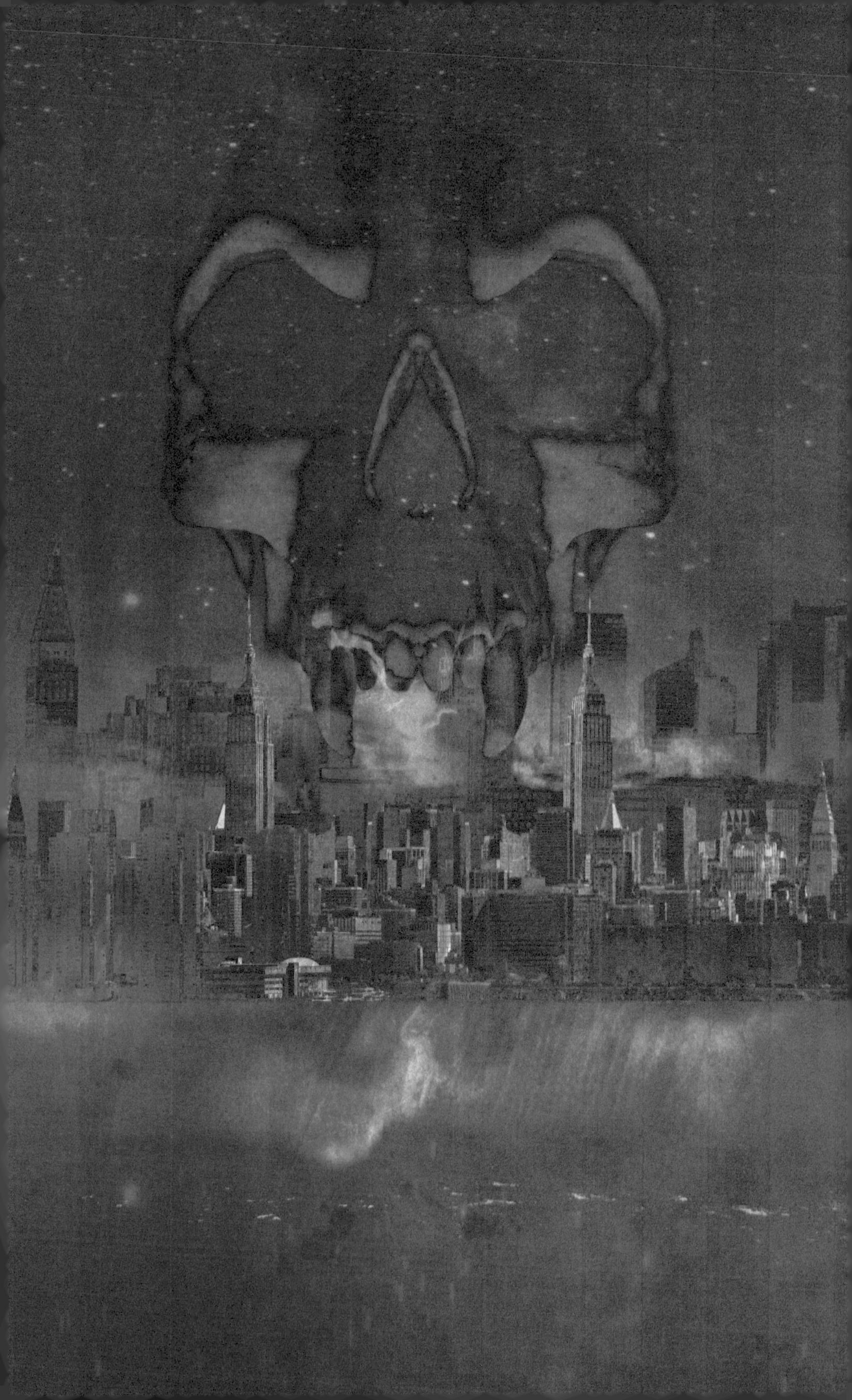

CONTENTS

A Need for Newer Boxes

Foreword by Don Webb

People outside of the book biz are (blissfully) unaware of its truths. So, on the off chance you've bought a small press volume (this one) and are not a writer/publisher/artist I am going to lay Truth upon you. First Truth. Nobody reads introductions and forwards first. At best after you have read the contents of the book and picked it up off the bathroom floor you will read the introduction as you sit and—er—meditate. Hey, it doesn't bother me. I have (by now) cashed my large check for introduction writing and spent it all on gold futures, champagne, and cocaine. But there you sit wanting to read something until you can stand and go buy a copy of my *Building Strange Temples* because you're enchanted with my wit and deft prose. Your expectation is that I'll talk about the stories in this volume and in my remaining time speak about... what's his name?

Oh yes, John R. Fultz.

We'll certainly I'll get around to that, but I want to explain Dan Sauer, the publisher, and his many errors. Firstly, it is well known that book buyers, including you, spend more money on non-fiction than fiction. Then if fiction is purchased (perhaps by misreading the Amazon product description) novels outsell short story collections by a great deal. I mean, it could have been worse. He could've published a poetry collection. But that leads to his second error. Short story collections are generally bought by completists. That means something like, "I've read John R. Fultz's fantasy novels. He has a deft hand with fantasy. I will buy a collection of his fantasy stories and be entertained thereby whilst waiting for him to do his job and crank out another fantasy novel for me." But, as you are aware—having read this volume (and turning in despair to this introduction)—only one or two of the tales herein could be called fantasy. Now as you know the reason Dan Sauer published the volume is because he likes to draw macabre pictures and this book gave him an excuse to do so. Having created the great cover, he now sits back and waits for the money to roll in. Of course, since he committed the unpardonable sin of publishing a collection of hard-to-categorize tales, it will be a long and dismal wait.

He had hopes that by titling the collection *Darker Than Weird* it will attract the "horror" reader. Some of the tales could be said to fit that description. The brilliant first story with its chilling description of a nightmare city (drawing equally from the horrors of living in a decaying metroplex, the fears of a parent seeing their innocent child destroyed body and soul, and a survey of trends in modern horror) certainly meets the bill. But most of these tales are much harder to classify. Horror, as we know, is the notion that the chaotic forces of imagination will invade the safe bubble of our homes, our livelihoods, our flesh. Although that note is hit in most of these tales, other ideas wander in. Some of the tales, such as "The Man Who Murders Happiness," are deft Kafkaesque fables that show Fultz as a mature writer that can reveal the nihilistic side of existence, as well as a master of his craft. Others take on a Dante theme but match it perfectly with Kafka, in one of most nightmarish after-life scenes you will encounter.

The big questions for humans now—the questions of identity and purpose—are dealt with in the tales collected in the "Welcome to the Urbille" section. I am sure that the average reader would label these as science fiction, but you (as I have come to know in the short time we've been hanging out) are beyond the average reader. These stories deal with three philosophical notions. If we replace our corporal selves with mechanical parts are we us? (The problem of the ship of Theseus invades the safe bubble.) If medical technology is an expensive commodity, is quality of life to be seen entirely as a manifestation of class? Will God/Nature resent our stealing of the divine fire to make (or counterfeit) Life itself? Fultz deals with these questions not with the endless speculation of excited freshmen taking Philosophy 101, but with images both gorily grotesque and ideas clothed in emotional context—in this case the love/hate relationship we have with medical science. Come for the horror story, leave with deep ontological questions.

The last section of the book looks safer for the human trying to shelve it—tales inspired by H. P. Lovecraft's Cthulhu Mythos. The first of these, in the tradition of Zealia Bishop's "The Mound," deals with the Lovecraftian Western. The "rules" of that cosmos blend the essential part of American thought, the great frontier, with the great nothingness at the center of the Lovecraftian cosmos. This deceptively pulpy story deals with themes such as colonialism and the imposition of Christianity upon native peoples with the tropes of cosmic dread and cannibalism. Again, we see the Fultzian twofold punch: Come for the horror, leave with deeper questions about history and metaphysics. I have no doubt that this little volume will garner great reviews in the magazines and webpages that review short horror, but the lasting taste here is not that of cheap soda (which most short horror gives us), but the bitter otherness of absinthe.

The paradigmatic tale of the book, the story that Fultz has been teaching us to read, is (perhaps) "The Embrace of Elder Things," a sort of comic book Rembrandt. The surface read will be appealing to a certain type of fanboy anywhere. It is not only a Lovecraftian homage, but also (Yidhra save us!) a Derlethian homage complete with star stones. Even pulpier, it is set on a lunar colony quite suitable for seventies sci-fi, back before the United States turned its back on the challenge of reaching other worlds. The setting and the background make this a sort of candy treat to humans that spent their teenage years reading Arkham House collections. But in the midst of this green cotton candy two very deep ideas emerge. Our hero's mother despairs of his fate as his otherness is discovered by the intolerant world. Mom's fears are connected with the frontier-ism of the other tales: If sonny can only make it to the mines of Mars, he can safely be what he (secretly) is. Fate, however, brings the tale's two big ideas to the very surface. Idea number one is that growing up, shaped and protected by human love, one learns to love not only specific humans but humanity as a whole. Idea number two—you can't run from what's inside of you. If you are Other, you are Other.

"The Embrace of Elder Things" is about accepting how deeply weird, how deeply Other you might be and reconciling it with the reflection of a mother's love. Here is the deepest of Lovecraft's fears (as seen most poignantly in "The Outsider"), the fear of not belonging, of being hated, of being one of "Them," reconciled with the nobility of human love in a cosmos where love and light are decidedly not the norms. This tale is exemplary of Fultz's magic—it can be read by humans that know how to make the Vulcan salute and thrive in SF nerdy coolness, but it can also be enjoyed by humans who have come to understand their very depth-of-thought sets them aside from humanity. Such stories will lack the vociferous support of the current intelligentsia, who prefer a trendy nihilism, but will in the long run actually be of use to the humans who will build the future. Not bad for a story with a rock from Mnar.

I see our time is done and you are about to shelve this little book. Having given you the critical tool to re-read these stories, I leave the re-reading as an enjoyable homework. But I leave you with my deepest wish that you introduce other readers to this little book (after all, it's hard to sell short story collections) by talking up its horrific wonders and NOT by talking up its philosophical underpinnings. Face it—a lot of readers aren't as deep as you.

When I shared this introduction with Fultz he asked if I was serious. I told him I was not Sirius but instead *Mu Draconis,* my wit being dry but spicy. For the few of you who google that you will discover that, yes, I am indeed nerdier than you.

—Don Webb
Austin, TX
2022

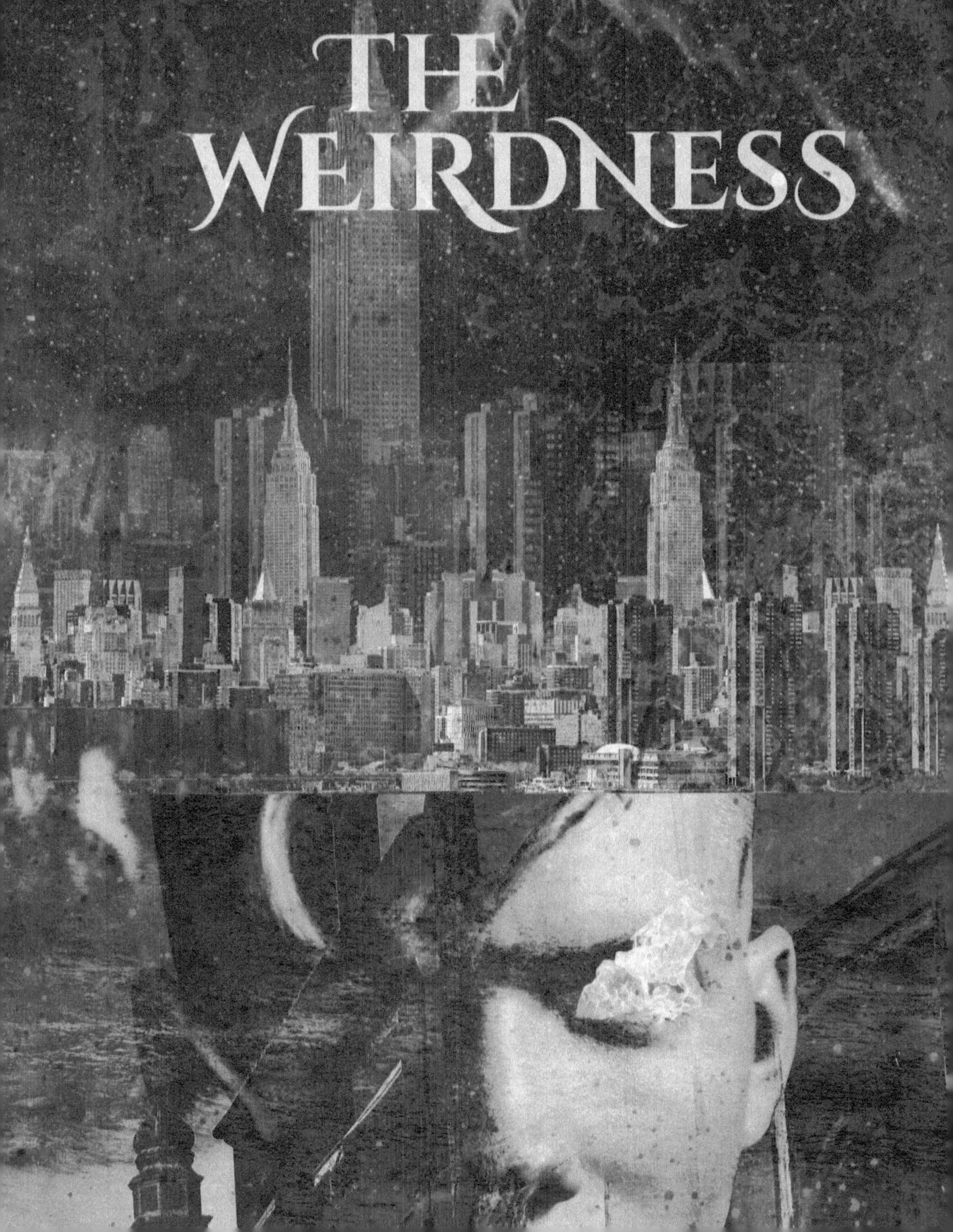
THE
WEIRDNESS

THE RIVER FLOWS TO NOWHERE

I hate the city.

I hate the nonstop rain and the blood-salted asphalt slick as snakeskin. I hate the smells of mildew, petrol, and despair. The acrid fogs, the vagrants gathered like clumps of fungi beneath rusting bridges. I hate the eternal night of the city, how the sun never shines there. It's an endless labyrinth of neon canyons, trash heaps, and the husks of dead factories.

It changes you in ways you never thought possible.

I hate the city, but I understand it. That's why I get hired for cases like this. It's the only reason I go back to the streets again, something I swore I'd never do. I've broken that vow many times. Every time the money runs out and the booze runs low. Every time some desperate client with a hefty bank account wanders into my office.

The clients talk, sometimes they cry, and I just listen. Usually it's a remorseful father, the kind who spoils his kid relentlessly and can't figure out why junior ends up hating him. Sometimes it's a lady. A mother or a sister. Out of her mind with worry or guilt.

The last thing anybody wants to do is go into the city. So they show me a picture, write me a check, and one more time I break that promise I made to myself. After an hour or two at the bar I head for the old highway. Far sooner than I'd like, I'm staring at a jagged skyline. The city steams like a technicolor volcano beneath a black shroud of smog. It's always night in the city.

I take a one last look at the setting sun, slip the border guard a sawbuck, and drive into a maze of endless twilight. Walls of rusted iron and rotting stone rise up to swallow my vehicle.

I take a good slug from the flask of Old Kentucky nestled inside my jacket. I'm sweating and nauseous. That's the way it always goes when I come back here. I hate the city.

But I've got a job to do.

....

Her name is Dorothy, if you can believe it. I'll try to keep the Oz jokes to a minimum. Dorothy McIntyre. Nineteen years old. Beautiful girl. Her mother hired me for the usual reason: no other options. Dorothy's story sounded all too familiar. Ms. McIntyre explained it from behind a tear-stained handkerchief. Dorothy's father had been out of the picture for some time. Ms. McIntyre didn't talk about him or what his line of work had been. I could've guessed.

"Dorothy was a good girl until she met that...*boy*," she said. "They call him Roach. A horrible name for a horrible person."

"Any idea his real name?" I asked. She didn't know a thing. They never do.

"First, he got her hooked on drugs..."

"Junk?"

"Yes, I believe that's what they call it."

"Anything else?"

"No," said the mother. "At least I don't think so."

"So Dorothy and this Roach never drank?"

"Oh, yes, there was drinking...I thought you meant—"

"It's all right. Go on, Ms. McIntyre." I offered her a glass of bourbon, the dregs from my last bottle. To my surprise, she drank it down in a single gulp. Momma had done her share of drinking.

"She started staying out all night with him. Coming home a mess. A few days into it I caught him in her room. They were doing drugs. Junk. Dropping it into their eyes. I remember the veins on my daughter's arms pulsing and throbbing. Her eyes rolled back in her head, she barked like a dog... I thought she would die right there. I drove that boy out of the house with this..."

She opened her purse and showed me a handgun. Antique six-shooter. Probably wouldn't have fired at all. But I'm sure "Roach" didn't want to take that chance.

"He came back for her two nights later," the mother said. "Dorothy refused to listen to me, she walked the halls all night long. She couldn't sleep or eat...she was so thin."

"Withdrawal," I said. "Very common in these cases. Nothing to worry about."

Sometimes a good lie is all it takes to make a client feel better.

"He broke through a window and took her. Or she broke the window and climbed down to him. I'm not sure. But I saw them running through the hedges. Him in the black leather jacket with the skull stitched on the back. I'd have known it was him even without that silly jacket."

"What was Dorothy wearing?" I asked. A few more procedural questions followed. She gave me a picture of Dorothy. It was taken a year ago, before Roach came into the picture.

The picture showed sunlight, green grass, and the blossoms of a cherry tree. Dorothy stood beneath the branches in a yellow sundress. Her hair was long and wavy, the color of ripe corn, her eyes black as midnight. She was smiling. The kind of smile that makes you feel good, yet also a little sorry for her. I believed Ms. McIntyre when she said her daughter was a good girl.

Good girls are prime currency in the city.

"Promise me you'll find her," my client said. "Bring her back to me..." A fresh welling of tears ran down her cheeks. Dorothy's mother was a looker too. I could see her beauty beyond the patina of pain and worry that marred its surface.

I knew better than to make a promise I couldn't keep.

"I'll do everything I can," I told her. "I have some experience in these matters. Go home and get some rest. I'll contact you in a few days."

Ms. McIntyre paused at my office door and looked back at me.

"Do you think...do you think he took her...*into the city*?"

I nodded.

She nearly fainted. I grabbed her shoulders and she fell into my arms.

"Don't worry," I told her. "I know the city. Leave it to me."

I cashed her check as soon as she left.

··•·•···

The picture of Dorothy lies on the passenger's seat next to me. Neon lights seep through the windshield to glide across its glossy surface, painting her face in shades of hot pink, cherry red, and bruised violet.

Most of the outer streets are lined with the burned-out husks of old cars or service vehicles. You can only drive so far into the city before you have to get out and hoof it. Luckily, I have a good parking connection.

A pack of red-eyed starvelings eyes me as I glide by. A bottle of piss or alcohol smashes across my windshield. I hit the gas and take a few corners fast enough to leave them behind. It's not far to the alley that slopes beneath a crumbling tower.

At the bottom of the ramp is a steel door like the kind you used to see in bank vaults. I hit the brakes then lay on the horn.

A couple of armed guards appear from nowhere. I pass them my investigator's license and a pair of neatly folded fifties. They hand me back the license and the vault door opens. I glide through the rows of vehicles, most of them left to rot here years ago. But there are a few clients like me, a few machines left in working order. I pick a spot near the exit, pay the attendent, and get my gear from the trunk. All of this is going on my expense report.

A longcoat hides the hand cannon strapped beneath my right arm. The picture of Dorothy slides into my right pocket, along with my silver flask. The hunting knife slides neatly into my left boot. Sometimes you have to work quietly in the city. That's when a good knife comes in handy.

The door I use to exit the parking vault is hardly visible from the street. I hit the asphalt and head toward the glittering chaos of the inner city. The light rain is steady and warm. Gusts of wind kick up swirls of dirty cellophane. Sheets of hanging moss dance like restless ghosts. Seven blocks later I spot an old woman with a black suitcase walking directly toward me. There's nobody else on the street. I'm in a canyon whose walls are pocked with glassless windows. Firelight flickers through rectangular orifices. The telltale signs of squatters and drug dens.

The woman with the black suitcase is closer now. I see her wrinkled face, the sway of her wide hips. Her hair is long and matted, her eyes hidden by the brim of a moth-eaten hat. She wears a raggedy longcoat over a tattered dress and army boots. She clutches the suitcase to her breast with both hands and walks with a slow limp, like she's never been in any kind of hurry. One of her hands rubs the surface of the case like petting the back of a lizard.

I cross to the other side of the street but she stops, head turning to follow me.

I reach the far sidewalk, step over a junkie who's either sleeping or dead in the gutter, and keep my eyes trained forward. The woman with the black suitcase laughs behind me. It sounds like a death rattle, like her throat's been cut and later healed into a mass of scar tissue.

I turn the corner and leave the horrid laughter behind me.

Up ahead I spot the globe of crimson neon blinking above *Frankie's Utopia*. A crowd of anxious junkies waits outside, quivering like snakes, waiting for their chance to gain admission. I walk to the head of the line, show my ID, and pay off the bouncer. He lets me inside.

Down a set of filthy stairs, through a reinforced iron door, and the pumping bass of the club rattles my bones. The sheer volume makes conversation near impossible. The lights flash and strobe, a mass of half-naked bodies writhes like some great amoebic organism. The room reeks of sweat, cheap perfume, and sex.

A dozen clashing colors of smoke rise from the crowd. Overtaxed veins pulse beneath shallow layers of skin. The place is a junkie's paradise. Hence the name.

At the bar Frankie recognizes me. She winks, pours me a shot of bourbon. Her mohawk haircut is covered with glitter, and her contacts sparkle in rainbow hues. Looking at her makes me dizzy.

"How's it hangin', D?" she yells in my ear. "Been a while…"

I nod and show her the picture of Dorothy McIntyre.

Frankie frowns and looks at me like I just spoiled her evening. She picks up the photo, examines it, then shakes her head.

"Nobody like *that* in the city," she shouts above the assault of the bass.

"At least not anymore, right?" She smiles at my little jest.

I ask if she knows a guy named Roach, wears a skull on his back.

She grins, points across the teeming dance floor. And there he is, Mr. Roach in his skullface jacket, nodding his head, sweating and jerking to the industrial funk. I leave some money on the bar, drink the shot, and make my way through the crowd.

··········

"I swear, I don't know where she is!"

It's hard for Roach to talk through his broken teeth and bloody lips, but he manages. He squirms across the puddles of piss and petrol. I grab him up again, slam him against the alley wall. His veins pulse like tiny snakes trying to burst free of his skin.

I drive a knee into his stomach. He pukes. Starting to sober up.

"Tell me another lie and I'll get mad. Dorothy McIntyre. Who'd you sell her to?"

Roach wipes blood and bile from his mouth. He's crying now.

I slap him. "Don't cry. Be a big boy. Who has Dorothy?"

The punk coughs and shivers. "I can't say anything…they'll kill me."

I bring my face real close to his. I let him see the big knife, feel its point on his eyelid. "I'll kill you. After I take your eyes. Tell me now and you'll have a chance to run. Get out of the city. If you don't, it'll kill you anyway. Just a matter of time."

Roach stiffens, too scared to breathe.

"Who has her?" I ask again. Neon glints off the naked blade.

Roach's eyes swivel toward either end of the alleyway. He whispers like he's afraid of his own voice.

"The Man…" he stutters, coughs. "The Man in the White Limousine."

I put the knife away, let him fall back into the mire.

"You stupid waste of skin," I tell him. "Now you better run."

He takes my advice, scurrying like a rat into the shadows and piles of trash.

When I leave the alley there's a boy with a sideways face picking up bottles in the street. He looks at me like I'm a tasty morsel, flashes the fangs lining his vertical mouth. I pull out the hand cannon, let him see the glimmer of its metal. He hisses at me, moves on down the road, disappears among a jumble of rusted-out vehicles.

I stand for a moment in the street, getting my bearings. The White Limousine never comes to this part of town. I've got some walking to do. Maybe I should just go home, forget about Dorothy McIntyre, write her off as another unsolved case. Just another victim of the city.

I take a good shot from the flask and look at her picture. She comes from a world of sunlight. And now she's lost in darkness. The rain picks up, turning from steady drizzle into dedicated downpour. Warm and oily. Like blood.

Damn it.

I shove the picture back into my pocket, turn up my coat's heavy collar, and start walking.

··········

On 459th street I pass the Man Who Speaks With Shadows. He's always there, like a phantom shaman who haunts the block. He stands on a pyramid of rusted shopping carts, waving his arms in the rain and muttering gibberish. His face is black with grime and madness, his gray beard a tangled crow's nest. His long robe is a stitched-together quilt of every color that has faded to no color at all. I pass by as far as possible. I can only reach the River District by going down 459th. All the other streets heading this direction are blocked by toppled skyscrapers, mountains of scrap, or barriers of rubble.

"The River flows to Nowhere!" shouts the old man. He's looking down at me now, bathed in the orange flicker of alley-fires. "To Nowhere!"

I keep walking. He's harmless.

"Give up the skin and you give up the heart!" he bellows. "What are we without hearts? What are *they*? The current carries us all toward oblivion! The River flows to Nowhere!"

Farther down the road I can't hear his ravings anymore. The rain lightens up, but the road is still waterlogged. Steam rises from grates, along with hollow moans of agony. I hear screaming somewhere down below. The city sewers are another world altogether. Couldn't pay me enough to go down there.

This close to the river nature has started to take back the city. Green vines with black leaves crawl up through the pavement to hug the facades of dead towers. Weeds grow waist-high from cracked asphalt, and sheets of purple fungus smother the concrete. Sometimes things like bloated eels crawl out of the sewers and go hunting up here. They feed on each other when they can't find rats or stray junkies.

Now I turn off the main avenue. The snipers up ahead will spot me soon if I keep going that direction. The only way I'm going to get close to the Man in the White Limousine is by navigating the Intestinal, a maze of alleys that leads eventually to the River District. I take out the hand cannon. The weight of it in my hand makes me feel a bit safer in the dark and narrow places. A bit.

Bits of bone and fabric line the alleyway, broken glass, the occasional skull, sometimes a gnawed skeleton. Two-headed rats skitter away at my approach, then reconvene to finish their feast when I pass. I take a right, a left, then two more rights, following tiny signs graven into the brickwork. Anybody else would be totally lost in here. Knowing these kinds of things is why I get paid so well.

Eventually I come to the Alley of Ecstasies. The girls here crawl like serpents across the slimy ground. Forked tongues flicker from their bright red lips, and they whisper filthy secrets. They offer me obscure pleasures as I step carefully between them. Their heads twist to follow me. Their bodies are covered with mud and green-gray scum, but otherwise perfectly proportioned. They're not exactly human, despite their spot-on female anatomies. My stomach turns as they caress my thighs with their long fingers, begging for my favor.

I stop right in the middle of them when I see the man lying at the far end of the alley. Two of the girls crawl across his naked body. His mouth hangs open, head resting on a pile of cast-off clothing. They do unspeakable things with his body, contorting him like a rag doll. He moans and cries out. I turn away, take out the picture of Dorothy and stare at it until the moaning stops. The man stands up, pulls on his clothes, and looks at me with naked embarrassment. He runs from the girls hissing at his feet.

They've given up on me, sensing I'm somehow immune to their charms. They bare yellow fangs, warning me to beat it. I drop a few bucks into the slime and make my way quickly to the alley's end. The maze continues, only now there is a second maze of conjoined fire escapes rising above me. I've reached the part of the Intestinal where the buildings still support life. Hunched figures move and scramble through the network of back iron, like fat spiders in a web. Sometimes garbage drops into the allies from above. I watch my step.

I follow the hidden signs, the ones I learned long ago when I was young and reckless. Back then I saw the city as a challenge, an adventure. I owned nothing back then, and so I had nothing to lose. I spent years in this place before I discovered a way out.

Something to live for besides hustling.

Her name was Carolyn.

··········

On my way out of the Intestinal I see the woman with the black suitcase again. She sits on a pile of crumbled stone, cradling the suitcase, watching me pass into the River District.

"Do you know where you're going?" she asks in that rasping, scarred voice.

I pause, for some reason I can't name. Maybe the urgency of her question.

"Yes," I tell her. "I know."

And she laughs at me again. I leave her laughing as I walk into the road beyond the maze.

The streetlights glow white and orange, rising on iron poles from the avenue at regular intervals . The folk here wear dark clothing and heavy cloaks. Their skulls poke through the skin of their faces like fingertips through worn-out pairs of gloves. They shamble about drawing rickshaws or hand carts loaded with cages full of chickens, hairless cats, or snuffling mutant things without names. The people of River District are meat-eaters.

I blend into the crowd along the Street of Succulents, moving between the stalls where hocks of pink meat glisten on hooks. Hooded vendors shout the merits of their products. The smells of animal shit and barbecue smoke fill the gloom. A couple of stands offer tentacled creatures pulled from the river, and a few even display old-fashioned fish with silver scales. Gourmet food.

Several of these places offer fresh human limbs for those with truly discriminating tastes. I might look into these places in my search for Dorothy McIntyre, but I knew better. If the Man in the White Limousine had bought her, she wouldn't end up in someone's stew pot. She'd be in for something far worse than a slaughterhouse death.

The crowd here reminds me of *Frankie's Utopia*, but without the blaring lights and noise. And there's no joy here, not even the simulated kind that junkies are always chasing. No, here the citizens speak in hushed voices, until an argument breaks out and someone gets stabbed or strangled to death. An undercurrent of rage and fear runs through the lives of everyone who lives in the River District. They know who their masters are here, and they're closer to them than anybody else in the city. They have good reason to be afraid.

The Children Without Mouths march through the crowd, which splits immediately to make way for them. I move to the side like everyone else, keeping out of their direct line of sight. They're almost cute, these little enforcers. They might be 5- or 6-year-olds if they were wholly human. But like the Girls Who Crawl the Alley, there's not much human left in them.

Fifteen of the little fascists stalk by my position, turning their tiny heads in every direction. Their big, round eyes scan the crowd and the stalls, looking for who-knows-what. Their tiny fists clutch curved knives and barbed whips. They wear dirty rags beneath cloaks of gleaming silver chain mail. Their faces would be adorable if not for the complete lack of lips or mouths, and the raw menace bleeding from their eyes. A smooth layer of waxy flesh covers the lower half of their skulls, beginning just below their tender little noses.

When the last of them passes by, I resume my walk. I hear the cracking of whips behind me, the shouts of alarm. They've found a victim, someone to haul away for whatever mysterious reason drives them. I used to think they worked exclusively for the Limousines, but I learned better. There are other powers in the city. The Children Without Mouths are mercenaries. Like everyone else in the city, they're for sale to the highest bidder.

At the far end of the avenue I reach the riverwalk. Black water stretches away from the shore, and dark shapes swim in its depths. The fogs hang thick above the rippling surface, so dense that the far shore is impossible to see. The big venus flytrap flowers growing along the riverbank yawn wide as I approach. Sometimes they capture a stray pigeon or some other bit of vermin. They'll take your arm off if you get too close.

Here on a platform overlooking the rainswept water, the Women Who Dance with Fire begin their nightly performance. Thirteen of them, naked as savages, swirling lit torches through the air, juggling them back and forth with hands, feet, and knees. Tattoos of ancient fire gods writhe across their backs and breasts. Their smooth skin is marred and scabbed over in places where the fire has caught them over the years. Their faces are invisible behind masks of polished bronze carved into the likeness of leering demons. The demon-masks are vaguely Asian in design, yet the Woman Who Dance with Fire are of no specific race or nationality. They come from all over, drawn to the fire like addicts are drawn to the Junk.

I lean against a light pole, watching the cross streets. Waiting for the White Limousine to come by. I know it will be here eventually. Waiting is a part of my job.

The fire-women undulate to the rhythm of drums from hidden speakers. The twirling fires mesmerize me, make me less conscious of my surroundings than I should be. I sip from the flask, and the taste of Old Kentucky makes me remember what it should be helping me to forget.

I remember Carolyn. I met her here, twelve years ago, on this same street. We watched the fire-dancers and took a barge along the river. We ended up in her father's penthouse, looking down over the whole rotten, steaming city. I had never been up that high. I knew I didn't belong there, but it was Carolyn who made me feel like I did.

Days later her father found out she was seeing me. He did what any father would do: forbid his daughter to hang out with a no-good street hustler. Next time I went to meet her I wound up tied to a chair in a burned-out warehouse. Her father and his goons stood over me in their pinstriped suits, looking at me like I was an insect. I was certain they were going to stomp me then. But they just worked me over good, broke my nose and a couple of fingers.

I remember her father's face close to mine. The sour hell of his breath, his crooked nose.

"Do you know who I am?" he asked.

I nodded. My lips were too swollen to speak.

"Stay away from my daughter," he said, "and you'll stay alive."

I nodded again. I would have told him anything to stop the beating.

They threw me in the river, and I barely crawled out of the frigid water before something ropy and hungry could pull me to the bottom. I vomited riverwater and was sick for a week. I promised myself that I'd never see Carolyn again. But eventually I went looking for her.

She wasn't hard to find. She had been waiting for me here, by the fire-dancers. We decided to run away, leave the city and her father behind. She stole some money from his safe, bought a used vehicle, and we bribed our way across the border.

We built a life together in the sunshine, made a little home surrounded by green living things. Had a baby. Best time of my life. I almost forgot about the city.

Six years we were happy together. Safe. Content.

But all of it ended when the White Limousine found us.

··········

Before I realize the flask is empty, I'm already half-drunk. The city has that effect on me.

The fire-women are still spinning, and the drums are making my head throb. I think about finding a flophouse to spend the night. I might have to come back here tomorrow and resume my watch.

Before I move away from the light pole, something slips about my neck, pulling me backwards. My skull slams against the pole, and the wire digs deep into my esophagus. A black bulk rises before me, blotting out the flame dancers. Dark glasses reflect twin images of my panicked face. A pair of black-gloved fists on either side of my neck, straining, pulling.

The man before me removes his glasses, and I look into his eyes. But they're not eyes at all, just pulsing orbs of translucent mucous, glistening like toad flesh. He croaks at me, and the last of the air rushes out of my lungs.

Sleep or death comes now. I'm not sure there's much of a difference.

·········

I wake up to a spash of icy water in the face. Deja vu strikes me like a fist to the teeth, followed closely by an *actual* fist to the teeth. My head jerks back. I spit blood from swollen lips. The skin of my neck burns and bleeds. There will be a nasty scare there if I survive. A big "if."

Three men with bull-necks stand about me. Their coats are long and black, although one of them has shed his outerwear. His shirt is gleaming silver silk, his well-tailored pants charcoal gray. His fists are covered by black gloves, and the gloves are covered with my blood. His eyes are gleaming toad-flesh.

My arms are locked about something, secured behind my back. A metal chair.

"Hit him again," says a voice from the shadows. It echoes in a way that lets me know this is one of the hollowed-out factories that line the River District.

Thunder rolls into my skull again. A tooth flies from my mouth.

It takes a few seconds for me to come back from this one. My vision is blurred, the ribs of the chair are cold against my naked back. At least they left my pants on. And my boots.

"Die with your boots on," they always say. Makes a kind of weird sense.

The sound of a purring engine fills the dank air. Twin points of light draw near, defining themselves as two headlights. The White Limousine pulls up close, its windows black as tar, revealing nothing of who's inside. But I already know.

The door opens and Carolyn's father steps out. He's every bit as tall and broad as I remember. A granite statue with a few more wrinkles carved into its face. His suit is immaculate. A silver skull pin decorates his lapel, like the kind Nazi SS commanders used to wear. He walks with a cane, fat fingers wrapped around its platinum head.

He comes to stand in front of me, silent as death. I spit more blood and force my head up to meet his eyes. They're cold, like blue ice. Carolyn's eyes were the same color. I bite back the hate and the sickness in my gut. Force a smile across my inflamed lips.

"Son of a bitch," I mumble.

He doesn't smile.

"I warned you, D," he says. His voice is the sliding of a tomb door. The crush of a gravel ton as it grinds your bones. "Told you never to come back here. This is no place for you. Never has been."

"I'm looking for a girl."

Carolyn's father shifts his weight, sighs. Someone brings him a chair. He wipes the seat with a handkerchief from his breast pocket and sits down in front of me. Leans in real close.

"Carolyn's gone, you poor bastard," he says.

"Not her," I tell him. "Dorothy McIntyre. Her mother hired me."

He looks at me like I'm speaking some language he's never heard.

"She wants her runaway daughter back," I say. "Sound familiar?"

He glances at the gloved thug. I take a couple more shots to the jaw before the bruiser backs away. Carolyn's dad leans in close again.

"Do you know who I work for?" he asks. "Do you even begin to understand my business?"

"Flesh trade," I say.

He smiles. It's a terrible, gargoyle smile. Unnnaturally white teeth. He even laughs. Turns to his thugs, who chuckle. I have no idea what's so funny.

"The flesh trade," he repeats my words. "There is that. But there is so much more. The flesh is only the beginning, boy. I work for *The Skinless Ones*. We all must serve somebody, so I serve *them*. The flesh is weak, but limited. There are so many other ways to suffer. So many alternatives to blood and bone. I think you came back here because you want to discover these things for yourself."

I shake my head, wince at the pain it causes.

"I only want the girl. The mother is well-off. I can arrange a ransom."

"It's too late for that, D." He turns around in the chair and motions to one of his goons. Someone brings him a small box of dark mahogany with an emerald clasp. He settles it on his knees. Rings glitter on his big fingers.

"You displeased me when you stole my daughter," he says. "You ruined her. Gave her an illegimate child. You took what was mine. I should have killed you then. But you reminded me of myself...when I was young and stupid. So I gave you a warning instead. Now you leave me no choice."

I flex my calf and feel the knife buried deep in my boot. I have no chance of reaching it. Not with my hands chained behind the chair.

"Unlock these chains," I ask him. "Give me a fighting chance."

Carolyn's dad laughs again. His fingers run across the clasp of the box. He opens the lid, stands, and turns it upside down. A dozen or so black worms fall across my head, shoulders, and laps. Cold and slimy, bristling with short black hairs.

"These are the Worms That Feed On Dreams," he says. "They will feed until there's nothing left of you but an empty shell."

"I loved her." I tell him. "Why did you have to kill her?"

"She was worthless. She disobeyed me. So I gave her to my masters. I'll do the same with you, once you're properly hollowed out."

"What about my baby? Your own grandson..."

"I am not entirely without mercy. I pitied Carolyn's little bastard," he says. "It's out *there* somewhere. On the streets."

I scream long and hard as the worms become tentacles invading my mouth and nostrils. But worse than that, they send fire coursing through my brain, filling my skull with flame. I'm twitching and straining, but the chains hold me tight.

The worms strip away my memories one by one: my mother, who died when I was a boy. I'll never know her face again. My time in the alleys of the city...the gangs, the drugs, the fights...all gone. Carolyn...no, that's the memory I can't bear to lose. It will kill me as surely as a shot to the head.

I feel them tearing at it now...*what was her name?*

Some kind of commotion begins around me. A rush of blurred images. Something quicker than the eye moves between the thugs. Red fountains spray across the concrete floor, across my face. Something rips the worms away from my head, one by one, tossing them into the shadows. I realize then that my screaming has stopped.

For a moment I black out, clinging to the memory of Carolyn's face.

What color were her eyes?

Then I'm back in the real world, and someone is unlocking the chains on my wrists. Something snuffles and snorts and chews nearby, digging into the spilled guts of the big bruiser. He lies on the concrete, body split apart like an overripe melon. What is the thing devouring him? It's like a canine, but more like a spider. Its lucent skin steams and smokes. Bloody light spills from the eight eyes set about its head, most of which is a fanged snout. It squats and feeds, suckles on the goon's viscera, then moves quick as lightning to the next body and continues its feast.

The chains fall away. I hear the squealing of tires and the roaring of an engine. The White Limousine races away, rear fender striking sparks as it leaves the scene of carnage.

A lean figure stands before me now, dark face staring from beneath a mildewed hat. Next to her a black suitcase sits open and empty. A strange animal musk fills my nostrils.

"Do you know where you're going?" she rasps at me. When I don't respond, she turns and whistles. The smoking dog-spider-thing scampers into the big suitcase, licking its chops. The old woman leans over and closes it tight. She clicks it shut and turns to face me.

"What is that thing?" I ask, rubbing my wrists and wishing for a shot of Old Kentucky.

The old woman glances at the black suitcase.

"My son," she says.

I try to stand but fall to the cold floor instead.

What was her name?

Carolyn? Dorothy?

Her eyes were...

"Do you know where you're going?" asks the old woman.

"He works for the Skinless Ones..." I mumble. "*He gave her to them...*"

The lights dim. The wet concrete becomes a comfy pillow.

"I know," says the old woman.

She touches my cheek with gentle fingers.

And I'm out again.

···•·•··•··

I wake up fully clothed. My shirt is torn, stained with blood and grime. My face is swollen, my head ringing. My tongue probes a hole in my gums where an incisor used to be. I'm a mass of aching flesh and bones. Somehow I'm alive.

Flickering firelight warms my shivering body. I'm lying in an alley somewhere on the edge of town. The woman with the black suitcase sits on the other side of the fire. Mounds of trash and rubble form a crude stockade about us. Rain drizzles across a latex tarp suspended above the flames, drips through tiny holes to sizzle on the embers.

My companion offers me a bottle. I struggle to a sitting position and sniff at the liquid. Old Kentucky. I drink deep, letting the warmth of the booze rush through my limbs, settle in my belly. Always takes the pain away. At least for a little while.

I pass it back. Her eyes are pools of darkness beneath the brim of the broad hat. The big suitcase sits close to her knee.

"What's in the case?" I ask.

She answers my question with a question.

"Do you know where you're going?"

I blink at her, rub my eyes.

"I'm looking for a girl," I say.

"What is her name?" she asks.

I stare at the heaps of trash about us as if there might be a clue hidden there. I run my hands across my battered body, looking for pockets. Looking for answers. I discover a big knife in my boot and a hand cannon strapped under my arm. In the pocket of my jacket I find a parking stub and a photograph.

The girl is beautiful. Blonde hair, dark eyes, soft skin against a green backdrop. A cherry tree, a sad smile. Right away I know that I loved her. Love her.

"Carolyn," I tell the old woman. "Her name is Carolyn."

She reaches over and takes the picture from my hand.

"That's not Carolyn," she says. "I'm afraid you're too late."

She drops the photo into the flames. I watch it wither and curl and turn to ash. She gives me another slug of the whiskey. I drink it down.

"The River flows to Nowhere," she says, and turns away from me. She caresses the surface of the black suitcase, which seems to throb as if breathing. She might be sobbing. It's hard to tell.

I force myself to stand up. My head spins. The parking stub says there's a vehicle waiting for me somewhere. I stagger away from the woman with the black suitcase, wincing with pain at every step. My belly feels hollow, empty, but I know better than to eat city food. Anyway, the emptiness feels deeper than hunger. I've lost something. The city has taken it from me.

I follow the address on the stub and regain my wheels. I drive away from eternal night and endless rain, putting distance between myself and a thousand secrets.

And I swear I'll never go back.

I hate the city.

BEHIND THE EYES

They say the eyes are windows to the soul. I can tell you this old sentiment is true beyond any doubt. As a passerby inspects a luxurious home by peering through its lucid panes of glass, a man studies his lover's soul by gazing into the liquid depth of her eyes. But every window has *two* sides. The house's owner looks out at the world through those same windows. Here the analogy ends: the *door* of any house provides entry and exit for its owner each day, but the door that permits a soul to leave its body opens only at death. However, there are exceptions to this rule. Times when doors and windows open and close blindly. Times when something terrible looks out from behind those glassy, blood-veined orbs.

Despite her legendary strangeness, I never truly believed that my grandmother was a witch. I first went to stay with her as a six-year-old, my mother driving me along a winding dirt road until we reached the dilapidated farmhouse. Granny Armaya was my father's mother; the father who had left us when I was a few weeks old. He'd grown up here, on this farm that had seen better days. There were only a few cows and a single horse left on its twelve acres of thinly wooded hills. We drove by a ramshackle structure that used to be the barn, now a slowly dissolving mass of rain-rotted wood. It reminded me of a piece of candy I'd left lying out in the sun the week before, melting in upon itself until it became a shapeless lump of nothing.

Barbed-wire fences enclosed the farm, and I saw a pale horse chewing the grass of a sun-browned hillside. Granny sat on a wooden porch swing, watching as my mother parked her station wagon. She wore big, horn-rimmed glasses, the first thing I noticed about her. That and her hair, still black as night in her old age—a persistent reminder of her Romany heritage.

Granny was a full-blooded gypsy, I learned later. Mother said she had come over from the Old Country in the thirties, her family spending the last of its European wealth to buy this little farm. Her husband, the grandfather I never met (just like my father), died less than a year after their immigration, leaving his wife and three sons to work the farm. One by one they slipped away, like restless shadows heading for the city, and the farm fell into ruin. Now Granny lived alone in the old house, surrounded by a family of crooked, black trees. Sometimes her other two sons would visit, but my father never came back to the farm. Not even my mother knew where he had gone. To her he was only the coward who left her to raise an infant alone in the city.

Although she was strange to me, I did not fear Granny Armaya. She welcomed me with a warm smile and a hug, and won me over with fresh-baked cookies. She let me run about the farm all day, playing among the twisted trees and trying to coax the horse near enough to let me pet it. My mother left me there all summer while she went back to the city to finish earning her college diploma. She would be the first one in her family to graduate from a university. Fifteen years later, I would be the second.

Granny Armaya cooked big meals for me, with plenty of sweets. Sometimes we fished in the little creek that ran through her property. But the most enduring memory I have of my time with her is when she took me up into her attic. My young brain reeled at the cluttered antiquity on display here.

Animal skulls hung along the walls, dried herbs swung like black chains from the low rafters, a thousand candles of all shapes and sizes sat across the floor, strategically placed among painted images that boggled my mind. Granny showed me her cauldron, an iron pot sitting on a hot-plate, the place where she brewed medicine to cure her arthritis. I watched her work among the candlelight, fascinated by the weird environment. Often I wondered about, combing through ancient chests full of velvet fabrics, antique clothing, gypsy-carved dolls, trinkets, jewelry. Occasionally I found a grainy, yellowed photograph of some sharply-dressed ancestor. Granny could name anyone whose picture I found in these trunks, but their names were Romany and I could not pronounce them. Several of them wore old-world military garb, with spiked helmets and curved sabers held against their chests. Once I squealed to find an ancient war dagger, preserved in a sheathe of moldering leather. Granny said it belonged to my great-great-grandfather, and she let me keep it.

The potions she brewed in the attic smelled horrible, but I didn't mind. There was so much to discover in that dust-blanketed treasure trove. By the second week of my summer vacation I spent more time browsing through the attic than playing in the fields. There was only one area of the attic that was off limits to me. It was a small alcove, or closet, in the very back of the room, closed off with a curtain of dark purple velvet.

"What's back there?" I asked Granny. She was stirring up the medicine in her iron pot, adding a pinch of something like powdered bone. At my question, she ambled over to me, grabbed me by the arm, and brought her wrinkled face close to me. She smelled minty, like the ointment she rubbed on her joints at night.

"Don't *ever* go back there, Stefan" she said, pointing to the curtain. Beyond its hem I saw a sliver of blackness peeking through. "That's where the *eyes* are."

She reached out and pulled the curtain aside with one liver-spotted hand. Inside was a visible nothingness: a rectangle of infinite darkness, where the candlelight could not go. A few days earlier I had stared into the black depths of the farm's stone-rimmed well, and could see no trace of the water that must lay far below. But this darkness was deeper, more solid, more impenetrable than even the subterranean gloom of the well. I felt that I might stumble and fall *into* that alcove, into that absolute dark, and I realized that I wasn't breathing. I sucked at the smoky attic air.

Before Granny let the curtain slide closed, I saw two orange pin-points of light staring out from the darkness. Narrow, burning things that made my skin crawl.

The eyes.

I was crying then, and Granny scooped me up into her arms. I sobbed into her shoulder as she carried me downstairs. "It's all right, Stefan," she whispered into my ear. She carried me out onto the porch, where the brilliant sun fell on my face, dried my tears. I sat on the swing watching a light breeze play through the leafy branches of the trees, and she brought me cold lemonade and a slice of cake. Soon I was my old self again. We never spoke about the alcove, or the *eyes*, again.

Three more weeks I stayed at Granny's house, spending most of my time outside. Eventually I coaxed the pale horse near enough to the barbed wire, offering it a red apple. I petted its soft nose as it ate the fruit. Granny seemed proud of me, though she warned me not to cross the fence into the horse's running ground.

In the evenings I watched cartoons on her big, floor-model television set, while she went about the house hanging strands of herbs, or painting odd symbols on the windows. She sang odd little songs to herself in the old tongue as she hung talismans and bone charms along the roof of the porch. These were the behaviors that caused the children who lived on neighboring farms to call my Granny a witch.

Sometimes I played with these kids on top of the green hills surrounding the farm, but they wouldn't come down into the witch's realm. I tried to tell them how nice she was, tried to bribe them with promises of candy and cookies, but none of them would visit me in my grandmother's house. I had to go up to meet them if I wanted to play. Eventually I decided, with the simple wisdom of a child, to let them think what they wanted to think about her. But I never believed it. Even after I saw the *eyes*, I never believed it.

When my mother came to pick me up, I cried. I would miss Granny, her wonderful meals, her willingness to indulge me, the wide playground of the lazy farm. I'd miss the pale horse, who I had named Dancer. But it was time to go. That year I entered third grade, and I soon learned once again to enjoy life in the city. I saw Granny one more time before she died, though. I was eleven.

The farm looked very different than I remembered, now that winter had claimed it. The hills were white, covered in a shroud of pristine snow. The horse was gone, sold three years prior along with the rest of the cattle. The trees were barren, grotesque giants bending ice-gloved claws toward the earth. The creek was a silver pathway of ice winding through the colorless landscape.

Granny's house sat unchanged beneath its snow-crowned roof, with a black coil of smoke rising from its chimney. My mother and I had come to visit her for the holidays, probably the only ones who cared to do so. But she didn't come out to greet us. I carried her present, wrapped in a crimson bow, up to the door. Our knocks went unanswered, but the door was unlocked. Although the house was warm, and fresh pastries lay along the dinner table, Granny was nowhere to be found.

"I'll check out back," my mother said. "See if she's in the attic."

At once I remembered that alcove where I had seen the eyes. I didn't want to go up there. But I was older now, and reluctant to tell my mother about my fear. So I walked up the creaking set of stairs into the fog of Granny's candle-smoke. The iron pot bubbled with some noxious brew, but where was my grandmother? I called out her name. She had to be here somewhere. I avoided looking toward the back of the attic until I heard footsteps.

Granny pushed back the dark curtain, walking out of the alcove, out of the infinite darkness. She squinted at me through the gloom. "Stefan?"

"Merry Christmas, Granny," I said, full of improvised cheer. She smiled and came toward me. But as the curtain fell across the darkness, I found my own eyes drawn to that black pit—I expected to see those evil eyes glaring back at me. I almost screamed. But there was only darkness, thick and invulnerable to vision. Then the curtain hid even that from me. Granny hugged me, and I helped her down the stairs where we celebrated the holiday and enjoyed one of her immaculate dinners.

I always regretted not visiting her again, but we lived so far away. Once I entered high school I stayed busy with sports, clubs and academics. Then I attended State College, earning a degree in English. Soon I was teaching middle-school and my next goal was to find a woman worthy of marriage. So I spent most of my time working or trying to please a seemingly endless procession of vapid, self-centered women.

My mother eventually got remarried and took a job up north. I stayed in the city where I had grown up, and was perfectly happy to spend the rest of my life there, looking for an ideal mate and teaching kids to read. But the recent news of Granny Armaya's death took me once again into the country.

It wasn't really a funeral, since I was the only mourner present. It seems all of Granny's progeny had vanished, like my father. The pastor said a few words and the undertaker lowered her coffin into the ground of the local cemetery. It rained. Granny had left me the tiny farm and her old house, but the estate taxes and burial expenses had to be paid. Only by arranging to sell everything could I avoid going into debt. I decided to visit the old farmhouse one last time, to salvage what I could for posterity before I sold it.

Fall was in full swing when I drove down the winding road, still unpaved after all these years. A swirl of saffron leaves filled the air behind my car as I approached Granny's house. It was quiet as death on the farm, ruled now by the trees that wept dying leaves across the earth. No smoke rose from the chimney, and the porch had caved in on the east side. I noticed one of the living room windows was broken, and as I neared the front door a black raven flew out of the shattered pane, startling me. Remembering the Poe poem, I smiled grimly.

The power had been shut off so I brought a flashlight from my car. Inside the house, the smells of a half-forgotten childhood filled my nostrils, the lingering scents of sugary baked goods, homemade candy, and charred firewood. Beneath it all, the barely perceptible tang of Granny's medicine. It appeared the house had been looted, the couch and chairs were overturned and ripped as if with a hunting knife. Anything of value had been taken. I found an old photo album laying on the floor of Granny's shattered bedroom, that was all. On my way back to the living room, I passed the door to the attic.

Even as an adult, I did not want to climb those stairs. But I remembered the treasures Granny used to keep up there, and I knew it might be the only way to gather momentos of any worth, sentimental or otherwise. Dismissing my childhood terrors, I ascended. The attic was largely unmolested. Granny's implements of supposed witchery lay scattered across the floor, or hung from the peeling walls. All the dead candles were burned to stubs, and the iron pot lay cold and bare, turned on its side.

Like steel drawn to a magnet, I walked toward the back of the room. The purple curtain still hung there. I forced myself to stand before the alcove, trying to get up the nerve to move that fabric aside and shine my flashlight into that interminable darkness. I reached for the curtain. My fingers trembled. I tore it aside and a battery-powered ray of light sliced through the darkness.

The alcove was lined with dozens of shelves, each one loaded with glass jars of various sizes. Exhaling, I entered the tiny space, holding my flashlight before me like a crucifix. Its light shone through the dusty glass of the containers, and my flesh crawled like it did when I was six. Within each jar lay a pair of round objects. There must have been hundreds of them, glistening like pallid marbles dotted with ruby, sapphire, or onyx. A vast collection of preserved human eyeballs.

Some of them were dry and yellowed, while many retained a perfect whiteness surrounding the prismatic irises. They seemed to stare at me, uninterested, lifeless, unconcerned. Entombed behind dirty glass. Granny had hidden her bizarre collection from me, no doubt for good reason. I remembered the eyes I had seen as a child, glaring out at me from this room. Just as I knew for a certainty that these were all *human* eyes, I knew that those feral things were *not*.

The batteries of my flashlight gave out. The light fluttered once, then died completely. Darkness fell over me like a smothering blanket. My breath caught in my throat, and I no longer knew the way out of this room. I could see nothing; or nothing was all that I could see.

Dizziness filled me, and I felt as if I would fall. But I no longer felt the ground beneath my feet. I groped outward, but I could not feel any shelves, my flailing arms disturbed no glass jars. An immense pressure filled my ears, as annihilation filled my eyes.

Suddenly, I saw flames. Soundless vision filled my brain. Flames leapt, and stars glimmered beyond them in a black sky. Murky faces stared at me through the flames. I looked down and found that my body was not my own. I was naked, and a woman. Ropes of strong hemp bound me to the tall pole at my back. The flames licked at my flesh, and I watched it curl and blacken. I was screaming in agony, but I could not hear myself, and I felt no pain. I knew then that it was not me who burned, but the poor woman whose eyes through which I now looked.

The faces beyond the dancing flames spat at me. I saw them clearer now. Garbed in the black and white garments of a Puritan society, they stared at me with hate-filled eyes that mirrored the color of the flames. I looked out from behind the eyes of a witch as they burned her living body into ash. I gazed on, deaf and mute, until the eyes through which I saw burst and melted. Then I plunged back into darkness.

Another flash of light and I was a man again. Or at least I looked *through* the eyes of a man. He wore the uniform of a colonial soldier, and carried a long-barreled musket. Again, there was no sound, only vision. I imagined the man to be a glass jar, myself a bodiless pair of eyes trapped inside, looking out helplessly.

I trudged through the snow, feeling neither the frostbite of my hands and feet, or the bloody wound in my right arm. Ahead, through a curtain of falling snow, I saw the wall of a wooden fort, with comfortable smoke rising from the peaked roofs beyond. I paused to wipe the cold sweat from my brow, almost home.

A black shape leapt from the snow. Its fangs ripped into me, painlessly, soundlessly. It was a lean, dark wolf, ravenous and desperate. But I recognized its smoldering orange eyes that glared into mine as it ripped my body apart. Those were the *eyes*...the ones that had stared at me from the ultimate darkness. The wolf tore out my own eyes then, whosever they were.

Once again I floated in the infinite dark, panicking. Then a flash and I looked through the eyes of yet another person. I was a woman again, or a girl. I walked along a deserted road, far from the lights of the city. Looking down at my own body, I saw a plaid skirt and high heels. Turning my head, I saw the smoking wreckage of a crashed car, its front end wrapped around a huge oak tree. I stumbled along the road, light-headed, until headlights came into view. Flagging down the car, a red Chevy Nova, I spoke a few words to the lone driver, who beckoned me inside. As I sat down, the man smiled at me, and turned his head. His eyes were those of a slavering beast, and he smiled. Before I could fumble the passenger door open, he pressed a gleaming blade against my throat. He whispered something I could not hear as he drew the knife across my flesh. And darkness came again.

I spun, tossed by invisible winds out of some primal void. I knew nothing else to do, so I called out my grandmother's name. This time I heard my own voice, echoing through the nothingness.

I looked then at my own six-year-old self. I wrapped my arms around the little boy, smothering him with my genuine love. I realized that I now looked out from behind my Granny Armaya's eyes, when she had still lived. My arms were hers, thin and spotted, my dress was an old, threadbare green, the one I always remembered her wearing. I watched the little boy that used to be me wander about the attic, prying into chests full of old junk. And I turned back to my cauldron, where I dropped in a batch of herbs. I saw the sigils scrawled across the attic floor and somehow, now, I understood their meaning. There was one particular symbol that sat within a crude pentagram, studded by lit candles. It drew my attention powerfully.

Vingaal.

I knew that word. I knew it meant "enemy." I knew it meant "devil," or "evil thing." And I knew it represented everything I stood against. It was the murderous owner of the *eyes*.

Time passed, and I saw my grandmother work many strange spells. Only then, suspended behind her aged eyes, did I come to accept that she was a witch. But that wasn't the correct word, for she battled the evil that was the Vingaal. To defy it was her purpose in life. It had claimed the life of her husband since it could not claim her own. It also took her children one by one, my father among them.

I learned that the name "Armaya" means "cursed" in the old tongue. I learned that Granny Armaya had come here far earlier than the thirties, and was *far* older than anyone would dare to guess, her life sustained by her arcane potions. I learned that the *thing* called Vingaal roamed the world feeding on the suffering and blood of innocents. If it could not murder directly, it seduced other innocents into murdering for it (like the Puritans who burned alive the innocent girl accused of witchcraft). I also learned what my grandmother was really doing all the time she spent weaving magic in her attic.

She followed the Vingaal, anticipating its victims, climbing behind their eyes and alerting them to its danger. She saved the lives of thousands in this way, spoiling the creature's blood-play. For this it would never forgive her. It longed for her blood now more than any other.

I watched through my grandmother's eyes as she entered her alcove of darkness yet again, sending her mind through the void, settling into the brains of those the Vingaal was stalking. Urging them to avoid the dark path after midnight, or to sidestep that particular alley where doom waited with an eager knife. Sometimes she even took control of the person's body, physically driving the victim away from the Vingaal.

She wasn't always successful. The Vingaal was clever, and determined. But she saved those she could. In the end, she even saved herself. But her potions could only hold off a natural death for so long, as her body continued to grow frail. It was a heart attack that finally took her life. I saw it strike her, in the middle of a conjuring, saw through her eyes as she staggered down the attic stairs to die on the living room floor.

Then I was alone in the darkness again.

I felt empowered by this knowledge of my grandmother's sorcery. On impulse, I concentrated on my own body, willing myself to return. I had to get back to my living self, or be trapped in the void forever. There was a rush, a fresh falling sensation. Then I looked upon my adult body, standing in the dark alcove among the jar-lined shelves. I knew instantly that something was wrong.

How could I *see* my own body if I had re-entered it?

As I watched my own head turn to look straight at me, I realized I was looking out from inside one of the jars. I looked through a pair of those dried, preserved eyes kept in my grandmother's alcove. And the smiling face that stared back at me *was* me, yet it was *not* me.

It had *my face*, but its eyes were blazing orange like hungry flames; narrow, bestial things that I recognized at once. I had none of my grandmother's powers, and I had left my body standing defenseless in the alcove.

I had left it empty, and the Vingaal had filled it.

The wicked *thing* stared at me from behind my own eyes, grinned at me with my own mouth.

It reached out for the jar in which I lay, and instinctively I jerked backward, into the void once more. I was a bodiless, homeless soul adrift in an ocean of starless night.

I thought of the city, the thousands of people living there. Maybe there was someone who could help me. It was the only chance I had. I *willed* myself toward them.

I emerged from the dark behind the eyes of a cab driver, looking out his windshield at the rushing lights of traffic. I don't know how long I looked helplessly upon those rain-soaked streets while he picked up one fare after another. Still I could hear nothing, say nothing, do nothing. *How* had my grandmother managed to take control of another's body? If I could only do that, maybe there would be hope. Somehow, maybe I could reclaim my own body. But she had practiced her hidden craft for centuries...how could I hope to duplicate her mastery?

It was well past midnight when the cabbie picked up the last fare of his shift. He looked into the rear-view mirror at his passenger, asking for a destination. Helpless to do otherwise, I looked along with him. There, smiling in the back seat, sat myself with orange wolf-eyes. The Vingaal, using my hands, reached up and slit the cabbie's throat with one of my grandmother's kitchen knives. With *my* tongue he lapped up the spilling blood like a thirsty dog. Then I was free of the dead cabbie, hurling through the dark again.

I found myself looking through the eyes of a police officer, responding to a domestic abuse call in some less desirable neighborhood on the city's south side. I watched his gloved hand knock on the door, hearing nothing. I knew who would answer it. As the door opened, the *eyes* looked back at me from my own face. I watched myself (the Vingaal) stab me (the cop) through the gut, wrenching the blade upward until it reached the heart. Behind me, the cop's partner was going for his gun, but I knew the Vingaal's knife would be faster. Then blackness.

Several more times I tried to find sanctuary behind the eyes of city dwellers. But every time the Vingaal came for me with his blood-smeared blade, his cruel smile that was a twisted perversion of my own, and his wicked eyes. Every time, someone new died. Then I realized what was really happening.

The Vingaal wanted *me*. Just as it had wanted my grandmother. She had cheated it by dying of natural causes. Wherever I went, it would follow me. By inhabiting anyone, I was condemning them to death at the hands of the immortal *thing* that wore my body.

So I stopped searching for eyes to look through. I couldn't bear the thought of more deaths on my conscience. My intervention would only bring more slaughter. There was only one way to avoid the Vingaal now.

I floated in the empty space between souls, caught in that infinite darkness. I could neither see nor hear. Blackness cocooned my disembodied consciousness. It was either this, or dive behind someone else's eyes, and so draw the Vingaal to take their life.

I know that I will be remembered as a murderer in the world of the living, and there is no way for me to tell anyone that it is *not me* killing all those people. That is not me walking in my body.

All I can do is float here in this ultimate dark, sinking ever deeper, drawing further and further away from the world of sunlight and living beings. I embrace the nothingness, wanting only to become a part of it. Let it dissolve the last bit of my guilt-wracked soul. Let there be an end.

I fall away from a string of violent deaths, into bottomless oblivion. The Vingaal will never follow me here...the lure of murder and pain is too powerful...it will not abandon its blood-play to descend into this nameless, formless void.

And yet, there is *something* here...a *presence*. More than one. They come to swim about me like shadows against darkness, invisible, but somehow I sense them.

They stare at me with burning, hungry eyes, like shapeless wolves.

There are *millions* of them. Millions of wicked *things*, one of whom is called Vingaal in another world so impossibly far away. They envy his freedom, they *all* want what he has.

I understand now that this non-place, this dark oblivion, is where they dwell. It is where they are born, dreaming of succulent living flesh.

They whisper to me. Telling me secrets.

Soon you will be one of us, they say.

I sink deeper, dissolving, the tattered threads of my mind spinning into the dark.

Now you are one of us.

Open your eyes...

THE MAN WHO MURDERS HAPPINESS

HE DRIVES A CAR just like yours, the one you polish and shine on Saturdays. Nondescript. You'd never notice him parked across the street.

His eyes are hidden behind a pair of square-rimmed glasses with mirror-bright panes. His hair is black and slick, heavy with Vitalis and cigarette smoke.

You'll never hear him coming. You might see him step from the shadows. Or watch the butt-end of his cigarette hover like a firefly in the night fog. He could be anybody, but you know who he is the moment he sets his eyes on you.

In the alley outside Big Pete's, two vagrants were torched to death last night. Six blocks away a police cordon surrounds the body of a girl who leaped from the roof of her apartment building. Somewhere in the big maze of post-war housing, someone is dying from a stab wound. Someone else waits patiently, watching the blood seep out.

The man shows up when you least expect him. You never realize it when you're having a good time. That's the danger. Suddenly your senses are more alive, your skin abuzz with electricity, your heart beating faster. Suddenly there's hope in the world and a reason to keep on going. At this point most people ask themselves: "Is this happiness?"

Then they look up and the quiet man is standing there. The man and his gun, a black metal extension of his gloved fist. He's the man who murders happiness, and he's caught you red-handed. Blam. Your time is up. On to the next fool.

They say his job pays immensely well.

On Tuesdays the factory boys come pouring out of the industrial park, checks in hand. The dive bars and strip joints fill up for the weekend. Drink will flow and blood will spill, all the usual shit. Behind the truckstop an aging prostitute buys smack to feed her habit for another day. Her hungry baby wails as she slides the needle into her arm. A drunkard with a bloody face sleeps in the gutter outside the liquor store. There's an amputated leg sticking out of the dumpster. It wears a thousand-dollar shoe.

The man drives by in his nondescript automobile, unmarked and unnoticed, just another motorist. Directions come through on the radio. He hates the way it interrupts the music, but it's part of the job. Mostly he listens to rockabilly, sometimes jazz. But the music dies every time the hollow voice of authority blares from the speakers. Direct communication with the boys upstairs, the secret infrastructure behind the official infrastructure. The one that knows where all the happiness is, and the one tasked with eliminating it.

He usually gets a name, and the name of a town. That's it. He drives, sometimes for days at a time. It's all flat farm-country now, and not much else. He drinks hot black coffee at nameless diners and bottles of cold soda sprung from gas station automats.

They say he can actually feel it as he gets closer to his mark. He feels the happiness like a bloodhound scents his prey. Drives into town like a shadow, finds the right neighborhood, parks his car somewhere nobody will ever notice it. Nobody ever does.

He walks along a sidewalk littered with dead leaves. Autumn wind moves cool and damp through the lanes. Each little house is exactly like the one next to it, and so on, all the way to the end of the street. And all the other streets here are just like it. Tiny green lawns, covered porches, a single old oak or elm rising in the front yard. Old folks sat on porches nursing shotguns. Lazy dogs lay a their feet. Children dig worms from the ripe grass, collecting them in old jelly jars. The sounds of television cop show themes blare from open windows.

He feels the happiness like warmth now, the heat from a blazing conflagration. As if the fifth house on the right was an inferno. On fire with joy. Sheer, raging happiness that will ignite the houses on either side unless it's stopped. The doors are locked, and heavy curtains block the windows. He slips in through the back door. He carries tools for the opening of locks, and he's very good with them. His primary tool is the gun now back in his hand. The soft moans of a woman drift from a back room with roaring fireplace. He moves closer on noiseless feet.

At first they're only shadows. Locked in a tight embrace on a shaggy rug by the fire. He watches them for a moment, removes his square glasses. His eyes are blank and colorless, like dead fish scales. But he sees the happiness. He watches it spill from their sweating bodies, rippling waves of color, invisible to the human eye but glaring to his own. Their naked joy mesmerizes him, and he cannot look away from the sheer beauty of it. The awesome beauty of the awful thing he was made to root out and destroy.

Happiness. The man and woman have found it together somehow. The quiet man's fascination turns to outrage. He's never seen such an intense bliss. Suddenly he's ashamed of himself for watching. He pulls the trigger.

It's fear that makes him do it. Time and time again, he pulls the trigger out of sheer fear. He accepted that long ago. He imagines what it would be like to be happy, to lose himself in those blazing energies he's witnessed so many times. To spark like comet and burn yourself to nothingness, existing as pure ecstasy.

To be happy.

It is a horror he could never endure.

That's why the government has agents like him. To keep its people from the threat of bliss. To keep the entire population from being devoured by voracious joy. Happiness leads to oblivion. To keep mankind alive, he must keep it suffering. The next stop he makes is at the lakeside, where a man with long hair mediates by the water, coming perilously close to bliss. The quiet man approaches, making no sound in the wet grass, and shoots him in the back of the head. Nobody notices. They never do.

In a rust-eaten trailer park three children play with a stray dog. Their faces are dirty, their clothing little more than rags. He shoots the dog and walks away while the children weep, poking at their dead friend with a stick. On the other side of the trailer park a man hangs up the phone. He's going to meet someone later that night—someone he can't wait to see. His happiness is like a flare in the dark. It draws the quiet man toward him, and the gunshot echoes above the squalor.

On his way out of the park, he shoots down an old lady feeding pigeons. The birds scatter as her blood stains the yellow grass to red. If her deep joy had spread any further than the pigeons, it might have infected the entire town. He considers shooting the birds, but they've already lost themselves in the gray sky. Not his problem anymore.

That night the radio calls him back into the city, where a young father celebrates the birth of his first child. Far too happy, especially for the urban district. Even with a permit for a birth celebration, the new father's happiness had been blazing in his heart for a week, exceeding his allotment. Too much happiness. Expired permit.

The quiet man intercepts the new father in a parking lot, and shoots him in the leg. He doesn't always have to kill. Sometimes a maiming shot is enough to restore the balance, squelch the gout of happiness. Close the psychic wound. The father howls in pain, bleeding on the concrete, until his co-workers drag him away. He doesn't thank the quiet man for sparing his life. He's no longer happy, but he'll be fine walking with a cane from now on.

After midnight the quiet man sits at an all-night diner, drinking black coffee. Long day. He tries not to think about the couple on the rug, the vortex of ecstasy that almost smothered him. It had been close, but he'd pulled the trigger. Restored the balance. He would never understand how they could be so terribly happy, so insanely elated. Some cases weigh on his mind, and he realizes this will be one of them.

He doesn't see the girl come in and walk toward his booth. He's looking at the plastic menu, lost in thought. She slides into his booth with a rustle of her silk blouse, and before he knows it she's looking right into his eyes. Her face is exquisite.

It's a face he's seen in his most secret dreams, the ones he can't even admit to himself. Her eyes are dark with secrets, brighter than stars. Staring at her, he cannot reduce the magnificence of the moment to the stumbling weakness of words.

His heart beats madly and he smiles at her. It's all he can do.

She raises the gun.

"Is this happiness?" he asks.

She pulls the trigger.

LOVE IN THE TIME OF DRACULA

"There is no greater glory than to die for love." —Márquez

WE NEVER SHOULD HAVE come to New York. The skyline was jagged, like broken fangs against the sunrise. The streets were deserted. The vamps were all sleeping deep in their holes, their slaves locked in underground pens during daylight hours. That Big Apple landscape in the morning, all those magnificent towers like sparkling mountains, it messed with our heads, made us think for a minute that there was no danger. We knew better, but still the splendor of the ruins made us careless.

There were about seventeen in our group at that time, strapped with rifles, crossbows, and silver blades. A few carried pistols. We were young and fearless.

Sunlight flared against the shattered skyscrapers, and the wind howled like a ghost chorus. Rats scuttled between heaps of rusted-out vehicles. Mounds of skulls overflowed a line of dumpsters.

"We can't stay here," I said. "Too many places for vamps to hide."

Mudder had been a sharpshooter before the plague. He agreed.

"Sewers and subways full of bloodsuckers," he said. "A whole city of 'em down there. Thousands of prisoners in the breeding pens."

The others looked from me to Marion. As usual, they waited for her to make the final decision. She shielded her eyes from the sun's glow and scanned the empty streets.

"We came here to find transport," she said. "So we'll be here until we do. For now, we find an old hotel with some intact beds. " Our bus had broken down a hundred miles west, and we'd hoofed it since then, sleeping mostly in abandoned basements.

"What we need is a good boat," Mudder said. "Sail away from all this shit."

"To where?" I asked. "Everywhere else is just as fucked up."

"Boys," Marion said. "You're missing the point." She rested her big gun across her shoulder and lowered her shades so I could see her green eyes. Deep green eyes, like the summer leaves I remembered from childhood. Green, fresh, and full of sunlight. The most beautiful eyes in the world. "We're not leaving until we find something to drive. So we might as well make ourselves comfortable."

We found a big luxury hotel that hadn't been completely stripped by raiders. Getting into the building was no problem, and we climbed to the thirty-third floor before we found a suite that was pretty much intact. We built a fire in the stairwell to cook some squirrels we snared in Central Park. We slept with our bellies full as the sun went down.

So far the search for a functioning vehicle—and the fuel to power it—had been fruitless. Most of the cars and trucks we found were burned out, trashed, or rusted to immobility. And we had yet to find any gas. The vamps had secured all of these resources and tucked them away underground somewhere. We heard rumors of blood-warrens, underground cities where vamp hordes lived for years without ever coming up for moonlight. I had hoped we'd never find one of them. I should have known that Mudder was right. We were camping on top of the new New York—the one that only came to life in the dark. The NYC underground used to belong to the rats, but now even they served the master.

Sleeping with Marion in that fantastic hotel room—a relic from the world we both remembered—I dreamed about the slave-pens. Half-starved families stuffed into tiny cages, kept alive in the dark until their time came. Then the hooded ones came to choose the victim. The vamps would feast and the shriveled bodies were burned, or dumped into mass graves. In the dream I lay among the dead bodies, thirsty for the blood that was drained from my withered body. I suffocated and choked, and finally fangs grew from my mouth, and I rose up as one of them. That's when I woke up shivering and sweating, like I always did. Always that same damn dream. Marion held me tight, and her whispers brought me back to reality. The first time I ever told her that I loved her was after one of those nightmares. She had gotten used to them over the years.

"Let's get out of here," I said. She hushed me with a finger to my lips. We made love, and the fear faded as it always did. Fear can't stand against love. It never could.

"It's all right," she said. "It's all right." She knew what had happened to my parents, my sister. She knew I never wanted to talk about it. But I couldn't help dreaming about it. I told her again that night how much I loved her.

"You better," she said. She kissed me.

That night we couldn't hear anything from the streets below. There must have been vamps down there, roaming about looking for strays. Or maybe they stayed in their underground city enjoying the comfort and privilege of their status. The next day we searched another sector of the city for transport. We found some tires that were still in good shape, but nothing to put them on. A few old car batteries that were still operational, but not a drop of gas.

"Tomorrow let's hit the docks," Marion said.

"Yeah, let's find that boat." Mudder said. He drank from an ancient bottle of whiskey. Marion laughed. We sat around the stairwell fire, eating canned beans.

"Where you wanna go, Mudder?" she asked. "Europe?"

"Yeah," Mudder grinned, his dirty face lighting up. "Par-ee, the City of Lights!"

"Paris is a graveyard," I reminded him.

He gave me a dirty look.

"The whole world's a graveyard," Marion said.

The others didn't talk much. In our band talking could get you killed. We had learned to be silent, to the point that it had become our greatest habit.

Torres found an old flat-screen television. Nobody thought it would work, but he plugged it in anyway. The electrical grid had fallen apart years ago. To all of our amazement, the stairwell was suddenly full of blaring voices. Colorful images sprang to life on the screen, rabid pixels assembling into faces and figures.

"Holy shit," Mudder said.

We gathered around the tube and watched as Torres turned the sound to a bearable level. And there he was, staring us right in the face: Count Dracula, Master of the World. It was some kind of talk show hosted by vamps, interviewing Drac like they used to interview heads of state. His voice was soothing, his face handsome beyond belief, his eyes miniature suns, red as blood and impossible to ignore. He wore a black suit and red silk tie, a golden amulet bearing his family sigil hanging at his breast. His hair was black as night, groomed to perfection, not a single strand out of place. About his golden chair lay or squatted his Brides, half-naked vamp women like lazy cats, rubbing their cheeks against his knees and hands. His shoes were black patent leather, and his fingers were long and expressive as he spoke directly to the camera.

There was too much interference and static to hear exactly what he was saying, but his smile held us all at attention. His ivory smile and his blood-bright eyes. Snatches of conversation emerged from the static: "...Old Romania is new again...", "...human stock being managed toward optimum levels...", "...after thousands of years the world's true order has been restored...", and something about "...carrying the wisdom of our blood to the stars..."

An audience of vamps shouted and applauded onscreen. A crowd of slaves were led into the TV studio by their neck-chains, and the pleasant talk-show atmosphere became an orgy of bloodletting. The vamps drank deep from the throats of their victims, while the master watched from his high seat. His eyes were still smiling.

"Turn it off," I said.

Marion sat transfixed by the spectacle, along with everybody else.

"Turn it off!" I screamed. I grabbed the set and tossed it down the stairs. It exploded in a shower of sparks and lay still.

Marion looked at me. "Never seen him before," she said. "Not his face."

"Me neither," said Jenny. She was only sixteen, the youngest member of our group. Another survivor from a massacred family. Sandy and Colleen, both in their 60s, sat in quiet contemplation. Drac's irresistible beauty had scarred their minds.

"Marion?" I slapped her face gently. "Snap out of it."

She looked at me and the spell was broken. She smiled.

"Hey, man," Torres said, as if waking up. "You broke my television."

·········

Marion was too quiet that night. I knew something was wrong.

The next day we searched the harbor where the wrecks of trading ships lay like dead gargantua, slowly rusting into oblivion. There wasn't much international travel these days. No more airlines either. Vamps didn't like to cross water much, and they had no real reason to travel for the most part.

We found a small trawler—a fishing boat with a working motor. A few hours later we liberated six barrels of fuel from a wrecked warehouse and fired up the engine. The sun was low above the ruins as the boat's engine disturbed the air. I knew the engine was too damn loud. It must be echoing off the stone walls of the city, seeping through the cracked streets into the blood-warrens. Into the places where the vamps slept, waiting for sundown.

"It's getting late," I told Mudder. "We need to get back. The boat'll be here tomorrow."

"Why not set sail right now?" Mudder said. His face turned to Marion—the question was really for her. The dusk light was golden on her braided hair. I should have grabbed her right then and ran, taken her far from that place. But that wasn't how it worked. The group followed her, not me. I didn't care to be the leader. Didn't want the responsibility.

Marion stared at the dark water as night rolled in above the waves. "Yeah, we better get back," she said. "Unless you want to be caught on the open ocean with nowhere to hide when the vamps wake up and start flying around. Leave now and we won't get very far."

Mudder couldn't deny the wisdom of her words. We had all seen vamps sprout wings, or melt into the shapes of giant bats. At night they not only ruled the earth, but also the skies above it. Never forgetting this was key to our survival.

We killed the engine and hid the boat behind a wrecked battleship. We stocked it with the barrels of fuel we had found and planned to return the next day. We reached the hotel just before sunset, but dark shapes were already moving through the rubble as we crept indoors.

Everybody in the group was excited, nervous about the nautical adventure we planned. "What if we found an island out there?" Mudder said. "Somewhere there ain't no vamps? Would could hide there forever."

Marion said nothing.

"If we stay here," Torres said, "it's only a matter of time until they find us. Drain us dry. We have to try this...it's the only possible way to escape hell."

"I agree," I said. I waited for Marion to add her own agreement. She stared at the fire, and I wondered what she was seeing. I remembered Dracula's blood-red eyes glaring through the TV, spanning space and time, unholy photons gliding from the screen to caress her eyeballs and brain. Invading her soul.

"Lemme sleep on it," she said. I tried to get more out of her, but she only kissed me and distracted me with lovemaking. Afterwards I heard her whispering to the other women. I lifted my head and called out to her. She came back to kiss my forehead.

"Sleep, Danny," she said. Her hand was cool against my forehead. "No more dreams. Just sleep..."

I should have tossed away the dirty blanket and demanded to know what was going on. Instead, I fell asleep in that comfortable bed. I don't remember having my usual nightmares that night. I don't think I dreamed anything at all. I woke up with the first rays of sunlight seeping through the window. I rolled out of bed and stretched my limbs. Outside and far below the broken city spread for miles, a kingdom of rust, dust, and vermin. At first I didn't notice that Marion was gone. She usually woke up earlier than me and let me sleep for awhile. But she wasn't in the stairwell stoking the fire or making coffee. None of the other men were awake yet. Then it hit me.

The women gone. All of them.

I ran down the stairs, screaming Marion's name. I ran all the way to the street, when Mudder caught up with me and dragged me back into the shadows, trying to calm me down. Slowly it began to sink in. Marion was gone, along with Jennifer and the two older women. At some point in the dead of night they had abandoned us.

"Where are they?" I asked. "Where did they go? There's nowhere to go."

"Yes there is," Mudder said. Our eyes locked.

"The boat."

Now there were only thirteen of us—ten grown men and three boys between 10 and 14. They might as well have been full-grown men after growing up in such a world. We stopped thinking of them as kids once they had killed their share of vamps. Now we all ran through the cold bright morning, clutching our weapons and packs, hoping that we hadn't really lost our women, that they would be waiting for us at the boat. That they had come along early to prepare for the exodus.

We reached the docks and saw that the boat was gone. Not a sign of it.

I sat down on the wharf's edge and stared at the sparkling blue ocean. Somewhere out there four women were gliding into the unknown. Why had they done it? Why had they forsaken us? A couple of the men began to weep. Others started beating on each other to release their anger. Mudder sat down next to me, almost as heartbroken as I was.

I reached into my pocket for cigarette and found a letter from Marion. She had written it with a ball-point pen from one of the hotel desks, on stationary printed with curling lavender flowers. I didn't need to read it to know what had happened. I already knew it in my heart. I read it anyway.

She started with an apology, then told me how much she loved me, how good I was for her. She went on about how grateful she was to have known someone like me. She saved the real message for the end of the letter:

The master calls, Danny.

He whispers in my dreams.

Even when I'm awake, I hear him.

I didn't know until I saw him. Until I saw his face on that TV, I mean. I didn't understand. But now I do. I know you're going to hate me for leaving, but I am sorry. I had no choice.

I saw it in his eyes.

I belong to him now. We all do.

I've spoken with the other women and we've all agreed. Together we stand a better chance of crossing the water and reaching Romania. It's where we belong.

Stay here and keep yourself alive, Danny.
Please forgive me.
There's nothing I can do to resist him. Not since I've seen his face.
I belong to him.
Don't come after me.

There was more, but that was the gist. His insane power drew women to him and made them his willing slaves. It worked even through broadcast media. Or maybe that old TV had never really worked at all; maybe it had been some kind of spell. Dracula's dark magic, cast across the world from his icy mountain, summoning fresh concubines to his castle. Now he had Marion. Or he would, as soon as she reached his mountain, looked into his perfect face again, bared her neck to his fangs. To him she would be another piece of livestock, another slave to satisfy his needs both carnal and bloody. Just another stolen soul, another Bride of Dracula.

Unless of course she died on the long journey to Romania. I knew she would make it. I didn't know if I could survive without her—if any of us could survive without her—but I knew she would make it to that castle. I knew Drac would admire her strength as he made her his slave. He would taste it in her sweet blood.

"Whadda we do?" Mudder asked.

He and Torres looked to me for an answer. So did everybody else.

"Let's go back to the hotel," someone said. "We need to hide."

"No," I said, watching the sun reach its zenith. "No way in hell."

"Then whadda we do?" Torres said.

"Find another boat," I said.

And just like that I was their new leader. I didn't ask for it, didn't really want it, but the guys just followed me. I guess they figured I had been the closest to Marion, so I would have to do now. Or maybe they were just scared shitless and needed me to pull them out of it.

The vamps came for us that night. We heard them coming up the stairwell, so we had time to prepare. Mudder greeted the first blood-sucker with a Molotov cocktail in the face. I knew he'd regret losing the booze, but it was an effective method. The vamp went down in a blaze of flames, wings and skin blackening to ash. They poured through the doorwell, trampling the burnt one's body, hissing open-mouthed at us like cobras, ripping at our throats and bellies with their filthy claws. We opened fire until our ammo was gone, then the bladework began. It was Marion's go-to strategy. She had turned our haphazard brutality and survival instincts into focused teamwork. Automatic weapons were good to have, but ammo never lasted.

It always came down to cross and blade. Wetwork.

We lost two men that night. I don't remember their names. Admitting that still shames me. In my defense, they were new to the group. Next day we found a new hiding spot. That's the trick of surviving in a world of vamps—stay invisible unless the sun is out. Any sign or whiff of you in the night, and they'll track you like bat-nosed hounds. The sound of the trawler's engine before sunup must have tipped them to the presence of wild humans in the city. They had followed Marion's trail right back to the hotel. In the process of leaving us behind, the women had also revealed our location.

I didn't blame Marion for it. She was under his spell. She loved me as much as I loved her. She couldn't help the call that made her leave, but she had still tried to spare me. It's why she left that note for me.

It took us weeks to find another intact fishing boat and scavenge a few more barrels of fuel. Sometimes we tussled with roaming bands of vamps, but we managed to sail out of NYC harbor before its subterranean hordes came pouring out to devour us. We sailed past Lady Liberty, something I had never seen with my own eyes. Blackened by fire and scored by dozens of mortar wounds, she looked more like a Goddess of Death than a symbol of freedom. Someone had spray-painted a pair of crimson fangs protruding from her lips. I wondered if vamps had a sense of humor after all. Maybe some stray resistance fighter had done it to make a final statement. I never got an answer.

On the open ocean we retched and puked and clutched our bellies. Twelve of us living on canned food, bottled water, and a stash of beef jerky Mudder had found in a burned-out supermarket. Only one of us had any real experience at sea. His name was Gimble, he was from Florida, and he hadn't said a word in six years. Not since his own family was wiped out. He'd been in the Navy back when one existed, and after that was he was an avid boater. He wrote messages to me on little pieces of paper he carried around with one of those stubby little pencils.

"Our lives are in your hands," I told him. The boat rocked beneath us as the coastline faded away. I held onto the rail and tried not to dry heave again. Gimble shook his head. He wrote something down and showed it to me.

We can't hide out here.

When sun goes down we're fucked.

"You got a point," I said. I stared across the waves, watching the sunlight dance like diamonds. "But they may not follow us over the big salt. They don't like the water one bit."

Gimble wrote again. *Do you think they went after Marion?*

"No," I said. "I think they wanted her to go. She's going to him. They all are."

Sorry, Gimble wrote.

"Can you get us to the French coast? No bullshit." I had only half-believed him when he told me the first time. I would risk anything to go after Marion. I'd have made the voyage myself in a goddamn rowboat if I had too.

I can do it, Gimble wrote. *Unless something kills me first.*

I showed him the automatic rifle slung across my shoulder.

"We have plenty of ammo and real sharp eyes," I said. The boys had stocked up at an abandoned department store before we left. More guns, plenty of bullets.

I don't trust guns. Not against vamps, Gimble wrote.

I pulled the silver blade from its sheathe. It sliced the sunlight into tiny rainbows.

Now THAT I trust, Gimble wrote.

He pulled out a sharpened iron cross that he used as stake. He'd staked hundreds of vamps with it. We all carried something like it. Gimble's other hand scribbled with the little pencil.

That and this.

During a month at sea we saw three minor storms and ran completely out of provisions. We tried fishing, but the things we pulled out of the ocean were not fish. They weren't quite squids or urchins either, but something like a combination of the two. They bit a few fingers off before the men stopped fishing altogether.

I sat hungry in the bow of the boat, watching the flat horizon of neverending blue. The NYC vamps never did come after us. Maybe they wanted us gone. Maybe they knew we were headed toward the master. Or maybe they knew we'd starve and die out here, and we weren't worth the trouble of a chase. They had millions of slaves to feed on, mile after mile of underground pens. Vamps never went hungry in Drac's world.

I thought the sea would kill us long before vamps did. The long nights were the worst. We had been used to hiding and sleeping at night—living only during the daytime. It was the key to our survival on the mainland. But out on the ocean we couldn't sleep much. The rocking of the boat was constant, and even when it no longer made us sick, it still kept us awake. The threat of being exposed on the open water kept everybody on edge. We all knew that if we let our guard down, that's the moment something shitty would happen. So we sailed on, bleary-eyed and hollow-bellied, day after day and night after night.

Something huge passed over us one night. It blotted out the stars and I wondered how such a massive bulk could stay aloft. It must weigh tons. A mountain of black flesh glimmered with slime, which fell across the sea like a soft rain. Men rushed for the shelter of the cabin to avoid getting that scum on their skin. Samuel, the 14-year-old, took a glob of slime right in the face. His flesh dissolved into a steaming mess as he stumbled over the railing and fell into the sea.

The leviathan's wings made terrible winds as it passed over us. The lights of its roaming eye-clusters glowed like red moons. I thought it might swallow us whole, until I realized that we were actually beneath its notice. Just a tiny speck of metal bobbing on the ocean with a few tiny meat-morsels clinging to it. Torres wouldn't stop screaming, even after the leviathan rose into the stars. Or maybe it flew behind the moon. I couldn't really tell.

Mudder slugged Torres to knock him out, but when he woke up again he came at me like a rabid dog. His eyes spewed green mucous and clots of blood, his yellow teeth tore at my sleeve. Mudder shot him in the back of the head, and we tossed his twitching corpse over the rail. Jenkins said a few kind words, but we all knew Torres was better off dead than starving out here with us.

"How do you do it?" Mudder asked me. He drank from his last bottle of Tequila, drowning out the guilt of killing Torres. They had been friends. "How do you keep going? Why not just give up and die?"

"If you wanna die, then go ahead and die," I said. "Nobody can stop you. Me, I'm gonna find Marion."

That seemed to satisfy him. We finished off the bottle.

···•••••···

It's almost time to make that final climb. The sun will be up soon, and I won't have to hide in this crevice anymore. There isn't much time to tell you how we came to ground south of Paris and marched on foot across the vamp-infested countryside.

We found provisions in abandoned hamlets and bombed-out villages. Nobody starved to death. The French countryside was quiet, green, and beautiful during the daytime. At night we hid in old cellars, caves, and decrepit factories, always making our way toward Switzerland, then on into Austria and Hungary.

We even met a few resistance bands in those mountains, folks hiding away from Drac's world right in the shadow of his own kingdom. They helped us out more than once, getting us out of jams, offering us a place to stay, restocking our ammunition when we needed it. But we were outsiders who didn't speak their language. We never stayed more than a single night with any band of survivors. Somewhere along the way we lost Gimble, along with about half our number.

As we crossed the Romanian border a patrol of military vamps ambushed us. They wore the shapes of men with black-and-crimson uniforms, but the wings of demons grew from their backs. I could tell you every bloody detail of that fight. It still replays in my head every damn night. I watched them tear out Mudder's throat, and there was nothing I could do. I took out the vamp that killed him, but there were so many more of them. I could tell you that I killed twenty of the bastards, or even thirty. I could lie and say I was a hero that day. But I ran away. They tore the last of my friends to pieces as I slipped into a gulch and ran until the sun came up.

It was a coward's escape. But I was too close to die now.

Too close to Marion.

Day after day I watched the towers of Castle Dracula rising from the range ahead of me. I would reach it alone, weeping for those I had abandoned. Only when I came to stand before the mountain did I realize there was no more road to follow. No way up to the master's house. But I had come prepared for that.

For six days I've been climbing, and every night I write in Gimble's notebook.

But now it's time to leave it behind and do what I came to do.

Time for one last climb.

Time to find Marion.

••••••••••

I wrap the notebook in a plastic bag and stash it beneath a flat rock. A message for future generations, if there are any. A record of my existence and Marion's. A love note for the ages. The gun is too heavy and clumsy for this part of the climb, so I leave it behind with the heavy pack. Now it's just me, my ropes and crampons, my iron spikes. The wind screams in my face like a devil.

The sun comes up and the great wall of ice turns into a wall of fire.

I climb. Halfway up the ice-wall my hand slips, but I only fall a few hundred feet. The impact knocks me out, and I wake up hanging from the ice over a snowy abyss. Clutching my way back upward, I have to ignore the pain. Like the cold, it simply doesn't exist. Only love exists. Drawing me closer to Marion with every frozen inch.

I don't know how long I've climbed, but the sun is almost down when I finally reach the walls of black stone. The outer wall is far easier to climb than the icy slope of the mountain. I catch my breath, adjust my gear, and scale it quickly.

I stand before the dark towers as the sky turns crimson, and I don't have to wonder which tower holds Marion. I can hear her voice. She calls out to me on the frigid wind. A mass of bloated bats swirls into the sky. Flamelight glimmers in the windows of the fortress now. I follow Marion's voice. But I don't speak her name. Not out loud. Not yet.

In the courtyard below the wall vamps rise from their stone couches and rush to intercept me. They shriek at the iron cross as my silver blade cuts them down. I leave a trail of severed limbs and heads behind me. Another crimson trail made by the magic of cross and blade.

Daniel...

Marion's voice. Calling for me.

I am here...

Come to me...

No need to ask, babe.

By the time I crawl through the window of her bed chamber, my clothes are sticky with vamps' blood. The silver blade drips in my fist. I leap from window casement to a floor of exotic carpets. It's slightly warmer in here than outside. Silence replaces the moaning wind. She sits across from me, her eyes bright as lamps. A cold flame burns in the fireplace. Candles along the walls make shadows dance. I smell lavender, and blood, and that unique smell that was always hers. The lovely scent of Marion.

My heart beats faster, and my numb fingers begin to ache.

"Oh, Daniel..." She rises. "I told you not to come after me."

"But you knew I would," I say.

She only smiles, showing fangs bright as pearls. Her eyes are still green. Green and glowing. Her lips are bright as blood, her skin pale as snow. She wears a diaphanous gown woven from fog or dreamstuff.

"I love you." I say the words like a magical spell, feeling stupid and giddy.

She stares at the blue flames writhing in the fireplace.

"I belong to the master now," she says. Avoiding my eyes.

"No," I say. "You love me, Marion. I feel it."

She looks at me the way she used to. She doesn't deny it.

"It's not possible," she says. "You'll have to kill me."

Her eyes focus on the iron cross in my left hand. I drop it and the silver blade to the floor. More stains for the master's fine carpets. My hands tremble like an old man's.

"I could never hurt you," I say.

"Then why come all this way? What do you want from me?"

I tear off my shirt to bare my neck.

I don't have to say another word.

She knows exactly what to do.

I DO THE WORK OF THE BONE QUEEN

AFTER I DIED, I went wandering about the town. Stars littered the sky like diamonds, and the moon was a curved blade. I reveled in the freedom of ghostliness. No longer would a mangled and deformed body imprison me. I floated along the black alleys strewn with trash, past a crowd of rats gnawing a severed hand. One of the beasts looked threateningly at me as I passed by, its eyes gleaming like minute lanterns. I laughed and willed myself higher, rising above the cracked pavement and the black rooftops of condemned buildings. The town snored below me, a neglected, dying organism rotting in its own filth. A heavy rain fell, passing through my ethereal self, and distant thunder rolled across the flat, gray horizon.

Among the slumped roofs and crumbling towers stood the abandoned factory, a shriveled heart that had once pumped lifeblood into the town. When it had finally ceased operations, years after the industrial accident that crippled me, the town began to diminish. Then came the corpse-like rot. I looked out my window every morning at its boarded windows and rusted gates, wishing that it had closed down before it had ruined my body. Where it used to produce intricate copper components and bulky industrial machines, its only products now were dust and decay.

What surprised me were the watery lights shining from the factory's windows.

The light struggled to free itself from the fissured brick walls, seeping through cracks in the boarded windows. Floating in the heart of the storm, I realized a magnetic attraction to that dilapidated place. The sensation became a raging hunger, amazing to me since I no longer had need of any food or drink. It was a hunger of the soul. Who could be in the old factory lighting fires or installing generators to shed light down its decrepit hallways?

My phantasmal form slid through the rain toward the speckled walls as lightning flared. Like a wisp of smoke I glided through an ivy-smothered wall and entered the musty bowels of the factory. Orange flames belched from a line of soot-stained furnaces. Silent forms bustled about a collection of worktables. They wore black smocks with heavy hoods. Their faces were indistinguishable in the shadows of these cowls, but I saw that opaque goggles shielded their dim eyes. Gloves of dark rubber covered their hands, and they worked feverishly to assemble some arcane product that made its way down the line. Hundreds of workers lined both sides of the tables, and as I floated near crimson drops spilled from the tables' edges. They were not working with metal, this odd and faceless crew.

Had a new meat-packing plant moved into town? If so, shouldn't they have cleaned the rust, mold, and filth from the walls and floors? Weren't there federal guidelines for such things?

I looked over the workers' shoulders; they seemed completely oblivious to me. They were not cutting meat. They were *assembling* something, some unknowable architecture composed of variously shaped chunks of raw meat. At the next table black-gloved hands chose pieces from a pile of shattered bones. Blunt fingers shoved the jagged bone bits into the fleshy sculptures and passed their handiwork on to the next table, where blankets of blistered skin were stretched over the grotesque forms. When these misshapen sculptures of meat, bone, and skin reached the final assembly table, new personnel hung them from metal hooks on rusted lengths of chain. The chains did not hang from any ceiling, but instead depended from a swirling sea of darkness that tossed and heaved above the sculptors' heads. I expected the dark waters to fall at any moment upon them like a massive, oily tidal wave; but this never happened.

I hovered above the manufacturing tables, an unseen spirit watching the grisly work, and a deep horror surged to fill my bodiless form. What were these bloody sculptures and who were these faceless drones? What gruesome purpose did this installation serve? I imagined a work force of mass murderers engaged in the hopeless endeavor of reassembling the bodies of all those they had slain. But that could not be the case because the final products of their industry, hanging bloody from the hooked chains, came nowhere close to resembling human bodies.

Yet I did notice that after a time suspended in the charnel air of the factory, each of the meat sculptures began to *quiver* and *twist* on its hook. If they had mouths, I was sure they would be screaming in agony. Eventually, each of the twitching oddities was drawn upward on its chain and disappeared into the inverted sea of roiling darkness.

I could not watch this process any longer, so I willed myself to float out of the insane factory. Then I discovered that I could not pass back through the sweating walls. Passing *into* the factory had been easy, yet now I was trapped inside, and I wanted only to glide out into the churning freedom of the storm outside. I tried again and again, but I felt my airy form growing heavier and denser, and soon I stood on the gore-slick factory floor.

I looked at my hands, gleaming ghostly before my intangible eyes. My translucent wrists bore deep gashes, spiritual recreations of the fleshly wounds I had inflicted upon myself. I had used a shaving razor to make bone-deep cuts, and my life had flowed from these cuts drop by drop. At first, it was a glorious liberation, this death of mine. But now I felt drawn toward a terrible confinement far more horrible than the broken body that I had fled. Why could I not leave this scene of deathly industry? This was not what I wanted when I murdered myself.

A hand grabbed my shoulder and turned me about. One of the hooded assemblymen stood before me. His face was lost behind some sort of gas mask or antique breathing apparatus. He motioned for me to follow him.

"I don't belong here..." I told him. But he only motioned again for me to follow, and pointed toward a doorway where a set of cinderblock stairs led upward. He held something out for me to take, and I peered at his gloved hand. A red, glistening chunk of meat pulsed in his palm. It was a human heart, still living, squeezing the last few drops of warm blood from its interior chambers.

I don't know why, but I accepted the throbbing organ. As the blood ran down my forearm, I noticed that I was no longer transparent. My flesh had returned, and my body was no longer crippled. A dark thrill excited me, and the hairs along my new arms stood up. The masked worker signaled that I should mount the stairs alone, so I did.

Shards of mutilated bodies littered the steps: ears, eyeballs, lips, fingers. Each one twitched horribly as I made my way upward. I passed a tall, gleaming mirror. I stopped, staring at myself in the glass, but it did not reflect my newfound flesh. It showed only my grinning skull and the skeletal network that existed beneath my fresh skin. I watched, fascinated by my fleshless reflection, and dropped the beating, bloody heart into the center of my empty rib cage. A great ecstasy filled me, and the world swirled like dark waters.

The heart beating wildly in my chest, I walked *out* of the mirror and continued up the stairs. I stared again at my skeletal hands, glad to see that the deep gashes had disappeared along with my new flesh. The wounds had reminded me of my old body, and I had not liked seeing them. But now I was glorious—the purity of gleaming white bone without a single ribbon of flesh. Except for the red, pulsing heart that floated within my skinless breast.

My feet clicked against the slimy stone of the stairs as I ascended, emerging onto a wide balcony overlooking the production floor where the hooded workers feverishly assembled their sculptures of flesh and bone. I paused at the railing for a second, looking down upon the flurry of activity. Then I looked up, and saw a sea of darkness rolling and heaving right above my head. Staring into its whirlpool, I experienced a great vertigo, and suddenly I was staring *down* into those dark waters. Since I could do nothing else in this precarious position, I fell.

The darkness swallowed me, and I sank like a stone. Leviathan forms swam past me, and tiny eyes like drops of flame swirled about my skeleton figure. Far below, *which had once been above*, I saw the roof of a great palace rising from the sea floor. The sand about its base was black as obsidian, and the towers were curved and pointed like scimitars or hooks. A forest of chains floated upward from the many windows of the wicked palace, and some of them were being drawn down *into* the structure, hauling in the squirming creations of flesh and bone assembled in the deathly factory.

I sank to the dark sand before the towering gateway. It was built from tremendous ebony blocks stained with flowering fungi. The figures of smiling fiends were carved across the walls, arabesques of tortured victims writhing across the green-black stone. Two soldiers stood before the gates, fleshless skeletons like me, but wearing suits of ancient armor flecked with coral. Their empty sockets stared at me from beneath horned helmets, and they pulled the gates open, moving aside their hooked spears so I could enter.

A host of living skeletons stood within, some draped in the robes of ancient Rome, others garbed in Grecian style, some in stranger garb from unknown lands, while others stood naked with phosphorescent bones gleaming in the deep waters. They stared at me, applauding as I walked a path of crushed rubies. Their bony hands made no sound in the thick depths, but I sensed their approval, their welcoming. I was expected here, and they were glad to see me. Suddenly I felt important, yet completely lost.

The Bone Queen waited to receive me on her throne of skulls. She wore a crimson gown, and her grinning skull face was set with two great diamonds. Two superb eyeballs had nested there in ages past, bright as sapphires. Her crown was a loop of dancing silver flame, blazing eternally, even in these abysmal waters.

I knelt, and kissed the bare bones of her feet.

"Welcome," she said. "We have a special place for you."

Her beauty was terrible to behold. It pierced my throbbing, naked heart. She had no flesh to spoil the purity of her immaculate essence, nothing but bleached bone that seemed to glow with the glory of jade.

I knew her. How I had dreamed of her, all those years sitting crippled in my darkened room, ignoring the dead factory rotting beyond my sealed shutters.

"I am your slave," I said.

"As are *all* here," she replied.

"How may I please you?"

"I am told you have…industrial experience," she said. "We have a factory for you to run."

I screamed then, and tried to tear the hammering alien heart from my rib cage, but the skeletal guards grabbed me and prevented this. They carried me away from the black palace and the terrible beauty of the Bone Queen.

They gave me a dark smock, with a heavy hood, and gloves of black rubber to wear. They conducted me back to the assembly tables and showed me to my glass-walled office overlooking the production floor.

"Is this…Hell?" I asked.

In voices of grating bone, they reminded me that I had a quota to fill.

·•••••••••·

So I work, and I dream of her beautiful, fleshless face.

I keep the production lines moving.

And I remind myself:

Now and forever, I do the work of the Bone Queen.

THE TASTE OF STARLIGHT

Pelops wakes gasping and shivering inside the CryoPod. A thin layer of ice crystals coats his cheeks and hands, pricking at his exposed skin. Crackling and moaning, he raises hands to his eyes and pries their lids open, shedding ice shards like tears. The curving glass surface before him is cracked into a mass of spidery lines. Struggling to inhale the frozen air, he pushes against the glass. The door of the pod refuses to move. He is entombed.

He moans as he raises his right leg, shedding a cloud of crystals. Boot against the fractured glass, but without much strength. His muscles are still asleep, slightly atrophied by years of stasis. Again he kicks, and draws in a burning lungful of cryonic air. A third time his booted foot meets the glass and it shatters, toppling him forward in a shower of ice and fragments. Instinct pulls his hands up, and he lands on them instead of his face. Splinters cut into his palms and fingers, but he can breathe freely now.

Lying on the floor, he rolls onto his back and looks sideways along a flickering corridor of cryonic niches. Here stand the stasis pods of his thirteen fellow sleepers. Even the chill metal of the floor feels warm compared to the ultimate cold of the CryoPod.

Something has awakened him early. A mistake? An emergency? Staggering to his feet, he clings to the cables along the walls and checks the nearest pod. A calm face, eyes closed, just visible through the cloudy glass. Digital display reads "Thompson, J." and the indicator light glows green. No fissures. Pod intact. He checks the next one, and the next one, until he finds another cracked pod lid with the display reading "Tanaka, Y." No frost at all on this lid. A blue face stares at him from inside. Asian eyes open. Mouth slack.

Pelops tries the release lever. Nothing. He tears at the rim of the pod's lid. Finally, he kicks in the glass like he did his own, this time from the opposite side. Tanaka falls out, stiff and dead. She was a good woman, and fine physicist. She would have been an asset to the Dantus colony. Must have suffocated when her stasis was interrupted. Like being buried alive. He might weep for her, but his eyes still feel frozen. He knows he'll have to eject her body into space, but he'll wait until he regains his strength.

He lays Tanaka gently on the floor and checks the last few pods. Twelve remain intact.

The frost coating his skin and flight suit melts into cold water. Droplets fly from his beard and hair, grown to primordial length while he slept. What could have happened?

He stumbles along the corridor beneath the pulsing florescent lamps, follows the plastic maps posted at each intersection, and finally reaches the sealed door of the bridge. A gleaming hand plate accepts his touch. The nerve center of the *Goya* opens before him, a spacious cockpit of flashing neon display grids and blinking digital interfaces. Above it all, a vista of interstellar wonder, a great oval viewport looking out into the universe. He stares into the bottomless void, captivated by the glimmering of ancient stars. A purple nebula clouds the starfields ahead, and the sheer beauty of the galactic deeps overwhelms his waking senses. Sinking into a vast gulf of infinity. Distant fires grinning and sparkling, the eyes of a demon legion.

You don't belong here, the stars whisper. This is the Great Emptiness. The stronghold of Death. Soon it will consume you. Utterly.

Pelops tears himself away from the celestial vision and goes to the control panels. He is no pilot, no navigator, but he is a man of science. He has been on ships before. He scans the displays and finds that the ship's thrusters have gone offline. He switches the relays to instigate backup power.

A lurching and shuddering tells him the ship has resumed its full-speed journey. He falls into the captain's chair and punches his fingers at the keyboard, requesting a status report. A holographic display emerges, dancing before him like a ghost. It's the *Goya*, a gleaming bottle-shaped vessel surrounded by pinpoints of rushing starlight. A scarlet line enters the left side of the display, trailing a cloud of sparks. A comet. It crosses the forward hull of the ship, bathing the vessel in a cloud of scintillating motes.

He reads the print display below the hologram.

Radiation cloud. Unidentified in nature...

A short-circuiting of the ship's power grid, disabling the auto-drive.

Severe turbulence resulting in damage to two CryoPod units.

No shit.

Communications permanently disabled. No messages going out or coming in. Not until the com techs on Dantus install a new stack of relays. Absolute radio silence. The report ends and the curved panels blink silently. Course renewed. Power reserves engaged. Everything nearly back to normal. But now Pelops is awake. And completely alone.

He accesses the logs for time, date, and distance.

Time elapsed since launch: 6 years, 2 months, 3 days, 9 hours, 52 minutes, 39 seconds.

Time remaining to destination: 1 year, 4 months, 2 days, 7 hours, 18 minutes, 3 seconds.

Sixteen months. Alone on this ship.

He considers waking the rest of the crew. Walks back to the pod corridor and almost does exactly that, when it hits him: A terrible, gnawing hunger in his gut. And the realization...what is he going to eat? Nobody was supposed to wake until a few hours before touchdown. This ship isn't equipped for manned flight.

He finds his way through the labyrinth of steel into the airy cargo hold. The massive bulk of the twenty-five UV converter domes loom like black hills beneath plastic tarps. In the far corner he finds what he is looking for. Emergency Supply Kit.

A man-sized chest (like a coffin). Inside, a collection of boxes, tins, and tubes of dry rations. A map on the lid reveals the location of emergency water tanks. He breathes a little easier. There's enough water in those tanks to keep a man alive for three years. However, he's not so sure how long the food will last. He'll worry about that later.

Cracking open a plastic box, he tears through an aluminum pouch and devours the beef jerky inside. Famished and relishing every bit, the salty taste of it on his tongue, the familiar warmth as it fills his belly. In a few seconds the entire package is gone. He curses himself.

He'll have to ration this out if he's going to survive. He can't indulge himself in such feasts. He closes the lid and makes his way along the bay to the water tanks, where he turns a valve and fills a bucket with drinking water. He drinks his fill of the cold liquid.

He surveys and logs the emergency foodstuffs, planning out subsistence portions. Drops his pen and slides to the floor. Someone was supposed to load more emergency supplies than this. Someone did not. There's barely enough food here to keep him eating at a base survival level for 100 days.

Three months. If he does not wake anyone else.

If he does, that time will be cut in half.

Three months of food. Sixteen months until reaching Dantus.
Nothing else here.
Nothing to eat.
After three months he will begin to starve.

·········

Pelops carries Tanaka's rigid body into the airlock, says a quick prayer, and ejects her into space. He should be grateful. One less mouth to feed.

He races back to the two open CryoPods and tries to get them operational. Spends hours working on them, up to his elbows in grease and cryonic residue. But it doesn't matter. They're both totally out of commission, their transparent lids shattered. And even if they weren't, the pods cannot be put back into service once they've been opened. The only way to do that would be to introduce more cryogen...which can only be done by CryoPod contractors.

No way to re-freeze himself. No way to avoid the twelve weeks of bare subsistence and the slow, lingering starvation that will surely follow. He envies Tanaka her quick death.

He lies on the floor of the pod corridor, weeping, remembering his look into the void. The whispering stars and their message of doom. And he knows it's true. This is the realm of Death and he has entered it willingly.

He wails and gnashes his teeth and smashes the floor with his fists. Eventually he falls asleep and enjoys the mercy of a warm oblivion.

·········

Pelops wakes sometime later, trembling on the cold metal floor. He gets up and returns to the bridge. His stomach growls, but he denies it. He sits in the captain's chair and stares out at the numberless stars.

With Tanaka dead, he is the only one capable of getting the UV converters up and running on Dantus. And the future of the colony depends on those machines. Wolf 359 is a red dwarf star, and not enough crops grow in its infrared glow. The colony's population has grown too fast for its the agricultural systems to handle. Setting up the converter domes and transforming the star's radiation to ultraviolet light is the only way to boost food production and end the famine. The only way to feed thousands of brave families who settled there. Eleven thousand men, women, and children already, with an exponentially expanding birth rate. They're all depending on Dr. Andrew Pelops.

I have to survive, he thinks. All those lives depend on it. This mission has to succeed. Everything else is secondary.

Think about those people. Those children. Think about those hungry mouths, so many more than yours.

The mission must succeed.

········•·•····

For the first three months Pelops eats frugally and his body grows lean. The flight suit hangs loose on his frame. He cuts his beard and hair with a pair of infirmary scissors, but they always grow back into a hermit's nest of tangles. The boredom is deadly. He spends most of his waking hours on the bridge, staring into the glittering void. He charts constellations...Scorpius, Serpens, Hydra. He sails through a gulf of myth and darkness. At times he fears the demon-eyes of the stars, and at other times he laughs at them. He carves images of ancient monsters into the deck floor with a screwdriver. He sleeps.

Sometimes he talks to the sleeping crew, sharing his knowledge of photonic chemistry, tales of his failed marriage, and his dreams for the future. They lie cold and still inside their coffins and listen to his every word. They are the perfect listeners.

Sometimes he imagines they reply to him.

Whispering like the distant stars.

········•·•····

Pelops eats the last bit of the dried jerky from the emergency chest. There is nothing else inside. Only the empty carcasses of plastic and tin where the faintest scent of edible things lingers. For days afterward he endures the grinding of his stomach, drinks himself to bloating at the water tanks, endures the hunger pangs that stab in his guts.

He babbles to the sleeping crew, telling them tales of hunger strikes.

"You see the body persists on glucose energy for the first three days of starvation," he says, walking between the rows of frosty faces. "At that point the liver starts feeding on body fat as ketosis begins. Thanks to the natural reserves of the human body, you don't really begin to starve until after three weeks. Now the body extracts nutrients and substance from the muscles and organs. Bone marrow too. Here's where the real danger begins..."

He imagines himself gnawing the meat off a large bone, slavering like a hound.

"Most hunger strikers die after fifty days...but are incapacitated long before that. We can't allow that to happen. The mission is all that matters. It must succeed...at all cost."

He hopes they understand.

·········

After ten solid days of starving, he dreams of his father. The stars are bright and blinking above the Colorado mountains. He's twelve years old, and his father has killed a deer. Pelops helps skin and prepare the carcass. They roast the venison over an open flame and enjoy its wild, savory flavor. His father's eyes glisten like the stars as he smiles through a frosty beard:

You know what you have to do, son.

Pelops wakes remembering the taste of greasy venison.

He staggers to the infirmary and finds a laser scalpel. In the cargo bay tool cabinet, a trio of gas-powered welding torches. He picks one up and presses the switch. A blue flame emerges, dancing before his eyes like a beacon of hope.

The flame is hot and perfect.

I have no other choice.

He punches the release lever on Thompson's pod. A hiss of escaping vapor, a white fog rushing about his feet. He lifts the lid and looks at the man's sleeping face, blue-white with a mask of rapidly melting frost. As the eyes begin to flutter against their icy hoods, Pelops raises the hypodermic needle. He's found a powerful sedative in the infirmary cabinet. He injects the drug into Thompson's jugular and pulls him from the pod, slinging him over his shoulder.

I could use the scalpel on myself, he thinks. Cut my own throat...quick and painless.

Is it wrong to kill a few people to save thousands?

He already knows the answer. It sits in his chest like an iron weight, far heavier than a single human body.

On the infirmary operating table he lays Thompson out, strips him of flight suit and undergarments. Bathes his body with fresh water from the tanks. Removes most of the body hair with scissors and razor.

He has never killed a man before. His nerves are electric. His hands tremble, and he begins babbling again. He knows the unconscious Thompson can't hear him. He could wake him up and have a real conversation first...but that would only make it harder.

"During World War II this type of thing was fairly common," he says. "Take the Siege of Leningrad. Eight hundred and seventy two days. The survivors trapped inside the city ate all the pets, birds, and rats before they were forced to… So it's not as if this sort of thing is completely without precedent. The mission must succeed, Thompson. At any cost."

I'm so sorry.

He switches on the laser scalpel and draws the blade of light across Thompson's soft throat. A fountain of red flows across the table and drips onto the floor, where Pelops has spread a tarp and bucket to catch it.

He dons a surgeon's mask to avoid the smell and proceeds to butcher the carcass. First he separates the limbs from the torso, then the head. The heat of the laser provides partial cauterization, but not enough to keep blood from leaking through tiny holes like puncture wounds in the raw, pink muscle tissue. A wave of nausea and weakness claims him, so he leaves the segmented body for later and takes Thompson's lower leg into the cargo bay. With the scissors he lacerates and peels the skin from the hock of meat. Then he arranges the calf and foot on a metal spit, propped between two crates above the three activated welding torches. The blue-white flames cook the flesh nicely…the smell of it roasting both titillates and nauseates him. He wretches, but has nothing inside him to throw up.

It's only venison, he tells himself.

After a few minutes he turns the spit, browning the other side.

He catches himself drooling and wipes his lips.

He cannot bear to wait for it to fully cook, so he settles for medium rare.

Picks it up like a massive chicken leg and takes his first bite, sinking teeth deep into the tender flesh. Tearing a mouthful from the bone. He chews, remembering that trip with his father…sitting around the camp fire. Eating what he'd killed.

Veal.

The exact consistency of fresh and tender veal.

He takes another bite. Expects to wretch it all up but doesn't. He swallows the second bite, and a third. A great contentment settles over him. For the first time in six years his belly is full. He falls asleep on the cargo bay floor, the hock of gnawed meat lying on his chest.

He dreams of brown gravy and hot, steaming biscuits.

··········

Less than a week.

Less than a week, and the meat has all gone bad. Energized and renewed by a succession of hunger-free days, Pelops realizes his mistake. Once the pods are open they won't freeze again. There is no freezer on the ship—it was never meant to sustain awake beings for more than a few hours at a time. He has no way to keep the meat from spoiling.

The next few days he makes himself sick by eating the rotten flesh. Half of his kill has been ruined. He smashes a naked shinbone against the wall in frustration.

He checks the time log on the bridge again. Just over eleven months to go. Eleven functioning CryoPods. Eleven bodies to sustain him. But only if he does things differently.

It all depends on me, he reminds himself. Eleven thousand men, women, and children.

If he keeps eating spoiled meat, he'll die. So he shoves the rest of Thompson into the airlock and ejects it into space.

What a waste. Just like Tanaka.

He waits as long as he can for the hunger to catch up with him again. Stares at the cold stars beyond the bridge viewport. Gazing into an emptiness that mirrors the void in his belly. He abstains as long as he can possibly stand it...nine days this time.

He harvests the next pod.

Staggs, E. Male. Big, guy, good physique.

Pelops thaws him out, sedates him, and straps him to the operating table. He can't kill this one like he did Thompson. He has to keep the meat fresh.

He dry heaves into a plastic waste bin...there is nothing inside him to throw up.

Think of Dantus. All those people...all those hungry people.

Wiping his wet eyes, he starts with the left leg, severing it at the knee.

Like last time, he roasts it and relieves his initial hunger. This time his guilt and nausea are drowned beneath a torrent of sheer gratitude. The meat (venison!) is savory, red and juicy on his tongue. His teeth tear through it with gusto. This man was an athlete...lots of tender muscle. Protein...nutrients...flavor.

Thompson was veal. Staggs is prime beef.

He waits as long as he can between each meal. Finally settles on eating once every 48 hours. In this way, he calculates his meat will last until Dantus. Eleven months. Sure, he'll suffer from lack of carbohydrates and vitamin C...but men have survived on all-meat diets for longer than that and been just fine. After this ordeal, after the converters are installed on the colony farms, there will be vegetables and fruits aplenty. A bounty to replace what he has lost. And the crew of the *Goya* will be remembered as heroes.

He pumps Staggs full of fresh sedative on a daily basis. The man remains oblivious as his legs and arms disappear, replaced by careful tourniquets that prevent him from bleeding to death. Pelops cleans him, looks after his bodily functions, makes sure he stays alive. Preserves as much of the man's dignity as he can.

Later, when only the head and torso are left, Pelops has to be more careful. Tricky to harvest a torso without killing the subject. He starts with a crude appendectomy. Next, he removes the liver. Then the spleen and stomach. Eventually, when Staggs is truly dead, he cracks open the chest cavity and removes the fist-sized heart.

Filet mignon, he tells himself. That's all it is.

He cooks the heart a special way, cutting it open to butterfly the meat.

Eats it sitting before the viewport, gazing into the abyss of blinking stars.

It is the finest piece of meat he's ever tasted. The heart, he decides, must be the choicest morsel in the human body. The prime muscle. The lights of the console blink across his face as his molars grind the meat and it slips down his gullet into his grateful stomach.

Staggs' brain, sliced in two, provides a double meal.

Tastes like stringy roast chicken.

Gray matter. White meat.

···•·•••··

Pelops harvests the next pod in the same way, but runs out of sedative after ten days. First Officer Bernard Hoffman wakes up on the table, restrained and entirely legless. His panicked screams draw Pelops into the infirmary.

"Shhhhhh..." Pelops comforts him. Gives him cool water to drink. "Take it easy, Hoffman."

"What...what's happening?" asks the terrified man, his brown eyes pleading.

"Shhhh...it's all right. It's just a bad dream. The mission is going to be a success. We're only ten months from Dantus. Go back to sleep."

Hoffman writhes against his restraints, tearing at the leather straps. The stumps of his legs begin to bleed. "What the fuck are you talking about? You look...look...where are my legs? What happened to my legs?" More screaming. He's only just noticed his missing appendages.

Pelops breaks down. He apologizes and explains everything. Tells Hoffman about the comet, about the radiation, about the pods, the lack of food, how he must ensure the mission's success. Reminds him of the thousands of people depending on his UV converters.

But Hoffman doesn't get any of it. He just screams.

Screams and screams until he makes himself hoarse.

Pelops begs him to stop, but the screams go on and on. He knocks Hoffman unconscious. But the man only wakes up screaming again. Pelops stuffs a rag in his mouth and leaves him on the table. In a few days, he won't have the strength to make any more noise.

Pelops uses a local anesthetic now instead of sedative. Hoffman may have to be awake during his amputations, but he won't feel a thing. His eyes grow large as golf balls as he watches Pelops remove his left arm, then later his right. He finally stops trying to scream. Spends most of his time unconscious now. Sometimes he wakes and mutters nonsense, so Pelops sits in a chair next to him, his belly full, and listens.

He reminds Hoffman that this sacrifice makes him a hero. One of the Saviors of Dantus colony.

When he harvests the torso this time he learns to salvage the intestines, filling them with minced organ meat. He discovers how to make a week's worth of sausages in this way before Hoffman's heart finally gives out.

He decides to keep the white bones instead of flushing them into the void.

He'll bury them on Dantus, beneath a growing field of wheat. With stone monuments.

He comes to this decision over dinner.

···•·•···

The next pod contains a gorgeous blonde woman. Mewes, C.

After he gets her onto the table, he wakes her and talks at length about their situation. Lets her know the heroic role she will be playing in the mission. She weeps, begs, pleads with him. He sobs with her, sharing in the tragedy of the situation. He unbuckles her restraints and embraces her tenderly.

"Don't worry," he whispers in her ear, arms wrapped around her. "Don't worry. It'll be okay."

He chases her down when she slips away from him, but manages to corner her in the cargo bay and knocks her senseless with a crowbar.

I could let her join me, he thinks. It wouldn't be so lonely then. Maybe there's enough meat in the pods for both of us...

He smacks himself across the face. Stupid! He knows two people surviving the rest of this journey is impossible. There's simply not enough food. Both would starve and Dantus would die.

So it's back to the table where the harvesting begins. Still a good supply of sedative, so she won't feel any pain.

Somehow, she wakes in the middle of things and starts wailing. The sound pierces his ears in a way that Hoffman's guttural bellows never could. He has to gag her so he can finish.

Later, enjoying the last of her, he smacks his lips and remembers the lovely blue of her eyes. So delectable on his tongue, like tender Swedish meatballs.

· · · · · · · · · ·

The void persists, and so does his hunger. It returns like clockwork every 48 hours.

He doesn't bother looking at the name of his next harvest. He cuts out the tongue first to avoid any more conversation.

A few days later he goes to the table-bound crewman, removes the gag and offers him a taste of his own thigh meat. The man eats ravenously, saving his questions until his own hunger is sated. Then he stares at Pelops and tries to form words. The stub of his tongue rattles around inside his mouth. His mute eyes plead desperately. They remind Pelops of the blonde's blue eyes.

He eats them next.

The human body is indeed an amazing thing.

So many different flavors.

· · · · · · · · · ·

Five and a half months left, five CryoPods unopened.

With proper rationing, he will make it. However, the anesthetic is nearly gone.

This complicates things, but is in no way a barrier to success.

The mission is all that matters.

He has it down to a science now: Open the pod. Tie the sleeper's hands and feet with copper wire before they come fully awake. Drag them to in the infirmary, strap them to the table. Remove the tongue, put the gag in place. Ignore the screams. Ignore the blood. Slice. Tourniquet. Ignore the squirming, the moans of pain. The tears, the squealing.

Forty-eight hours later. Slice. Tourniquet. It's no longer a person, despite all the writhing and moaning and muffled screams. It's only meat.

Forty-eight hours after that. Slice. Tourniquet. They're usually too weak to scream much more after this.

Some are lucky enough to sleep through the whole process from this point on.

···•••••···

Three more crew members and thirteen weeks later. Only two months away from Dantus.

His next meal is the last female. But this fact barely registers; Pelops no longer sees them as women or men.

They're only meat.

All of us...charting the course of history...only meat.

Yet this one is something special. When he slices into her abdomen he finds her secret. The command board would have grounded her had they known. Or maybe she didn't know. Two months along before Cryo, he estimates. Her eyes are glazed by the time he discovers the prize inside her. Strapped, gagged, limbless, and unblinking, she stares at the antiseptic ceiling as he vivisects her. And there it is...

A tiny thing...only 18 centimeters. Barely recognizable as human. More like something amphibian...a vestige of our marine origins.

Miniscule arms more like fins, or flippers. The stubs of barely formed legs. Round head no larger than an orange.

So we begin...the seed from which all of us grow.

Expanding and developing meat on a rack of expanding and hardening bone.

He carries it to the bridge, shows it to the stars. He imagines the universe itself as one big womb...an inescapable uterus containing planets, stars, and galaxies.

In the end, it's little more than a snack.

Sweet, a bit crunchy. A fresh flavor.

Bit of a fishy aftertaste.

Its mother lasts another eight days.

···•••••···

In these months he's decided to put all those bones to good use. At first he carves them into tiny figurines: goblins, serpents, scorpions, or wholly new creatures birthed in his imagination. Then he decides on a project. A sculpture. He drags all the bones and skulls onto the bridge and works nonstop in the pale starlight, baring his creative spirit to the naked universe.

Directly ahead, a red star shines. Wolf 359. His destination, the color of spilled blood gleaming brightly in a mantle of eternal night.

A new god observes and blesses the success of the mission. Its lofty head is a ring of ten bleached skulls gazing in every direction. Its body is a tangled conglomeration of leg bones, arm bones, and rib cages. It wears a necklace of finger and toe bones. With screws and caulk and ductile adhesive he has brought it to life.

He sits before it in the captain's chair, discussing with it the secrets of the universe, watching the void outside and the red star that is their final destination.

His creation tells him things, terrible things that he has long suspected, now confirmed in the glaring honesty of cold starlight. He eats his meals before it, calling upon it to bless the meat.

He tears into his latest chop, red and quivering.

Fresh and raw, that is the only way to eat meat.

His new god approves.

·········

With two months to go and two CroPods left, Pelops gets careless.

The man inside (Harmon, Sgt. G.) revives while he's being tied, his frosty eyelids flickering open. Some fight-or-flight mechanism kicks in and he knocks Pelops from the opened pod, spilling out on top of him.

"Wha..." he stammers. "Whaaaaa..."

Pelops tries to club him on the head with a wrench but Sgt. Harmon is already too fast. He rolls away and pulls his hands free of the wire. He kicks Pelops in the side of the head. Stars swim crazily in Pelops' eyes.

Pelops regains his senses to find Harmon holding him against the wall, pressing the tip of a screwdriver against his neck. The sergeant is still cold and reeks of cryonic fluid. He breathes hotly in Pelops' face, the crystals on his beard beginning to melt.

"Who are you?" he asks. "And what the hell are you doing?"

He shoves the screwdriver painfully into Pelops' skin, drawing a trickle of blood.

"I'm Dr. Pelops," he says. "I had to...awaken you prematurely."

Harmon looks around the corridor. Sees the empty pods. All but one now missing its inhabitant.

"Where are they?" His teeth are gritted as his black eyes bore into Pelops'. "Tell me!"

"Dead..." Pelops admits. "There was a comet, or a meteor...some kind of radiation cloud...took out the auto-drive and the pods. I was lucky."

Harmon blinks, thinking. Considering. *He knows I'm not telling him everything.* His eyes fall upon the last functioning CryoPod.

"Why didn't you wake Captain Tyler?"

"I...I was going to," says Pelops.

Harmon grabs Pelops' throat in an iron grip. "Then why tie me up? Huh?"

Pelops says nothing. Gasps for air.

"You look like hell," says Harmon, examining him. Hair and beard a matted rat's nest. Face sunken, skin sallow. Nails long as claws.

Can he smell the dead on my breath?

"How long?" asks Harmon. Rams his knee into Pelops' groin. Pelops falls to the cold floor. Harmon bends and holds the screwdriver's tip to his eye. "How long?" he shouts.

"F-f-fourteen months!" cries Pelops.

Shock spills across Harmon's shaggy face. "Fourteen..." He looks again at the empty rows of CryoPods, stares down the corridor in either direction. Sniffs the air like a suspicious hound. "Fourteen months...how did you survive?"

Pelops clutches his throbbing groin and says nothing.

Harmon kicks him in the stomach.

"How? Tell me! Say it!"

Pelops tells him. Doesn't look at his face. Hears him start to wretch.

"All that matters is the success of this mission..." Pelops growls. "And I'm the only one who can get those converters up and running."

Harmon is strangely quiet.

"We've got two more months," says Pelops.

Harmon's boot comes down hard on his face.

Darkness.

···•·•····

"He's a sick fuck!"

Pelops regains consciousness, wrapped in a web of pain. No, it's the copper wire. He's propped upright inside one of the defunct pods. In the corridor Harmon stands arguing with another man. The inhabitant of the last pod, the ship's captain (Tyler, Capt. H.). A sinking feeling as he realizes that Harmon has revived Tyler far too early. He tries to move his arms and legs, but he's securely bound. He listens to their conversation, watching them in the corner of his eye.

"I know how you feel, soldier," says Captain Tyler, still wiping frost from his flight suit, rubbing a hand across the back of his neck. "But Pelops is the only one who knows how to set up those UV converter domes and get them operational. We can't just execute him."

"Execute? Who said anything about an execution? You don't execute a mad dog, captain. You put it down. And that's what we have here. He fuckin' ate them! Didn't you hear me?"

"I heard you, son." A weary sigh.

"Come on," says Harmon. "Let me show you the nice little present he built for us on the bridge. Once you see that I'm sure you'll agree to shoving him out the airlock at the least."

The sound of their boots tramping down the corridor.

Pelops waits.

Prays.

Mutters poems to his bone god.

Eventually the voices return, growing in volume, punctuated by the sounds of boots on metal.

"...even if we do this, we're still going to starve. There's no food left on board and we can't enter Cryo again. This is the end of the line for us."

"Then it doesn't matter, does it? Let me kill him. One last good thing before we die. Then we'll set the auto-destruct...go out in a blaze of glory. Better than starving to death."

Captain Tyler has no response to that.

The two men stand before the open CryoPod now, looking at Pelops.

"Captain..." Pelops says, "you know as well as I do—"

"Shut up, freak!" Sgt. Harmon's fist slams into his gut. The air rushes from his lungs, along with the words he failed to utter.

Harmon lifts a service pistol to Pelops' chin, the barrel digging into his jawbone.

"All of us may have to die," Harmon tells him, "but you're going first you cannibal fu—"

Thud.

A flash of silver above his head, a meaty sound, and Harmon goes down. Captain Tyler stands over him with the wrench in his hand. Its round end drips dark blood like syrup, and a clot of hair and skin hangs there.

Tyler drops the wrench and peels the coils of wire away from Pelops' wrists and ankles.

The captain is silent for awhile as Pelops rubs his limbs to get the circulation flowing again. Tyler stares at his fallen officer, leans against the wall. Tired. Ready to accept his fate.

"You did the right thing doctor," says Tyler. His sunken eyes turn toward Pelops. They are as black and glittering as the void. "The famine on Dantus could kill tens of thousands. This mission has to succeed."

Pelops nods. His stomach growls. He is ravenous.

"Can you still make it work?" asks Tyler.

Pelops stares down at the unconscious soldier. Makes a few mental calculations. Rubs his sore temple.

"Yes," he says. "With your help, the mission will still succeed."

Tyler helps Pelops carry Harmon into the infirmary.

·········

Pelops carefully rations out pieces of Harmon over the next few weeks. Tyler holds out for sixteen days but eventually joins him for a slight meal. Pelops insists.

"It's imperative to this mission that you stay alive captain," he says. "Just a little while longer."

Tyler won't go near the infirmary. The blow to Harmon's head inflicted some kind of brain damage, so he remains comatose as he's carved to bits day after day. Just as well. No screams to deal with, but still Tyler takes it hard. He sits on the bridge in his chair most days...staring at the red star growing ever brighter directly ahead.

Pelops thought the captain would dismantle the bone god...but Tyler doesn't seem to mind it. Or perhaps he's frightened of it. Too frightened of its power to risk desecrating it. He must know that it, not him, now rules the *Goya*.

Harmon would have lasted longer if Pelops did not share him with Tyler. However, Tyler ate so very little...only enough to keep himself alive for another month. Finally, when the last of Harmon has been consumed and his bones have been added to the god's intricate frame, Tyler comes to Pelops. A broken man, emaciated, begging to be put out of his misery.

"It's all my fault," Tyler tells him, weeping. Pelops listens. "It was my responsibility to make sure we had extra emergency kits. I didn't do it."

Pelops leads him into the infirmary.

Tyler babbles, weeping. "Trying to maximize profits...cut corners...it should have been a simple trip. I did it to save money, Pelops. I killed us all for money..."

"Not all of us, Captain," says Pelops.

Tyler nods, wipes his swollen eyes. He must be thinking of those starving families on Dantus now.

"I am sorry there is no more anesthetic for this Captain."

"Just do it," says Tyler. He unholsters his pistol, lays it on a nearby counter. "Get it over with. Kill me. For Dantus...for all those children. Kill me now..."

"If you wouldn't mind lying on the table first," says Pelops. Tyler complies.

Pelops straps him down securely and prepares the laser scalpel.

"What are you doing?" asks Tyler. "One shot between the eyes will do it. Make it quick, Pelops."

Pelops hesitates.

It seems the captain has misunderstood his role here.

"We've still got over a month of travel time, sir..." Pelops explains. "If I kill you now, I'm afraid you'll spoil before we reach Dantus."

Tyler's shock registers as a moment of silence. "No," he says, shaking his head. "No, you can eat for two or three weeks, and the last few days you can go without. You'll be fine...as soon as you touch down you'll have food on Dantus. You don't need me to last that long, Pelops!"

"I'm sorry, Captain," says Pelops. "But I don't like to go hungry."

He ignores the captain's screaming and writhing as he puts the gag on him. Same old reaction. Pulling against the restraints, wearing the throat raw with grunts and smothered screams.

"It's for the mission," Pelops reminds him.

He starts with the legs, as usual.

Tyler, once a strong and vital man, lasts nearly three weeks on the table.

•••••••••

In the end, with the last few scraps of Tyler gone, Pelops still has six days left to starve.

The red star swells brighter than ever among the starfields in the viewport.

Pelops sits in the captain's chair and stares into the shimmering void.

Everything from plants to mammals is fueled by the light of stars. Sunlight fuels photosynthesis, which feeds the plants that in turn feed the animals we eat on earth. Photons and atoms being constantly recycled and reinvented, a molecular dance of destruction and creation that never ends. Everything consumes and is consumed.

We are all made of starlight.

Brilliant starlight, pulsing bright as blood inside us.

It's all energy...and energy is neither created nor destroyed.

His stomach growls.

•••••••••

In the glow of a red sun, the *Goya* touches down atop a broad plateau littered with wrecked vehicles and rusting machines. Pelops stumbles from the open hatch into the ruddy glow. He walks with a single crutch made of bones. His right leg is missing below the knee, a fresh tourniquet wrapped tight about the stump.

He held out for two difficult days before the hunger won its final victory.

Still, he has made it to this place. A nice prosthetic limb waits in his future.

He blinks in the harsh glow of infrared daylight and stares across the plateau at the colonial city.

He stumbles through the wreckage toward the dilapidated walls. The wind hurls black sand against him, raking like claws across his flight suit and his exposed cheeks, coating his beard with dirt.

Where is everyone?

There should be a welcoming party to greet him. They've waited seven years.

The famine won here, he realizes. I'm too late.

He walks through dried fields where crops have died in geometrical rows. Now only the fossilized stubs of cornstalks rear from the smothering sand.

He sees the distant towers more clearly now. Skeletal and stark they stand against the purple sky. He walks with his crutch among the hulks of dead machines, until the sun sinks below the flat horizon. The ruined city looms before him. No signs of life.

Hunger did this. Is there anyone left at all?

He calls out. His voice echoes between crumbling walls, along vacant streets.

The bleak stars emerge to glimmer in the night sky.

We are all made of starlight.

Finally a group of thin shadows emerges from a ramshackle hut near a fallen tower.

Survivors. They converge upon him like wary dogs trailing rags.

He sees their young faces, smudged with dirt and lean as wolves.

They smile, showing rotted teeth. He waves.

They carry sharp knives that gleam in the twilight.

"Wait!" he says. "My name is Pelops—from the earth ship *Goya*. I've brought what you need."

"Yes," says a raggedy woman, brandishing her knife. "We can always use fresh meat."

It is impossible for him to run on a single leg.

Their knives sink deeply, a dozen whispers of metal.

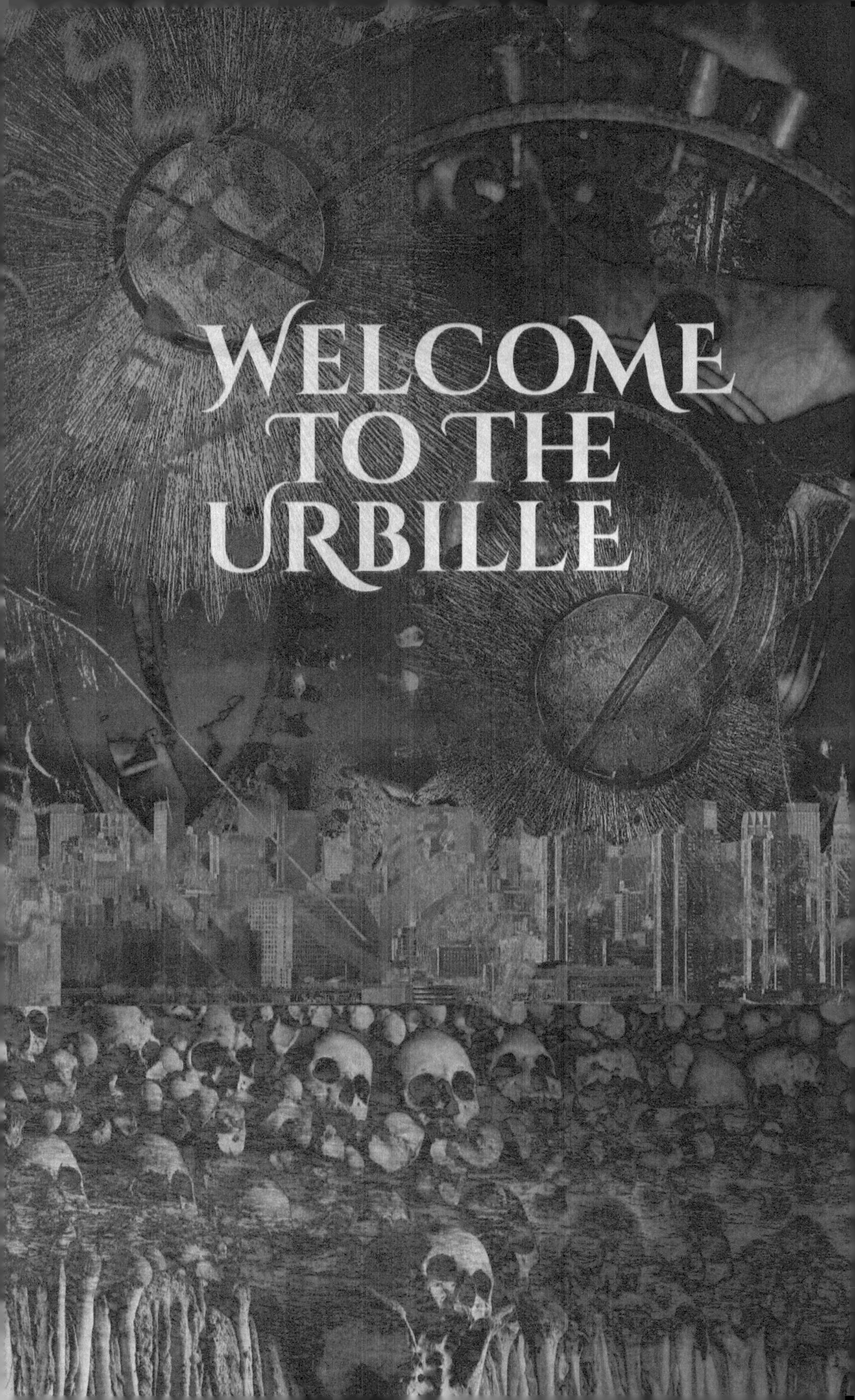

Welcome to the Urbille

THE KEY TO YOUR HEART IS MADE OF BRASS

Wake up. Something is wrong.

Greasy orange light smears the dark. Only one of your optical lenses is functional. The walls are slabs of corroded metal with rust patterns like dumb staring phantoms. You lie awkwardly across the oily flagstones of an alley where curtains of black chains obscure the night. Bronze lanterns hang from those chains, but most of them are dead. Lightless. Like your left optical.

Struggling to hands and knees, you realize your porcelain face has been shattered. White shards gleam on the alley floor between puddles of greenish scum. You lift a gloved hand to explore your ruined visage; the upper left side took the brunt of the blow. Your fingers brush across the silver skull beneath the missing porcelain.

This won't do at all. To be seen without one's face. It could damage your reputation.

It might even be illegal.

That same blow—the one you don't quite remember—must have dislodged your left optical. There it is now, lying among the porcelain fragments, a thumb-sized orb of blue glass. Removing your gloves, you wipe the scum from its glistening surface and carefully reattach it to the vitreous filaments inside your left socket. Much better. Your depth perception is restored. Inside its silver casement, your tender brain begins processing images from the repaired optical. You slide the blue orb carefully back into place, grateful it wasn't damaged.

Now at least you can see. And perhaps remember...

The girl...the Doxie...you remember her ceramic face, exquisitely formed with tiny lips painted crimson. The gentle amber of her opticals peeking through the beautiful mask. Her gown, a flowing affair of scarlet satin and black lace. The red fabric hugs the supple curves of her torso before spreading out to engulf her lower body. You met her in the alley, beneath the dead lanterns. By that fact alone, you know what she must be.

She is a Beatific, like you...but not like you at all. She's a prostitute.

Your bodies are sculpted to the same degree of slim perfection, your faces designed for maximum aesthetic value. Yet she is a creature of the streets, the gutters, a plaything of her nameless clients. It dawns on you with a sick familiarity that *you* are one of those clients.

You snap out of the vision, frightened by rushing memories. Your waistcoat is stained by the filth of the alley, but you brush off the grit as best you can. Near a receptacle of eroded copper tubing you find your top hat. Your expensive walking stick appears to be gone...stolen. Perhaps it was the bludgeon that shattered your face; the pommel was a bronze orb sculpted in the likeness of a grinning toad. A formidable weapon, but it had done you no good. Your attacker, however, had found it a useful tool.

The purple neon glow of the street is a watery vision at the end of the alley. Before you can go out there and find another face to wear, you must look presentable. There are certain rules of Beatific conduct, and you must adhere. Reputation is everything in the Urbille.

Checking your neck kerchief, you discover the emptiness in your breast pocket. A shock of panic runs through your lean limbs, and the gears of your joints grind like creaking doors. Your fingers invade the pocket, searching but finding nothing. The key to your heart is gone. Horror rushes down your throat like a bitter oil. The gentle whirring and clicking in your chest cavity is now the sound of ticking dread.

You sink to your knees, searching the alley. Where is the key? You remember inserting it into the narrow slot in your bare chest last morning, turning it full round ninety-nine times, enough to power the gears and cogs and wheels and springs of your Beatific body for another twenty-four hours. Winding the clockwork mechanism that is your living core. The key is made of shining yellow brass, and like all Beatific heart-keys it is one-of-a-kind, a customized symbol of your status.

It's not here!

You paw at your trousers and find that ironically your pocket watch has not been stolen. It is almost three a.m. You have six hours to get a replacement key made. The alternative is unthinkable...winding down to an inanimate collection of useless parts while your brain rapidly dies inside its silver casement.

The Doxie...she must have taken the key. But that makes no sense. She...or someone with her...clubbed you over the head with your own walking stick and stole your heart key. Why would anyone else want it? It will not wind the heart of any other Beatific. Its only value is the daily function it plays in keeping you, and only you, alive. This is the course of your existence: Wake, wind the heart-key, get dressed, and go about the business of your day.

You had never considered the possibility of a day without your key.

You have never considered what that would mean.

Duplicating one's heart-key is a High Crime. Beatifics have been dragged off to prison for contemplating it aloud. The Potentates' decree was *One Key for One Heart*. "We must preserve our individuality or risk becoming soulless copies of one another." The words of Tribune Anteus, as broadcast on high-frequency transistor during the last key duplication scandal.

Fear breaks the icy stillness of your reverie.

The key isn't here, so there is only one option.

You must solicit the Keymaker.

And you have six hours.

··•••·•••··

You pull the top hat down low to disguise your shattered cheek. At this late hour no one of any consequence is likely to be about. At least not in this quarter of the Urbille, where Beatifics seldom wander. Here among the decaying spires of ancient metal, the bulwarks of rust and corrosion, the moldering and brittle bones of bygone industrialism. Decrepit factories have become squatter's kingdoms, and iron bridges span brackish waterways where finned, scaly things slither and swim.

Lanterns gleam atop iron posts, the flames of viridian gas dancing in their soiled globes. This is the Rusted Zone, where the metals of previous ages have gathered like flotsam washed upon a dirty beach. You would never come here in the light of day. But you have needs, and your wife has been dead thirty years. A man...even a Beatific man...can only hold out so long.

As you shuffle into the deserted street your elastic skin tightens. The sign of a brewing rabidity in the atmosphere. A storm will break soon.

Your time with the Doxie comes back to you now. A shameful memory of fulfilling base desires. This isn't the first time you've crawled among the rust to seek the company of whores. You always feel pity for them, even as you enjoy the pleasures of their trade. You remember this one well...your gloved fingers against the base of her skull, the golden glow of her opticals behind the porcelain facade. Revulsion intrudes as you remember the slick softness of her thoughts...the way your consciousness slid hungrily into hers. You almost feel sorry for her, and all her kind, those who open their minds to the nearest paying stranger. Until you remember what she did to you...broke your face and stole the key to your heart.

Her psyche was a red and pulsing universe. You soared there like some winged beast, looking down upon the nooks and crannies of intellect from the lofty cloud-realm of her thoughtsphere. You did not consider the countless number of other men who had invaded her mentality. Somehow this never matters in the throes of psychic ecstasy.

You played with stray impulses, gnawed on the raw assumptions of her personal reality, dominated her cognition. Such a satisfying conquest of the female mind by the lusty intelligence of the male. She was sweet, this one...yet something untouchable lingered beyond the curtains of her memory...something she refused to share with any client, including you. Your thoughts slammed against those gates like battering rams...you wanted to know her every secret. You wanted to claim her utterly, never caring that you might discover what caused her to fall from grace, why this Beatific maiden became a Doxie trollop. In the heady grip of your blind need, you strove to penetrate deeper.

That's when it must have happened...someone in that dingy alley grabbed your bronze-topped cane and brought it down against your forehead with all force. The mental link was broken immediately as you lost consciousness. Your mind yanked from hers as your body fell to the filthy flagstones. She must have had a partner. But why? What could she...they... possibly gain by stealing your heart-key? If they wanted you dead, they could have killed you right there.

The wind picks up, pelting you with clouds of sandy rust. The twisting street (you never caught the name) is narrow, and few other figures move in the pre-rabid gloom. Outside the doorway of a ramshackle saloon a pair of Clatterpox ramble noisily. The neon placard above the door reads THE DISTENDED BLADDER. Three more Clatterpox lumber across the street ahead of you, heading for the tavern. Their cylindrical bodies rumble and clang, supported by thin iron legs and metal-slab feet. Their chest furnaces burn hot, exuding foul vapors and smokes from the various holes, tubes, and vents placed about their grotesque frames. They turn oval heads toward you as you walk past, staring with flat optical lenses of gray glass.

Poor souls. You do not envy their mean existence, hearts fueled by chunks of burning anthracite, their days spent working mindless jobs just to afford the black rocks that keep them ambulatory. They are the poor of the Urbille, the wretched working class. If they recognize you as a Beatific, they may assault you. Class distinctions are dangerous among the rust. If they knew you were the head of House Honore, what would they do? Tear you apart and sell your gears for scrap?

Now it comes to you: Could the Doxie have known? She might have been someone important at one time. She might even be an ancestral enemy. Someone your father or grandfather ruined in some forgotten business dealing. Could the theft of your heart-key be some form of belated revenge?

One of the Clatterpox shouts something as you hurry past, but you turn the corner without looking back. The sound of their rattling bodies follows you down the street, but you turn and turn again, finally losing them in the shadows of a lightless thoroughfare. Here the sky is clear, and you see the swirling constellations of night. Unfortunately, this welcome sight does you no good because the rabidity has arrived.

It swoops down upon the dark streets like some predatory bird of legend. A tightening of the air itself, a freezing and cracking of atmospheric forces. It keens in your ears like a wailing tea pot, and the wind takes your hat into the night. Fissures in the fabric of space/time erupt along the street. You've walked right into the heart of this one. The air splits open not six yards away, and you see another world revealed beyond the throbbing gash.

It's green and steaming...a jungle like the ones from ancient botanical texts. Colossal lizards feast on one another, tearing flesh, skin, and tendon with terrible fangs. The sounds of their shrieking flows from the vacuity. The gravity of that primeval world pulls at your lapels. If you let it, it will pull you through and your life will wind down in that nameless wilderness. The gears of your legs grind as you pull away from the hovering fissure. The wind screams. You walk against it and pass another vacuity, a rip in existence that pulses and expands, bleeding gravity. Beyond this one you see a night-dark sea and a distant shore lined with luminous towers.

Golden-skinned beings sail the waters in skiffs of pale wood. They must see the vacuity from their side as well because their glowing emerald opticals turn toward you as you walk past. The vision dies as the vacuity begins to shrink.

You stumble into the dying wind as the storm subsides. A dozen more vacuities glimmer in your vicinity. You ignore them. At a meeting of four streets ahead, you see a Clatterpox staring at one of the fissures as it closes completely. Then his round head turns toward you with a fresh burst of vapor and a hissing sound. Is it the same one, who called after you? He stares uncertainly in the post-rabidity calm. You step toward the windows of an all-night merchant on the corner.

Above the doorway the name HOFFSTEIN'S gleams in torrid blue neon. You walk inside and find yourself hemmed by rows of crowded shelves. The proprietor is a handsome Beatific, but he greets you with a suspicious glare as you approach the display of porcelains. No time to be choosy. You pick the first masculine face on the stand and carry it to the counter.

"You're out late, Sir Honore," says the proprietor. "Some wild party, eh?"

"Something like that," you say.

"Must have gotten a bit rough..." He nods toward your busted face.

You say nothing, avoiding his glare.

"Anything else?"

"No," you say. "Yes...a hat. That one." You pick a simple black topper. It's been nearly an hour since you awoke in the alley. You must move quicker.

"Seventeen brilliants," says the merchant.

"Put it on my account," you say. Earlier tonight you emptied your pockets to pay the Doxie.

"Very well. Have a good morning, Sir Honore."

You cast your old face into the store's dustbin and replace it with this splendid new one.

New hat sitting firmly on your head, you head back into the street.

Making for the Steeple Road, you notice a shadowy figure trailing a block behind you. You stop near a pile of metal sculpted into a hideous beast and stare back at the pursuer. A Clatterpox, of course. Now you can hear his hissing, rattling locomotion as he draws nearer. He carries a club or a dark blade in one of his metal fists...you cannot tell which.

Now you run. The Rusted Zone becomes a blur of gray, brown, and dirty neon, and you ache to put it all behind you. The Clatterpox could never move as fast as you. Soon you see the Steeple Gate, and the faces of its stone gargoyles glare at you like old friends. You speak the word of command and the gate opens. On its other side the streets are well-lit with spherical lanterns kept shiny and clean. As the iron gate closes behind you, you realize the Clatterpox might know the command word as well. So you hurry, shuffling between the houses of ornate stone and their lawns of crushed glass until you see the spiked fence of the Keymaker's estate.

A great brass bell hangs at the gate, and you hate to ring it so late. Your pocket watch says 4:03 a.m. But it can't be helped. You ring the bell once. Wait. Again. No lights go on inside the stone mansion. You ring it a third time and notice the front gate is ajar. You pull it open just enough to creep inside. The lawn is immaculate, filled with sculptures of glass and stone in the shapes of skulls, fantastic machinery, and abstract forms recalling the Organic Age. Your shoes sound far too loud as you walk across the crushed glass toward the Keymaker's door. He will be annoyed to be awakened so late (or so early), but you will offer him whatever price he demands to cast a mold of your chest lock and make a new key before 9:00 a.m. You have little choice. His workshop is attached the mansion, a domed miniature factory of green stone, possibly jade. Certainly you cannot be the first panicked Beatific who has come to him after hours with a lost key emergency.

The front doors are hanging open and a single lantern burns somewhere inside. Something is not quite right here. The estate is not large, but the nearest neighbor is several hundred yards away. Perhaps someone out there heard you ring the gate-bell, or perhaps not. But the front door should not be open.

You almost stumble over a lump of metal at your feet. A two-headed canine lying on its side. A lean body of iron and bronze covered in fuzzy, elastic skin. Both its necks have been broken, and the inner workings of its guts have been torn out. A scattered mess of cogs and gears litters the foyer.

You walk cautiously toward the dim light, already knowing what you will find. Ahead lies the parlor where the Keymaker keeps his bookshelves. You were here twelve years ago for a party honoring his fourteenth decade of service. You remember his great easy chair, where he sat and entertained his guests with stories of his youth. Now you slip into that curtained room and see him sitting in the same chair, dressed in a satin night-robe. The lantern flickers unsteadily on the table beside him. He is headless, his body reclining on the cushioned velvet, gloved hands resting on his lap. His head lies a few feet away, fractured porcelain cheek against the burgundy carpet. Scattered bits of copper and wire spill across his chest and lap. Once again fear steals your ability to move.

The Keymaker is dead.

You press your ear to his breast, but you hear no mechanized whirring, no clicking of cogs or sighing springs. The lantern oil burns low; this happened hours ago. You know his brain has died inside that severed skull. He is gone.

You stumble backwards until you fall into the soft embrace of a couch.

The Keymaker was not a true Beatific...he did not inherit his title...he worked to earn it. He was a laborer, basically. He had no fortune or noble lineage. But he was a man of honor. And he was the only man who could save your life.

A noise breaks the silence of the dead man's study. Something heavy, moving on the terrace. No, in the foyer. You glance around for a weapon, an exit, something, anything...an ancient cutlass hangs on the wall, blade eaten by rust. You pull it down and brandish it, fists wrapped around the hilt. You have no idea how to fight with blade or pistol.

The sound moves nearer. Heavy footsteps. Now the hissing of steam through a vent.

You remember the sound of the Clatterpox following you, and sure enough he stands in the doorway of the parlor. A terrible thing of corroded iron, leaking pistons, purple vapors, and swiveling joints. He stares at you with his flat gray opticals. His mouth is a horizontal slit, dividing round chin from oval head. He sighs at you...no, it's the sound of hot air leaking from his heart-furnace. The grill of his chest emits orange light where the anthracite burns hot.

"Honore," he says, voice flat like the ringing of tin. "We have something you want."

Now you recognize the weapon he carries in his left hand.

It is your walking stick with the bronze toad head.

••••••••••

"Who are you?" You wave the useless cutlass at the Clatterpox like some protective talisman. But you know it offers no protection.

"My name is Flux."

"You're with the Doxie."

"Yes."

"You assaulted me and stole the key to my heart."

"Yes."

"Why?"

The Clatterpox shrugs its rusted shoulders. Something *pings* inside its whirring guts.

"Because you have wealth. We need it."

"Extortion...the device of cowards." Your words sound brave. But terror swims in your chest cavity, runs along your plastic skin like spilled oil.

"That may be, but we have your brass key. We want a hundred-thousand brilliants. Bring them to the Well of Bones at sunrise. Or we will drop your key in the well and you will never find it. You'll wind down. Your brain will rot and die."

You consider this. Your ancestral fortune is vast. You won't miss a hundred thousand brilliants. Besides, there are no other options.

"You...you killed the Keymaker."

"Of course," says the Clatterpox. "Don't be late." He thumps across the foyer and out into the courtyard, then beyond the gate and down the road into the Rusted Zone.

You lay the ancient sword down at the Keymaker's feet. There is no time to mourn for him. The sun will rise in less than two hours.

You run along the winding avenues of the Good Hills, ignoring the stone domiciles of your fellow Beatifics. Rarely do any lights glow in the oval windows at this rude hour. You dash north, heading toward your manor house, and the fractured moon rises above the palace of the Potentates at the top of the great hill. Its crumbling walls and crenellated towers are older than the Urbille itself, and large enough to house a second city, which according to rumor, it does. The Potentates live inside its walls of mossy stone, and not even Beatifics are allowed to sully its precincts with their presence. Once per year the Potentates emerge for the Parade of Iniquities, carried by clockwork horses through the streets of the Urbille, wrapped in their dark robes and chains of gold, their bulbous heads veiled, the dark shadows of their opticals scanning the populace in silent judgment. They are terribly tall, the Potentates, hence the immensity of their stone citadel. Rumors speak also of the labyrinth below that towering fortress...a dungeon into which only the most evil and unrepentant of lawbreakers are cast. You imagine the Doxie and her murderous Clatterpox cast into that dark maze, pursued by terrible ancient things.

The Honore Estate lies three miles from the outer wall of the great palace. You reach it an hour before sunrise and race through your front doors toward the sealed portal that guards the lower vaults. Once the house was full of servants, semi-organic toadlings imported from stabilized vacuities. They kept the manse from disintegrating and the cobwebs from accumulating. Now, many years after Siormah wound down and left you, your outer garden is a hideous collection of weeds and vine. Your walls are clammy and the stone crumbles a bit more each year. You often sit here, in the heart of your inherited power, and contemplate the transitory nature of things. At times you can almost feel the pillars and the stone slabs of your walls decaying slowly into blackened sand. Stone is no more permanent than metal. You realized this long ago. Your stone mansion will one day collapse, as will all the Beatific dwellings, and eventually the stone palace itself will tumble down upon the bloated skulls of the Potentates. Will anyone still be alive when that day comes?

At the bottom of the spiral stair you speak the Word of Lineage and the round vault door swings open. Inside a hung lantern lights itself automatically and a world of clashing colors fills the chamber. The floor is hidden under pile after pile of brilliants, precious stones in all the shades of ruby, amber, emerald, topaz, sapphire, violet, opal, and diamond. Here is the great fortune that your ancestors built. And on the four walls of this chamber, emerging from the gray stone in bas-relief, are the faces of those ancestors.

Your father, your grandfather, your great-grandfather, and a dozen more, going back a thousand years to the last Organic Age. Their opticals open and stare at you with flame-bright lenses. Somehow, as you wade into the room and begin scooping brilliants into an iron chest, their stone lips move and they speak in whispering voices. You try to ignore them, you know their cruel wisdom. You've long passed the days when you would come down here for advice. You learned eventually that your ancestors were just as ignorant of the world as you. Their accumulation of wealth and title was their only virtue.

"What are you doing, René?" asks the stone face of your father.

"You fool!" seethes your grandfather's visage. "Wasting our wealth again!"

"I need this…all of it," you say, not bothering to meet their radiant opticals. "Leave me alone."

"Leave him alone, he says!" Your father again. "Still haven't learned to respect your elders?"

"What are you doing?" asks another face, some older predecessor. Each succeeding member of the family lived longer than the one who came before. "What could be so costly?"

"I've lost the key to my heart!" you shout, overcome by strange emotions. "I have to buy it back."

"By all the Gods That Never Were," swears your grandfather's face. "That old scam again. You are being taken for a rube, boy."

Another stone face speaks, someone from terribly far down the line of ages.

"All of these stones are worthless, you know," says the face. "Bits of worthless glass. The Potentates manufacture these by the million."

"Nonsense!" says your father's visage. "Their worth is what made us a great family."

"No, he is right," says another ancient face. "The last true jewels were lost ages ago. This is all fakery. Our wealth is an illusion."

You scrape more armloads of the brilliants into the chest, hurrying. To stay in this chamber too long will drive you mad. Don't listen to their babble. They are liars and fools. And they are dead.

"René," says another nameless face of stone. "*All* wealth is an illusion. When you join us you will understand."

"Join us," says another face. "You are so close already."

"Join us," says another, through stone lips.

"Shut up!" you shout.

The faces grow still, but their fiery opticals stare at you.

You close the chest of brilliants, heft it to your shoulder, and leave the vault. The door slams closed behind you like the thunder of a collapsing empire.

You race up the stairs and check your pocket watch.

Less than an hour until sunrise.

You run out the front door, cross the overgrown courtyard, and head down the hillside.

Early risers are lighting their lanterns as you pass the gates of Beatific mansions.

Once through the Steeple Gate you head into the Rusted Zone, directly toward the Well of Bones, clutching the chest in your tireless arms, a precious ransom of a hundred-thousand worthless brilliants.

··•••••···

Along the Avenue of Copper Lungs you nearly stumble into a fizzleshade as it manifests in a haze of wispy hair and antique clothing. It stares at you with transparent opticals, pleading for help. They always want the same thing...the completion of unfinished business. Something left undone before they perished.

*Please...*this one moans...*my name is Enri...I left two children behind when I died. Will you find them and tell them about my hidden gold?*

"You died three-thousand years ago," you mutter, shuffling along under the weight of your burden. "Your children are long dead, too."

The phantom follows you, blinking in and out of existence, losing its purchase in the living world.

*Pleeaaaasssse...*it wails. *The children will starve! You must help me. I bled to death in this gutter...don't leave them alone.*

"Piss off!" you shout, a stab of guilt in your clicking chest.

Behind you the fizzleshade blinks into nothingness.

The light of pre-dawn limns the corroded skyline with an amber glow. The exact shade of the Doxie's opticals. You scurry along the streets of twisted metal, avoiding crowds of Clatterpox on their way to the factories. Gendarmes in black trenchcoats and stove-pipe hats patrol the streets now. Their faces are clusters of optical lenses, swiveling in multiple directions at once, observing the early morning activity, always alert for anything out of the ordinary.

Suddenly you realize that *you* are out of the ordinary. You are exactly the kind of anomaly the gendarmes look for as they enforce the laws of the Urbille: a lone

Beatific carrying a heavy chest through the pre-dawn rust. And if that chest were to be inspected, a fortune in brilliants. You walk quietly now, hoping to avoid their attention. If there were time, you might tell them of your blackmailers' plot and let the Potentates' justice fall upon the Doxie and her confederate. But by the time they investigated your claims the sun would rise, your heart-key would be lost forever, and you would be dead.

No other course now but the Well of Bones.

You rush past steaming grates, the crooked frames of aluminum huts, and cross a bridge painted with the sigils of feuding Clatterpox gangs. Luckily, at this hour only working citizens will be up and about.

There it is. The walled plaza containing the Well of Bones. You walk through the open gate, glad there are no guards here. Who would care to guard a worthless pit of bones? This place is haunted by the lowest of scavengers, those who climb the sheer walls of the pit for miles deep and crawl back up with a bag of bones to sell for a few copper bits, or trade for drugs. Bone used to be highly valued in the Urbille, but nobody wants it anymore. It is a relic of the organic times.

Now you stand before the great pit, among the piles of scrap metal and the crude huts of bone-divers. There is no time to think about how completely vulnerable you are in this place because the sun has broken the jagged horizon, and you see the Doxie and her Clatterpox enter the plaza.

She moves gracefully across the muddy scrapyard, as out of place as yourself. Today her fine gown is green, the color of damp moss. Her black hair is a tall oval, secured with a spiral of copper wires. Her face is the one you remember: superb with its tiny red lips, arcing painted eyebrows, and the delicate curve of perfect cheeks. Her opticals glimmer at you, although with malice or amusement you cannot say. The Clatterpox named Flux shambles beside her, filling the air with his noxious exhalations.

"Sir Honore," she greets you, her voice that of a high-bred Beatific. You would never guess she was a mind harlot if you met her on an avenue in the Good Hills. "So glad you could make it."

You sit the chest of brilliants at her feet. You don't bother to return her greeting, or to remove your hat. She deserves no respect from you.

The Clatterpox opens the lid of the chest and looks inside. He nods his bulky head, and the Doxie reaches inside her cleavage. She produces the brass key that means your life. She offers it to you in the palm of one white-gloved hand.

"Why?" you ask, taking the key from her. You need to wind your gears soon, but you have about two hours left. And you must know...if she will tell you.

As the Clatterpox lifts the chest in its metal arms, she reaches to caress its grimy cheek.

"You would not understand, Honore."

"I doubt that I will," you say. "But I've paid a heavy price. I deserve an explanation."

The Doxie smiles and turns her amber lenses toward you again. "I did it for my lover," she says.

Your neck gears nearly slip. "You love this Clatterpox?"

"Yes," she says. "So you *do* know the concept of love…"

"I am well versed in matters historical, Madame. As well as the poetic arts."

She nods, the morning light glinting off her delicate nose. "But do you know that love is real? Have you ever felt it?"

"You mock me."

"No, Honore," she says. "Not at all. Extort yes, but never mock. I, too, am a Beatific."

"Your behavior suggests otherwise."

"We are this way, you and I, only because we could afford the process."

The process. Beatification. You recall it, three centuries past. A *rite of passage*, your father called it. The shedding of useless organic bulk, everything but the all-important brain, center of the living intellect.

"Beatification is open to anyone," she reminds you. "Anyone who can pay a Surgeon's fees."

She looks at the Clatterpox Flux again, and he seems to smile, though his iron jaw will not permit such an action.

"You did this for *him*…" you say it for her, accepting the preposterousness of it. "You wish to Beatify him…so you two can be together."

"You are wise, Honore," she says.

"It is…abominable," you say.

"According to whom?" she asks. "Once Flux's living brain rests inside a Beatific body, he will be no different than you or I. We really cannot thank you enough, Sir Honore."

She turns to walk away with her Clatterpox lover and your stolen brilliants, and you want to say something. A last comment or condemnation…but your mind is blank. You squeeze the brass key in your hand, taking comfort from its firmness.

The Doxie's head erupts like a burst lantern. A shower of porcelain shards, silver fragments, and brain tissue assaults your waistcoat and shirt. The Clatterpox drops the chest and it cracks open, spilling brilliants across the muddy ground.

You stand there numb, paralyzed by shock and confusion, as the black-coated gendarmes rush into the plaza, leaping from walls and gates. Bone-divers scamper from their illegal habitations and climb the walls like pale spiders. The gendarmes carry pistols and rifles, one of which has ended the Doxie's life.

The enforcers turn their clustered opticals toward the Clatterpox. The rusted monstrosity falls to its knees before the dead Doxie, cradling her headless corpse. Inside the open hollow of her neck, gears and springs pop and grind into stillness. The Clatterpox pulls something from his side…a key that he inserts between her sculpted breasts. The gendarmes believe it a weapon and begin firing. You leap to the ground to avoid the hail of bullets. Lying there, so close to the Doxie and her lover, you watch him turning her heart-key, trying to restart her life. But her head is ruined, her brain—the center of all life functions—spread across the ground, a litter of shredded blue flesh. Yet why is there is no blood or cranial fluid? Her Beatific brain wasn't alive at all. The organ was dried…congealed…preserved.

Is every Beatific brain like hers—nothing but dead, decayed flesh?

The implications of this question run through your mind yet refuse to take root.

The gendarmes' bullets bounce off the Clatterpox's iron body, or create holes like ruptured pustules. He turns the heart-key again and again, heedless of their assault. Eventually, they stop shooting and approach him on foot. The vapors from his vents and exhaust pipes flow black and heavy now. They tear him away from the Doxie's corpse and secure his arms with titanium shackles.

You start to rise, but two tall gendarmes lift you sharply to your feet. One of them stares at you with his cluster of opticals, nine blue-green lenses bright with the caress of dawn.

"Sir René Honore?" the gendarme asks through some mouth aperture hidden below his high collar.

You nod, still too stunned to speak.

"By order of the Tribune, you are under arrest."

"What? I have done nothing. I was blackmailed…"

"We understand," says the gendarme, his anterior opticals already scouring the rest of the plaza. "To blackmail a Beatific is a High Crime. As is the paying of any funds to blackmailers. You broke the law. You will face justice."

You watch as they gather up the body and assorted remains of the Doxie and cast her into the Well of Bones. You know she will fall for several minutes before she reaches the bottom. There she will lie among the antediluvian bones, until perhaps some bone-diver gathers up her parts to sell as scrap. All that is left of her are the shards of an exquisite face, a few slivers of porcelain lying in the mud.

The Clatterpox Flux wheezes and coughs as they drag him away.

The gendarmes leave the brilliants lying trampled in the muck. Mere bits of colored glass beneath their notice.

You remember what the elder stone face said about the jewels, and you laugh as they lead you out of the plaza and into the rust.

·········

You're still laughing when they haul you before the veiled Tribune on his high bench, and later when they drag you across the stone bridge and deep beneath the walls of the crumbling palace. In the endless dark of the labyrinth, your laughter draws nameless things closer.

Soon you will join your ancestors on the wall of the sunken vault.

A laughing face of stone.

FLESH OF THE CITY, BONES OF THE WORLD

The Surgeon's hands are his most delicate instruments.

From the slim silver bones of the ten fingers to the minute arrays of gears, cogs, and springs set for agility and precision, to the pale elastic skin that stretches over the whole array, his hands are marvels of science. The rest of his body is no less amazing, no less detailed in its construction, a silver skeletal scaffold filled with organs of bronze and copper sheathed in that same supple skin without blotch or blemish.

His patients take these things for granted, ignorant of the miracles of design that sustain their existence. But he is a Surgeon and he knows the secrets of human biology as intimately as he knows the body and mind of his own wife.

While prepping for the operation, he recalls her silver skull laid bare and glimmering as she removed the demure porcelain mask that is her public face. The memory is from last night. They had danced in the courtyard of glass sculptures, baring body and soul beneath a canopy of stars. Tonight they will celebrate the return of their son from five years at the Ministère de Education. In a few days the boy will enter this chamber and at last become a man.

The Surgeon's opticals blink and he returns to the present as his attendants wheel a youth into the Conversion Room. The Surgeon turns his porcelain visage to greet the nervous patient. It is the face he always wears for operations: lean and handsome with a strong chin and wide, warm smile. It was painted by one of the Urbille's finest maskers.

"Are you nervous?" he asks the young man. Fifteen years old, just like his own son. So much like Alain that it frightens the Surgeon, though he doesn't know why it should.

The youth nods, tears flowing from his soft opticals. He is a weak thing of flesh and blood, hair and bone...an outdated Organic construct. It is almost a miracle he has survived fifteen years in the Urbille...a miracle that *any* youth survives so long. The flesh is so vulnerable, so prone to injury, disease, and entropy.

"Will it hurt?" the youth asks.

"No," says the Surgeon. "You will never hurt again. No pain, no bleeding...no hunger, no sickness. Won't that be wonderful?"

The youth nods and trembles. They are always this way before Conversion.

"Relax," he tells the boy. "It will soon be over, and your new life will begin."

The Attendant administers a sedative and after a few moments the Surgeon begins his work. Fluorescent lights gleam blue-white as he makes his incision at the center of the forehead then carves his way about the cranium with a scalpel of sterilized steel. He peels back the shaven skin that covers the dome of the skull. Now the bone-saw, following the same track as the scalpel.

He removes cranial roof and the living brain glistens before him, a thing of beauty. A marvel that exceeds even the finest mechanisms of scientific design. Here lies the secret to immortality, creativity, humanity...the fleshy bottle that contains the very Soul of Man. He applies the topical solution and speaks the Incantation of Transferral, pronouncing each syllable with ingrained accuracy as he removes the brain from its bisected shell. He smoothly clips free the Organic opticals and carries the brain to a second table. There lies the youth's new body: a perfect example of Beatific aesthetics, a collection of ingenious machinery wrapped in a smooth elastic sheathe exactly like his own. The silver skull wears no porcelain face yet...the youth will choose one when he awakes.

The Surgeon slides the brain into its new housing, connects the vitreous filaments to the new opticals (his mother chose green lenses), and seals the top of the silver skull with a soldering torch. Finally, he pulls the hood of elastic skin over the back of the skull and secures it with a permanent adhesive. He signals the Attendant, who flips a switch, sending a current of cobalt energy leaping through the youth's new body. Gears groan and the body quivers until the charge dissipates. The Attendant hands a brass heart-key to the Surgeon. He inserts it gently into the keyhole in the youth's chest and turns it...cranking it round and round until the green lenses begin to glow with faint light.

As he primes the youth's new body, a trio of Transporters enters the room and gathers up the youth's flesh-and-blood remains. They will remove it cleanly and dispose of the carcass somewhere. Three or four such operations a day creates a lot of cast-off flesh. The Surgeon is glad the disposal of such remnants is not part of his job. He has never thought of asking where they take the fleshy rubbish. Perhaps they cast them into the Well of Bones. He does not care enough to ask.

The youth sits up on the table, his opticals shining bright as emeralds. He lifts his arms and bends his fingers, looking at his adult body for the first time. His bright skull is incapable of expression, but the Surgeon sees wonder in the flaring green opticals. He is used to this moment of enlightenment. It always makes him proud of a job well done.

"How do you feel?" he asks the patient.

The green opticals blink, stare at him. "Brilliant," says the youth. With some coaxing he stands on his new legs. The Attendant leads him toward the door and his expectant parents.

"You're truly a Beatific now," he tells the lad. "A man."

"Thank you, Doctor...?" he pauses at the door.

"Wail," the Surgeon says through his smiling mask.

"Thank you, Doctor Wail," says the boy who is now a man.

The Surgeon bows at the waist. His patient disappears through the swinging doors.

"No more today, Doctor," says the Attendant.

"Excellent," says Dr. Wail, stripping off his plastic gloves and surgical gown. "Summon a coach if you would be so kind."

The Attendant nods and leaves the room.

A few drops of blood are all that is left of the youth's fleshly body. Wail stares at the crimson stains. *What a piece of work is man*, he thinks. *How frail and tender, how prone to destruction.* "Not anymore," he says aloud to himself.

In the lobby the youth's family embraces him, their porcelain smiles wide and colored with cheer. Rose-tinted cheeks and scintillating opticals. The father is telling his son to keep his heart-key safe and clean, that he must wind himself back to full strength every morning. The son holds the brass key proudly in his hands. It is the key to immortality.

Dr. Wail exits through the main doors of the Ministère de Science. A black rain falls across the Urbille as his carriage approaches. A pale sun sinks beyond the silhouettes of rusted and jagged towers. The Ministère itself is a gleaming spire of glass and steel behind him, a monument to modernity rising from a landscape of decayed and crumpled metal.

Two clockwork horses draw the carriage through the muddy street. Above and behind them on the driver's bench sits a steaming Clatterpox, its barrel-shaped body patterned with rust and salt encrustations. Its rod-like arms pull on the reigns, bringing the carriage to a halt before the Surgeon, who has wrapped himself in a gray overcloak. Soiled rain drips from the rim of his top hat. The Clatterpox driver vents a gout of smoke from tubes along its bulky frame, a sound like six teapots gone to boil at once. It swivels its oval head and focuses smudged opticals.

"Coach for the doctor?" asks the Clatterpox, its voice a rasp of scraping metal.

Wail nods, and the driver leaps down to open the door. Its joints creak and Wail thinks the poor fellow might fall apart at any moment. Still, he climbs into the dry, velvet-lined interior and doffs his drenched hat and cloak. He loosens a few buttons on his waistcoat and watches the Rusted Zone roll by as the horses pull him through the squalid streets.

Crowds of Clatterpox wander the avenues, going from factories to taverns, ambling through the red clouds of rust and oily rain. The Surgeon long ago stopped asking himself how people can live like this. A group of naked children, five of them, splash ecstatically in a mud puddle at the mouth of an alley. A shouting Clatterpox (their mother? father?) drives them into a nearby hovel. Wail knows that those children, if they survive another ten or twelve years, will undergo their own Conversions. But unlike the privileged sons and daughters of Beatifics, they will become clumsy, lumbering Clatterpox. For those who cannot afford the services of a Surgeon, the only choice is the Mechanics.

"Should these people even be *allowed* to raise children?" his wife had once asked.

"Perhaps not," Wail had told her. "It doesn't seem fair."

But like everything else in the Urbille, it was not the Beatifics who made decisions. The Law came only from the Potentates, and The Law was incontestable.

As the carriage leaves the Rusted Zone and its rows of dilapidated factories, it passes into the rolling greenery of the Good Hills. Mansions of ivy-smothered stone dot the hills, one estate after another of sculpted gardens, cast-iron fences, and meandering avenues dotted with gas lamps in baroque shapes. Night has fallen and the windows of the great houses gleam with orange warmth, the light of blazing hearths spilling across lawns set with pathways of ground glass. These are the homes of Beatific families, ancestral estates designed with grace and beauty to house the Urbille's most graceful and beautiful citizens.

The carriage pulls through the gate of the Wail Estate and up the curving driveway. That same kind firelight flickers from the windows of the house. The Surgeon's heart gears speed up a bit as he imagines his wife and son waiting for him inside.

Home. He exits the carriage. The window's glow caresses his porcelain smile.

He drops a single ruby brilliant into the driver's iron palm and the Clatterpox approximates a quick bow with its bulky frame. The mechanical horses' hooves click against the cobbled drive, as the Surgeon opens the door that bears the Wail sigil in pressed gold.

In the vestibule and the parlor beyond there is no sign of wife or son.

"Kalmea? Alain?" he calls out, removing his hat and coat.

"Kalmea!" louder now.

The house is stonily silent. Then the rush of padded feet on the carpeted floor. His wife enters the foyer, a single candle burning in her hand. There is no joy in her amber opticals. She wears a face of sculpted ceramic sorrow.

"What's the matter?" he asks.

"He is...ill," she says, a hand on his shoulder.

They rush to the bedroom where young Alain lies under blankets, sweating and moaning. The boy's pale skin is covered in purple blotches.

The frailty of flesh...

Kalmea tells him of the carriage that brought Alain home from school. He seemed fine at first, but soon began coughing. He would not eat the meal she prepared, and collapsed in the den. "He has been lying here ever since," she says. "I sent a summons to the Ministère, but they said you had already left."

"Must have arrived just after I departed," he says. He examines Alain's pupils, pulling his soft opticals open gently. They are glazed and unhealthy. *What is this sickness?* He has never seen such symptoms. He mutters an Incantation of Health but it has no effect. Even as he watches, the dark spots grow larger on his son's flesh. He administers an Elixir of Prevention with a golden spoon. No response.

"What can we do?" Kalmea asks him.

The Surgeon sits quietly for awhile, staring at his poor Organic son. He remembers the day they received this bundle of joy. The Angel of the Potentates with its flaring feathered wings, its heroic shoulders, its smooth and featureless head. It had come to them as expected, on the middle of the Fifth Day in the Year of the Basilisk. They were in the back garden when it descended, shedding sunlight from its pristine limbs. In its strong arms lay a tiny being of pink flesh, swaddled in linen and sleeping peacefully. Alain.

The faceless Angel placed the infant directly into Kalmea's arms, as was the custom. They were so exhilarated by the baby's presence that they did not see the Angel rise into the sky and fly back toward the great hill where stands the Palace of the Potentates.

"What can we *do*?" Kalmea asks him again, grabbing his arm.

"Rid him of this weak flesh," says the Surgeon. "His Conversion was due in twelve days. I'll do it tomorrow instead."

"Is that legal?" she asks. He senses fear like poison in her voice.

"I'll write up a Special Permit tonight," he says. "Send a runner for a coach an hour before dawn. Conversion will save him from this wasting disease...whatever it is."

"Father?" Alain's blind opticals flicker open. They are blue, like his father's, yet so soft.

"I'm here, son." He squeezes the boy's limp hand.

"Help me."

"You're going to be fine, Alain. In a few hours you will be a man...free from this sickness. From *all* sickness."

Alain shakes his head. "The walls..." he mutters. "Skin on the walls..."

Wail looks at his wife, then back to his dying son.

"What walls?" he asks. Could this be some clue to the origin of his sickness?

Alain swallows, coughs. Bloody spittle stains his lips, which his mother wipes with a damp cloth. "On the Avenue of Copper Lungs...I had to stop...I'm sorry, Father."

"You had to stop where? For what? Tell me, son."

"The buildings...the rust, the metal...it was all covered over. Covered with...*flesh*. Some kind of *skin*, pulsing muscles beneath the surface. The Clatterpox were staring...some ran away in fear...but it grew larger as I watched it. I had to stop...I had to *touch* it."

The Surgeon's heart skips a cog. "What did you touch? Something on the Avenue of Copper Lungs?"

"The *flesh*..." mutters Alain. "Walls of *living flesh*, Father....flesh like *me*...how could it? *How could it?* How..." He fades away, consciousness lost beneath a wave of bodily stress.

"What is he talking about?" asks Kalmea.

The Surgeon shakes his head. "I have no idea. Stay with him. I must draft the Permit." He shuffles down the hallway to his library, where parchment and a quill pen await his efforts.

As he pens the document that will save his son's life, the boy's words ring in his mind, fireflies set loose in the Organic folds of his metal-encased brain.

Walls of living flesh...

In the morning his son's suppurating skin is the color of charcoal. There is a sickly-sweet stench about Alain. He appears to be...decaying. The Surgeon says nothing of this to Kalmea. Like her, he has donned a grim-set face. He hopes he will have cause to wear a smiling face again after this day.

After hastily winding their heart-keys they load Alain into a carriage by gaslight. Kalmea insists upon travelling with him to the Ministère, and he cannot refuse her. The driver is another Clatterpox, but the coach and horses might be the same ones that brought him home last night. The vehicle rolls through the green lanes and descends into the serrated mass of the Rusted Zone.

"Faster!" he shouts at the driver. The Clatterpox complies, but hits a mass of early morning traffic on the Street of Coils. The Surgeon curses the crowds of steaming mechanoids. Kalmea clutches his hand. Their son lies dying on the floor of the coach. Rotting...

In the smoggy glow of sunrise the coach finally reaches the Ministère of Science. The Surgeon calls for Attendants and they carry Alain inside, prepping the Conversion Room for an emergency procedure. Dr. Wail pacifies his huffing Supervisor by handing him the carefully prepared Permit. He does not wait to watch the man sign it, but rushes instead through the doors of the CR. A top-of-the-line body was commissioned for his son months ago. Using it now, twelve days ahead of the ordained time, should pose no problem. Attendants prepare it for the procedure as sedative rushes into Alain's purple veins.

The Surgeon works feverishly, but with no less precision than any patient demands. The Attendants mumble behind their impassive ceramic faces...the state of Alain's body horrifies them. His flesh looks like spoiled meat...it has already begun to dry...soon it will be only a desiccated husk.

The Surgeon works his bone-saw magic, then drops the tool as the cranial roof comes loose. The Attendants moan, or curse, he isn't sure. He cannot hear them. He hears only the terrible shrieking of his wife, who looks into the CR from a round observation port.

Alain's young brain is neither pink nor glistening. It is black and putrid...atrophied. Little more than a fist-sized lump of rancid meat. There is nothing left of his son to save.

The Surgeon falls to his knees. A keening sound fills the room, and he recognizes it somewhere in the back of his mind as his own scream. Dr. Wail is wailing...

Attendants carry him away from the CR while Transporters in special hazard suits carry away Alain's shriveled remains. Wail breaks free of the Attendants' supporting arms and slams his skull against the wall, shattering his porcelain face to bits. His silver skull-face continues to shriek as they carry him into an isolation room. He does not see what becomes of his poor wife.

If his opticals were Organic, he would be weeping. But he can only scream, until a gear in his throat slips. He lays in the isolation room, twitching and moaning until oblivion claims him. Sleep offers little help...he dreams of Alain rotting to death before him, skin falling in chunks from a skeleton of brittle white bone.

He wakes up and slams his head against the wall again, seeking to pulp the brain inside; but his miraculous body is made too well.

In the depths of more mad dreaming he sees faces of carven stone staring at him with diamond opticals. The stone is alive and the faces speak with eerie voices:

It's all a lie, they tell him.

The Potentates have bound you in a web of illusion.

To see the truth you must look beyond who you are...what you are...

How their stone lips can move and produce sound he has no idea. But this is a dream, so he accepts it. He does not like their accusations.

You are as dead as your son...who was not your son at all.

Conversion is Death.

The Beatific lifestyle is a sham...you are all walking corpses.

Accept this and know freedom.

Accept this and defy the tyranny of the Potentates.

Where does the new flesh come from, Dr. Wail?

Where does the lost flesh go?

All sense of time is lost while he dreams.

Someone eventually comes in, takes the heart-key from his pocket, and winds him back to full strength. By this alone he knows that twenty-four hours have passed. Wishing they would just let his body wind down and his brain expire, he fights against this, but four Attendants hold his limbs. The Supervisor tells him the key will be waiting for him when he feels better. When they leave he sits quietly for some hours.

Walls of living flesh...

The words of Alain are what bring him back to sanity. His grief transforms gradually into anger. What was it on the Avenue of Copper Lungs that his son touched? What was it that killed him?

Walls of living flesh...

When he speaks calmly again, Attendants summon the Supervisor, who interviews him for an hour, then decides to let him go. He gives the Surgeon back his heart-key, along with heartfelt condolences. He also insists on a six-week leave of absence. The Ministère de Science will pay for Alain's funeral. (The diseased body, however, has already been disposed of. They will have to use his Beatific body...the unwound one that never housed his brain.)

The Surgeon nods, accepts an impassive face from the Supervisor's personal collection, and says whatever he needs to say to get out on the street again.

"Go home and be with your wife," the Supervisor says. "She needs you."

He nods, shakes the man's hand.

Now Dr. Wail stands in waistcoat and top hat in front of the Ministère, but he doesn't call for a carriage. Instead he walks, weaving between the huffing exhausts of Clatterpox and steam-driven lorries. He slides his heart-key into his breast pocket, alongside the key that would have belonged to Alain.

He clutches a scalpel in his right fist (nobody saw him take it from the Ministère), and his booted feet carry him toward the Avenue of Copper Lungs.

··········

The streets grow less crowded but more dangerous as he walks through the lowering sun. Abandoned foundries crumble slowly into rust alongside the paved lanes. Clatterpox rattle in and out of drinking establishments and Doxie houses. Bloaters float above the crowds, siphoning stray thoughts into their spherical bodies through quivering, worm-like tendrils. The few Beatifics to be found on this side of town wear their collars up to meet their hat brims, scarves hiding all but their narrowed opticals. Some hide themselves deep inside hooded cloaks, the handles of clubs or blades visible on their hips. The corroded walls of metal seem to close in about the Surgeon as he walks. The sky has taken on a ruddy color, as if it too has rusted. Gangs of rowdy Clatterpox roam the alleys, exchanging cryptic tweets and hoots of compressed steam. Their hearts are miniature furnaces that burn tiny chunks of anthracite.

Finally he rounds the corner and sees the Avenue of Copper Lungs running east to west before him. Looking back, he can barely see the shimmering steel and glass of the Ministère of Science rising from the metropolis of ancient, tangled metal. Now the wind picks up as he steps out onto the avenue, which is strangely deserted. Shops have closed here, and taverns have nailed their doors. Something has driven everyone away. He walks into the emptiness and a whirlwind of rust blows tattered broadsheets down the sidewalk. One wraps about his foot.

He picks up the crumpled newsrag and reads the headline:

MYSTERIOUS FLESH GROWS
ACROSS SOUTHERN QUARTER

Part of the ensuing article is readable, the rest of it having been smeared to illegibility by some acrid puddle.

Foundries 17, 34, and 53 are suspending operations due to an unexplained phenomenon along the eastern flank of the Southern Quarter today, centering on the Avenue of Copper Lungs. Seemingly overnight, a vast blanket of what appears to be Organic flesh has grown rapidly to smother the three factories and surrounding establishments, including a vent shop, two taverns, and a bronzing outlet. Authorities were quick to arrive and cordon off the scene, but not before several Clatterpox investigated personally. Many of those first-hand witnesses claimed the flesh was "alive with muscular tension" when touched. Gendarmes arrested three citizens who refused to flee the cordoned area (all Clatterpox), and traffic has been indefinitely suspended along the Avenue.

Tribune Anteus had no comment when contacted about the spazmal, *as some engineers are calling this outbreak of flesh, but in a statement he promised the "swift and immediate execution of anyone foolish enough to*

The rest of the piece is a mélange of runny black ink that reminds the Surgeon of Alain's decaying skin. He casts the paper aside and climbs the new metal fence placed by gendarmes to block the street.

An electricity in the air glides about his face and limbs, a growing pressure that signals the inevitable rise of a rabidity. He half-runs down the street toward the closed factories. They seem hung with great, flapping sheets or tarps of a torn and ragged substance. Red lightnings flare among the dark clouds as he comes to stand before the great wall of rotting flesh. The sound of the manifesting rabidity howls in his ears...the sound of reality splitting like punctured elastic skin.

The wind tears at the huge curtains of necrotic flesh hanging from the walls of the avenue. This place was literally smothered by flesh...a *spazmal*. He walks against the wind, following the length of the dead flesh walls. They are putrefying exactly as Alain's own skin had done...withering and drying like his beautiful brain. Standing in the middle of the phenomenon, he takes it all in. These curtains of flesh grew like a rapid fungus over roofs, smokestacks, walls, alleys, pavements, and lamp poles. As if the Rusted Zone was trying to grow its own skin but got the process horribly wrong. He walks upon the putrid, jellied flesh that smothers the surface of the street. It squishes unwholesomely beneath his boots.

Rotten...all rotten.

Where did it come from?

He sees again the stone faces from his weird dream.

Where does the new flesh come from?

Where does the old flesh go?

This is the incident that fascinated Alain so that he had to stop his coach and get out to touch it. His own feeble flesh must have caught the wave of bacteria that causes this rapid decomposition. Now the flesh hangs here, quarantined like a plague virus, and his son is gone.

The rabidity reaches full force and the wind nearly knocks him face-down onto the rotting carpet of flesh. He steadies himself and watches a vacuity open in the air nearby. A split in the fabric of reality tears itself into being above the flesh-drowned street. A saffron glow emanates from within the fissure...some distance away, another vacuity emits a blue-green light, and farther away there are others, each a random portal to some distant reality.

The Surgeon's green opticals stare through the vacuity nearest him. The world beyond is an alien realm, a broad sweep of sandy plain with obelisks of rock rising into a mauve sky. Nine moons float about the zenith of that wild dimension, and clouds of golden dust move across the wasteland. Colossal creatures lumber between the spires of natural rock...things with horned heads and pendulous jaws. Even on this side of the vacuity he feels the rumbling of that other ground beneath the tread of the shaggy behemoths. Do they recognize this portal into a separate reality? Or are they dumb brutes, ignorant of all thought? Nevertheless, they stampede on through the golden waste. If one of them stumbles into the vacuity, it may burst into the Surgeon's dimension. If that happens, he will be crushed beneath its awesome weight.

He moves back, away from the sucking pressure of the multiversal fracture before it can draw him tumbling like a grain of sand into that forlorn landscape. The roaring wind flows *into* the vacuity, and he strains against it, using all the power of his grinding leg gears to reach a safe distance. Finally, the storm subsides and the vacuity snaps shut with a peal of thunder. All about the city, similar thunders roar as dimensional wounds repair themselves. The evening calm returns.

The Surgeon stares again at the immense blanket of rotted flesh encasing the Avenue of Copper Lungs. When all this rots away there will be nothing left that might answer the *why* of his son's death. How long before all this *spazmal* flesh is nothing more than muddy pulp to be swept into the sewers? He must take a tissue sample. Get it to the laboratory. Maybe he will find an answer...some clue as to why the flesh appeared...why it decayed...why it took Alain. With the scalpel he carves a rectangular piece of oozing, blackened flesh from a defunct gaslight, wraps it carefully in a silken handkerchief, and tucks it into his coat pocket.

As he turns to go, a blast of white light assaults his opticals. The sound of a steam engine grinds near somewhere behind the lights. Tall, dark shapes rush forward pointing rifles. Gendarmes. They grab him and hustle him toward a six-wheeled lorry, ignoring his pleas.

"I'm a Surgeon!" he shouts, but their grip is tighter than iron screws. They shove him into the back of the wagon and slam the doors. Two of them sit inside with him, the barrels of their rifles pointed directly at him. Below their black, stove-pipe hats their faces are little more than clusters of dark optical lenses, each of which swivels independently in various directions. They wear trench coats and gloves the color of midnight. The lorry rumbles across the fleshy street, through a barrier gate, and into the streets of the Western Quarter.

"I was only doing research," says the Surgeon. They ignore him. "Where are you taking me?"

"To the Tribune," one of the gendarmes finally speaks. His voice is a transistorized buzz, as if broadcast on some distant wavelength. "Do not attempt to flee. We will shoot to kill."

The Surgeon sits quietly, his fist wrapped about the handkerchief in his pocket and the decaying evidence wrapped inside.

··········

Deep inside the Ministère de Justice gendarmes haul the Surgeon before the golden bench where Tribune Anteus sits in judgment. The crimson and black banner bearing the Sigil of the Potentates hangs on the wall. The Tribune's official robes are white, as is the long veil that obscures his face. His ruby opticals gleam faintly through the fabric, twin points of rosy light. Above the veil a powdered wig hides the rest of his thin skull. His fingers are long and sharp, covered in jeweled rings, and one of them points directly at the Surgeon.

"You entered a zone of prohibition," says the Tribune, his voice deep with power. The Surgeon recognizes it from a hundred transistor broadcasts over the years. It carries far more weight in person, seeming almost to vibrate the walls of the chamber. "How do you plead?"

The Surgeon can only speak in a rasping whisper, thanks to the damaged gear in his throat. "I was doing research—"

"How do you plead?" asks the Tribune again. "*Guilty* or *not guilty*?"

"I had a reason..." begins the Surgeon.

"Your reasons are of no consequence," says the Tribune. "You broke a Tribunal Decree. This court serves the Potentates' Justice and that Justice will be served."

"Not guilty then," says the Surgeon.

The Tribune lifts his gavel. "The plea is noted. This court finds you guilty of criminal trespassing and sentences you to death."

"Wait!" A new voice rings through the chamber before the gavel falls. It is a voice the Surgeon recognizes. The Supervisor of the Ministère de Science stands nearby, escorted by a pair of private gendarmes. "May I approach the bench Your Honor?" asks the Supervisor.

The Tribune nods and the two personages confer in whispered conversation. The Surgeon stands anxious before the bench and wonders why the Supervisor is here. His hand clenches the rotting flesh encased in his kerchief. He still has the scalpel in his pocket as well. The gendarmes did not search him. Perhaps they have no fear of a mere Surgeon. Six of them, heavily armed, line the chamber walls.

Finally the Tribune nods his veiled head and speaks again: "Doctor Wail, you are hereby remanded to the custody of Supervisor Guillaume. Your sentence is indefinitely suspended, pending further reports. Do you understand?"

The Surgeon nods. The gavel falls upon the golden bench with a sharp crack, and the Supervisor leads Wail into an adjoining room where only his two personal guards are present.

"How did you know I was here?" asks the Surgeon.

"I have friends among the gendarmes," says Supervisor Guillaume. "You are very lucky."

The Surgeon would smirk if his porcelain face allowed it. He blinks instead.

"Forgive me," says the Supervisor. "You have suffered a terrible loss. But I believe in you, Dr. Wail. I believe in your talents." The Supervisor's face is a grim ceramic expression; a serious mask meant for entertaining serious discussions. His top hat is red, with a black velvet band.

"I am grateful," says the Surgeon. "But *why* did you intervene?"

"Because," says the Supervisor, "I was wrong in asking you to take a leave of absence. You're not that kind of man. I have a *job* for you."

"I'm a Surgeon."

"No longer. Now you will be so much more. A *scientist*."

"I don't understand...what happened to my son?"

"Come with me," says the Supervisor. "I will explain everything. You will see that there is hope...for you and your family. For us all."

"Where are we going?" asks the Surgeon, pacing behind.

"To the palace," says Supervisor Guillaume.

A carriage waits outside for the Supervisor, driven by a third private gendarme. Inside its opulent interior the Supervisor offers Wail a glass of transparent lubricant. The Surgeon refuses, but Guillaume insists. Wail lifts his porcelain mask and drinks the liquid down quickly. The carriage trundles along the cobbled lane, heading into the Good Hills and the great prominence at the center of the Urbille.

"Good for the gears and cogs," says the Supervisor, finishing his own glass.

"What is this all about?" asks the Surgeon.

"As you may have guessed by now, I am far more than a Supervisor," says Guillaume. "I work for the Potentates. Special Sciences Initiative."

"Why are you taking me to the palace?"

"To show you our latest experiment."

The coach travels up a long and winding incline. Through the octagonal window the Surgeon sees the twisted silhouettes of mighty trees, the Interior Forest surrounding the massive walls of the Potentates' citadel. Soon the vehicle leaves the moonwashed forest and enters a tunnel-like gate leading to an inner courtyard. The obscure shadows of iron statues pass by the window. At last the coach comes to rest, and the Surgeon steps out into an immense yard of mossy flagstones. The Palace of the Potentates rises before them, a sleeping leviathan of gray stone dressed in tapestries of moss and ivy. The size of those stony towers dwarfs even the steel spires of the Ministères. Inside this colossal conglomeration of granite there might exist a second city, one more ancient and mysterious than the Urbille itself.

The palace is a carven mountain at the center of *everything*, and the Surgeon stands humbled in its inky shadow. In the gloom ahead he sees a vision of those stone faces from his nightmare, looking out at him from the very walls of the palace. They speak to him again. Neither the Supervisor or his guards seems to notice.

The Potentates have bound you in a web of illusion.
To see the truth, you must look beyond...
Accept this and defy them.

The faces disappear as the Supervisor leads him through an iron gate into a drafty hall at the base of a soaring tower. Then a series of heavy doors brings them into a great round-walled hall with a ceiling high enough to be lost in shadow. Perhaps this entire tower is hollow.

Beatific technicians walk about the rows of intricate machinery, adjusting tubes of glass and electrode displays. A confusing network of wires and colored glass hangs like a stained-glass window above the contraptions, connected to the machines by coils of cable and rubber-bound cords. This room, the Surgeon realizes in an instant, is one giant machine.

"Welcome to Project Viande," says the Supervisor, doffing his red hat and gloves. He babbles on and on about the technological skill of himself and his technicians, but the Surgeon understands little of it. His opticals roam the intricate arrays of levers, gears, switches, and transformers. The great machine is as intricate as any Beatific body.

"...and two days ago we came as close to success as we have ever been," says the Supervisor.

"Two days ago?" asks the Surgeon.

Two days ago something killed my son.

The Supervisor motions to a great oval of glass nestled at the heart of the machine. "Through this multiversal lens we have discovered a world comprised entirely of living flesh," says Guillaume. "An Organic dimension!" The Surgeon focuses his opticals on the man's dull ceramic visage. "Our goal is to enable the successful transversal of this *world-flesh* into our own realm. So...we introduced a viral strain of this Organic matter into an area of the Rusted Zone."

"The *spazmal*..."

The Supervisor shakes his head. "We call it the Organism. It seemed to thrive for the first few hours, growing at a pace we hardly expected. Then something happened, some side effect of the transversal process. The Organism began a rapid decay."

Alain's words rang hollow in the Surgeon's skull.

Walls of living flesh...I had to stop...I had to touch *it.*

"We had no choice but to cordon off the affected area and place it under quarantine," says the Supervisor.

"Why?" asks the Surgeon. His fist squeezes the steel scalpel in the pocket of his waistcoat. "Why bring this...Organism...into the Urbille at all?"

The Supervisor stands silent for a moment. He turns away from the Surgeon and surveys the technicians at their work. "The Potentates have...certain needs, Wail. I'm going to tell you one of the Urbille's great secrets."

"Go ahead...tell me."

The Supervisor whispers. "The Potentates...are Organic beings."

Like every other citizen, the Surgeon has seen the Potentates in person once a year during the Parade of Iniquities, when all seven ride through the streets on great mechanical steeds. He remembers their bulbous skulls, their black robes and thick veils, the golden chains decorating their vestments. Their limbs were inhumanly long, their oblong heads balanced on thin necks. Only their shadowy opticals are ever visible to the parade crowds. Sometimes they wave with incredibly long (gloved) fingers at the populace that fears and adores them. No one would ever guess their fleshly secret.

"What exactly are you saying?" asks the Surgeon, though he begins to suspect.

"Organic beings require sustenance," says the Supervisor. "The Potentates are entirely carnivorous. They desire only meat of a certain grade."

Neurons blaze inside the Surgeon's fleshy brain. His opticals blink and his gears moan and creak as if his parts were suddenly aged and worn.

"This...Organism...this transversal..."

"Was an attempt..." says the Supervisor, "...*is* an attempt...to provide an endless alternative food supply for the Potentates."

The Surgeon has no words. If he could vomit up the contents of his clockwork guts he would do so...but he hasn't vomited since he was a child. A small boy, frail and covered in tender flesh.

"We are so *close*, Wail," says the Supervisor. "So close to perfecting the process. This world-flesh is the key...finding it was the real breakthrough. We need to assemble a process for countering the rapid cellular degeneration that our reality creates. The next piece of the Organism we bring through will have a better chance of—"

"You said *alternative*," says the Surgeon. "*Alternative* food supply."

"Yes, that's correct."

"What do they eat now?" asks the Surgeon. The Supervisor sighs. The Surgeon grabs him by the shoulders. A gendarme steps forward, but Guillaume waves him back.

"*What do they eat?*" asks the Surgeon in his rasping, weary voice.

"What do you think?" says the Supervisor.

The Surgeon remembers the Transporters, hauling brainless carcasses out of the Conversion Room. Three or four a day.

Again he sees the faces of living stone, hears their voices.

Where does the new flesh come from, Dr. Wail?

Where does the lost flesh go?

"All those bodies..."

"They come here, to the palace," whispers the Supervisor. "For...*processing*."

The Surgeon slumps, and the Supervisor helps him into a chair.

"Now do you see the value of our work?" asks the Supervisor. "How important it is? Have you ever wondered what causes the rabidities? Why these portals to distant worlds keep opening at random throughout the Urbille? They are side effects of this machine! It's all about Project Viande."

All our bodies...all our flesh and bones.

"I need you on this project, Wail. Your brilliance can help us find a solution."

"What about the babies?" asks the Surgeon, remembering the white Angel. Alain's tiny pink face. "Where do they all come from?"

"Harvested," says the Supervisor. "From other realities. Places where life has nearly expired. Bringing them into this world is a gift. Their worlds are ruined and dying. We bring them into the Urbille and give them life...families...immortality."

Where does the new flesh come from?

Where does the lost flesh go?

"Wail, don't you understand?" demands Guillaume. "If we succeed, there will be no more need for Conversions! A new Organic Age will begin. All we have to do is find another way to *feed the Potentates*..."

The Surgeon pulls forth the scalpel and drives it into Guillaume's left optical. Its steel tip enters the Supervisor's brain and the blade lodges there.

Technicians run for cover as the gendarmes fire their rifles. Thunder echoes through the tower. A bullet grazes the Surgeon's shoulder, tearing open his elastic skin. There is no pain. He leaps upon the nearest gendarme, turning him to take his comrade's next bullet in the chest. The explosive shell scatters bronze and copper debris across the floor.

The Surgeon runs into the heart of the chamber, winding between banks of machinery.

"Don't shoot! The machine!" someone yells, but the surviving gendarme ignores him. A console explodes as the Surgeon runs past it.

He flees through a random series of doors, losing himself in the dank corridors of the outer tower. He hides behind a ventilation grate as a squad of gendarmes march past.

Whispered voices lead him on. Eventually he finds his way outside, and in the light of the silver moon he creeps through the courtyard, passing the iron statues, and hides himself in the mud behind a green hedge. There is commotion within the tower, although the rest of the palace seems lost to silence and shadow. Somewhere within that ancient immensity, the Potentates are dining on the flesh of the city. He takes the rotted *spazmal* flesh from his pocket and casts it into a drainage ditch full of stagnant water.

When the courtyard gate opens, a gendarme-driven carriage rolls down the lane and exits the palace grounds. Nobody notices the Surgeon clinging to the back of the vehicle, his clothing soiled by dark mud. At the edge of the forest he drops off the carriage, rolling into a pile of rotten leaves. He rises, filthy and crouching like some beast from an ancient world of flesh and bone. He runs across the hills, trying to outrace the carriage.

Just before dawn he reaches the broken door of his estate. The tracks of steam lorries have left muddy ruts in the lawn. Inside the house he finds the corpse of his wife lying among the shambles of furniture. Kalmea's silver skull blossoms like a rose where the exploding shell hit it. Head shots were the gendarmes' specialty...the quickest and most efficient way to kill a Beatific. Their silver skulls could not protect the delicate brain from such firepower.

The brain...the last refuge of a stolen humanity.

A humanity fed to seven imperious carnivores.

He smashes a gas lamp and winds his heart-key in the light of the roaring flames. He leaves the mansion burning behind him. Wrapped in a black cloak and hood, an antique blade at his side, he follows the voices singing a clear high refrain in his mind.

Now you see the Truth.

Now you see Yourself.

He stalks carefully through several neighborhoods in the small light of early morning, until he finds the place. No family has lived in the overgrown estate for decades. The name on the iron gate is rusted and faded. The mansion beyond is little more than a ruin...shattered windows, fallen beams, crumbled walls of blackened stone.

In the distance, the mountainous bulk of the palace rises from its central hill. On the opposite horizon, the uneven skyline of the Rusted Zone straddles the lower world. The Urbille is a broken and decaying apparatus that runs on and on, fueled by ignorance and deception.

He lifts a fallen wall and discovers a stairwell that spirals deep into the earth. Far beneath the ruined manor he enters a chamber of damp stone. Along the walls, great carven faces stare at him with shimmering opticals. The floor of the vault is littered with glassy stones of every color, a vast fortune in brilliants left here to gather mold.

Some of the giant faces grin at him. Others frown.

The Ministère de Stone.

Now you see, one of them says. *It's all a lie.*

The Surgeon nods.

"What must I do?" he asks.

With granite tongues they whisper ancient wisdom.

THE RUDE MECHANICALS AND THE HIGHWAYMAN

IT WASN'T THE SEASONAL gravity maelstroms or the swarms of psychic predators that kept us away from the Great Thoroughfare. It was the widespread tales of the highwayman known as the Surgeon.

Rumors of his perfidy rippled like ultrasonic waves from the Greater Urbille to the outer Affinities. In those distant territories where the living and the undead mingled, where villages of despair rotted at the feet of carven mountains, we heard tales from wounded travellers and weeping merchants. He stood tall and lithe as any Beatific, they said, and wielded an ancient blade faster than death. A dark cloak wrapped him like a shroud, and he wore a cruel face of sculpted bronze. To look into his burning opticals was to see your own demise, or so claimed the survivors of his attacks.

One constant ran like a silver thread among the scattered tales of his infamy: Each robbery ended with a single execution. These victims, they said, were chosen specifically by the highwayman. Others claimed they were chosen entirely at random. This point was often debated with dreadful passion.

The leader of our troupe was Sala North, the master performer so famous among the Urbille's Beatifics, Clatterpox, and Goblinkind. We were fourteen in number: ten Beatific actors and a quartet of Organic apprentices. At the end of this journey we four adolescents would receive our long-awaited Beatification. We would trade in our spongy flesh-faces for the infinite variety of porcelain visages that were the pride of Beatific society. Our fragile calciferous bones would be replaced by gleaming silver skeletons, our living brains housed inside perfectly crafted skulls of that same bright metal.

Some travellers said the Surgeon had once been a maker of Beatifics, a certified Surgeon who served the Potentates of Urbille in perfect faith, until he went mad and abandoned his practice. Now he prowled the outer edges of the Affinities, preying on whomever he chose, sparing some and slaying others. He was a demon, a defiler, a tale to frighten travellers. I only half-believed his legend. Still our troupe took the Lesser Thoroughfare now, staying well away from the Surgeon's hunting ground. None of us expected to cross his path out here, not even the ones who believed he was real.

The Rude Mechanicals had crossed a hundred Affinities and performed sixty-seven shows since our outward journey began. Our return to the Urbille would be the highlight of the year. The Beatifics would welcome us in their thousands and open their ancient marble amphitheatre, the *Théâtre d' Ames Rire,* to the spectacle of our stagecraft. We looked forward to such a grand reception after months of performing in muddy plazas, crowded graveyards, and crumbling ruins. The living and the not-quite-dead, the human and the inhuman, we entertained them all. But there was no audience like a hometown crowd—an Urbille audience.

Several more Affinities stood between us and the city, yet these were the Empty Lands. There would be no more performances until we came to the center of the Celestial Nexus, where the Urbille thrived and pulsed with a thousand different kinds of life.

"What a dreadful place," Harmona said. She tossed back her cloak and glared at the twin suns dominating a scarlet sky. The gargantuan cacti on both sides of the road sprouted millions of purple-veined blossoms. The wind blew furnace-hot and without mercy.

"You don't like the desert?" I asked. Teasing her was irresistible. She had complained about the cold for the last three days. Now there was only heat and dust. And thickets of stubborn cacti.

"Is *that* what this place is?" Harmona said. "I thought we had stumbled into Hell."

We trailed at the end of the road-weary procession. Half our number walked ahead of the six-wheeled steam carriage. It puttered along rasping and wheezing, belching pale vapors. The rest of us walked behind the conveyance, which was piled high with barrels of oil and coal, crates of costumes and backdrops, and a few bags of dried fruit and meat for the Organics. We always kept the steam carriage in our middle, ever since the time we had lost it for seven days. It ran out of fuel in the middle of an electrical storm, and we crossed into an adjacent Affinity before noticing our machine was missing.

Eventually we backtracked and found it, but looters had stolen all our gear. Not much of a concern for the Beatifics, who required neither food nor water. But for Harmona, Brix, Chancey, and myself—we pitiful Organics—such provisions were essential. Another reason to anticipate Beatification: On the day we relinquished our sweaty flesh for gorgeous clockwork bodies of metal, wire, and springs, we would leave behind our such genetic frailty. On that same great day, soon to come, we would join the ranks of Sala's journeyman actors. Our apprentice training would be complete, and we would be true Rude Mechanicals at last.

"Which Hell?" I said. "Depending on which culture you study, there are apparently a great number of netherworlds."

Harmona blinked at me as a cloud of dust blew across the road. We could barely see the black asphalt beneath the drifts of yellow sand. The Lesser Thoroughfare stretched on before us like a disappearing dream, winding through the arid landscape toward the next porte, which lay somewhere far ahead. Our homeward journey would be so much easier and faster on the Great Thoroughfare. But we avoided that route only because of the highwayman. Some might have called us cowards, but the troupe was trying to protect its most vulnerable members: Us. The frail Organics.

"You're far too literal," Harmona said. "Pass me your canteen. Mine's dry."

I gave her a drink. The steam carriage diverted its course to avoid a boulder lying in the roadway. A lucid dome containing its human brain glistened with condensation at the center of the baggage strapped to its roof. The vital organ, attached to the coal-fired engine by a clever array of neural filaments, floated in a tank of bubbling nutrient fluids. The vehicle possessed enough intelligence to avoid obstacles, but not enough to sense when it was about to run out of fuel. Skiptrain checked its gauges every few hours and refilled its furnace with handfuls of black anthracite.

Not for the first time I wondered what crime some poor Organic had committed to deserve such a fate. Prestigious or wealthy citizens of the Urbille transitioned from Organic to Beatific, while the poor gave up their flesh for Clatterpox bodies—clumsy coal-powered, barrel-shaped frames. Yet even the Clatterpox were superior to our sentient steam carriage. Clatterpox had arms, legs, and voices. They had names and a society of their own based in the Rusted Zone. Our faithful and nameless carriage had none of these things. Perhaps it was the brain of a madman or an idiot. In either case, it served well as the bearer of our troupe's necessities. It had done so for longer than anyone could remember.

Sala North walked at the head of our humble train, as always. She wore her travelling face, a finely sculpted mask of gold and ivory. On stage she wore only the most delicate and intricate of porcelain faces, but such things were not made for trekking across the Affinities. She carried a staff of dark metal, lighter than iron, with a head of living green flame. The glow of this flame had guided us through Affinities of perpetual night, realms of everlasting fog, and lately the darkness of sudden dust storms. She was our Flamekeeper, our Stagemaster, our Foster Mother, and the ticking heart of our ensemble. The original Rude Mechanical, and the director of all our performances. We all loved her.

I loved Harmona too, and I believed that she loved me. We mingled our bodily fluids in bouts of spontaneous intimacy whenever we could find a private moment. My love for Sala North was that of a son for his mother, or a student for his mentor. My passion for Harmona was the all-consuming heat of Organic lust. We would outgrow these physical expressions of intimacy when we gained Beatific status.

Not for the first time, I wondered if our relationship would survive the transition. Beatifics blended their minds, not their bodies. Only disaffected Organics joined flesh to flesh, as such antics were wholly forbidden in the Urbille. But out here on the open road Harmona and I were free to indulge our biological urges. We kept our mergings discreet, and our Beatific friends did not chastise us for it. They had all been Organics once, some of them centuries ago. They remembered what it was like to be young and feverish.

"How many more Affinities?" Harmona sighed.

I shrugged. The troupe plodded along, a trail of red dust rising in our wake.

"Not even Sala can answer that," I said. "Keep your mind focused on the Urbille, and what waits for us there."

She turned her soft blue opticals toward me and grabbed my hand. Her skin was hot and damp against mine. I wondered if her new Beatific opticals, miracles of glass and wire and miniscule gears, would retain that same delicious color. Beatifics often chose a new optical color when they transitioned. The wind howled and dust raked across the road.

"What waits for us," she repeated my words.

"You're not...scared?" I asked.

She smiled. Her broad lips were chapped and sore. Still her beauty stunned me, even as beads of sweat rolled from her hair and streaked her dusty forehead.

"Are *you*?"

"Not at all," I said. "Our days of hunger and thirst will be gone. We'll be as durable and fantastic as Sala. Beatifics at last. The pride of the Urbille."

She spat into the dirt. "You know, if we weren't actors, we wouldn't be able to afford the surgery. We'd be forced into Clatterpox bodies. Lumbering monstrosities belching steam and smoke like this dull carriage."

Sala North had adopted four orphaned children ten years go. She taught us the noble arts that made us performers. Only our association with her qualified us to join the Urbille's elite class. Our Conversion surgeries would be part of the troupe's official recompense. A reward for ten years of service and dedication to craft. Nothing was more precious in the whole wide Urbille.

I nodded. "Would you still love me if I was a Clatterpox?"

She leaned over and kissed my cheek, then wiped the dirt from her lips.

"You think I love you?" she said. "Whatever gave you that idea?" Her grin was a crooked promise. She squeezed my hand in her own. She wouldn't be able to do that when our hands were no longer spongy flesh.

Brix and Chancey walked alongside us, while Hangdog, Specious, and Aristotle formed the Beatific rear guard. Brix and Chancey never complained. They were as fragile as Harmona and myself, their dirty faces wrapped in scarves covering mouths and noses. Half-empty canteens hung at their belts alongside poniards in leather scabbards. Sometimes I thought they grew jealous of my relationship with Harmona. We had grown up together, and they loved her too. But Harmona had chosen me. I had no idea why.

"Pylons!" The shout came from the front of the procession. Sala's right-hand man Albertus gazed at the horizon through a telescopic lens. He'd spotted our next porte. The troupe quickened its pace in expectation. None of us liked this lifeless desert Affinity, not even the Beatifics. They didn't feel the heat, but the atmosphere here dried out the oils that kept their interior mechanisms running smoothly. Spending much longer in this place would be dangerous for all of us. The blowing sand would clog their gears as soon as the supply of lubricating oils ran out.

A flock of winged fungi rose from distant dunes and swept toward the procession. Their bodies were writhing masses of tendrils attached to bulbous middles, and their wings reminded me of pale, leprous bats. I counted at least two dozen of the creatures. They lurked here to prey on anyone trying to use the porte. There was nothing else to lure prey in this desolate place. We hastened toward the pair of tall black obelisks that appeared on the horizon.

Sala North stopped and stood on the side of the road like a commanding general. She pulled back the hood of her cloak, exposing her gold-and-ivory face.

It sparkled madly in the double sunlight. She raised her staff high and shouted at us through the wind.

"Quicken your pace!" she bellowed. Albertus ran to stand beside her, pulling his long rifle and aiming it at the swarm. The steam carriage kicked itself into a higher gear and we ran alongside it. Harmona would not let go of my hand, so we ran in lockstep. I looked back and saw bolts of green flame flaring from Sala's staff. The blast of Albertus's rifle shattered the wind's moaning, and a fungal beast exploded in mid-air.

The black pylons grew taller and more distinct before us, great monoliths that narrowed as they rose toward the sky. Their three-sided tops were flat, and runic formulas were carved into their stony sides. Ages of wind and dust had eroded the formulae but they were still barely visible. For a moment I feared their power was spent. If so we would be stranded here in this place of dust and death.

I looked back again and saw the fungi swarming about Sala. She flash-fried clumps of them with gouts of jade fire. Albertus cast away his spent rifle and drew his sabre. He had chosen a grim face of iron for this journey, and his opticals gleamed red as blood in their deep sockets. It was a demons' face. A face made for killing. A mask sculpted to defy the dangers of any given Affinity. On stage Albertus was a master thespian, but long before he joined the Rude Mechanicals he had been a great warrior. Now and again he told us tales of ancient wars, and the horrid slaughter of battles long forgotten by the Urbille.

Watching him skewer and hack at the flying beasts, I realized he was still very much a warrior. This gave me hope that Harmona and I would still be ourselves after Conversion. Our love would endure the loss of our Organic bodies as Albertus's warrior spirit had endured Beatification.

Beyond the pair of obelisks the dusty road stretched on through the bleak wasteland. One by one our company ran between the pylons and disappeared from sight, shunting through the invisible vertical plane of the porte. They had already arrived in the next adjacent Affinity. When the steam carriage finally rolled through, nearly half our number had already passed over.

Harmona and I raced toward the porte. Only a few more steps to go. Behind us one of the fungus creatures attached itself to Chancey's head, its tendrils writhing about his face and ears, seeking any entry to his brain. It was difficult for the beasts to pierce a Beatific's metal skull, but Chancey's bone skull would give way far easier. Brix pulled his dagger and sliced at the creature. Black gore rained across Chancey's head and shoulders, but the creature released him. It fell to the ground squirming and bleeding. Brix and Chancey ran toward the porte while Specious stomped the wounded thing into the dirt.

Skiptrain fired his ancient pistol, thunder exploding from his raised fist. Harmona and I plunged through the porte. The sounds of battle ceased instantly as the fabric of etheric reality contorted for one brief second—no sound, no gravity, no heat or cold, only a gulf of eternal nothingness that could smother us like tiny flames beneath a tidal wave. Then it was over, and we stood on the other side of the porte.

Chilling rain spattered our faces as we kept running. The steam carriage rolled on before us. The road stretched gray and shining like a serpent's back across the flat ground. A forest of shaggy willows rose on either side of the Lesser Thoroughfare. Rainwater dripped from hanging branches, stirring ripples in pools of blackish slime.

"Wonderful," Harmona said. "Another swamp..."

She had wanted to take the Great Thoroughfare. We had endured one unpleasant Affinity after another, and there seemed no end to them. The main road would have been far easier, but Sala had insisted we avoid the highwayman's path at all cost. I trusted her decision, even if it meant trudging through a series of hellish landscapes. The Urbille lay somewhere ahead of us, and that's all that mattered. That, and Harmona's hand in mine.

They came through behind us: Sala, Albertus, and Skiptrain, the last to arrive. The fungi would not follow through the porte. Such creatures abhorred the spaces between the worlds. Rarely would any threat follow a caravan through the portes. The trick was surviving long enough to reach the next pair of pylons. We had done well enough so far.

"Did everyone make it?" Sala asked. The gears inside her chest popped and creaked as her interior cogs slowed to their regular speed. The opticals behind her gold-and-ivory face stared through the rain as she counted our numbers. She nodded. The steam carriage had stopped to wait for us. The quartet of Organics gathered about the green flame atop Sala's staff, huddled like moths about a guttering gaslight. We had gone instantly from dry, scorching day to shivering in the cold, wet night. Such extremes were common when moving between Affinities. Beyond the tops of the willow trees constellations of strange stars lay hidden behind the scudding black clouds.

"Set up the big tent," Sala said. "We'll camp here until morning. Perhaps the rain will stop by then."

"I don't like the look of this place," said Albertus. He peered into the gloom of the marshland. Whatever looked back at us from the sodden wilderness must have surely trembled before his killer's face.

"Oh, *let's take the Lesser Thoroughfare*," Specious said. "It'll save us from *the horrible Surgeon...*" The opticals in his aluminum face rolled with a mocking expression, and his fingers wiggled in a parody of fear.

"The highwayman is real," Skiptrain said. "And it was Sala's decision."

"Right," said Specious. He removed his face and wiped a spatter of fungal gore from its surface. His naked silver skull gleamed dully in the glow of his opticals. He replaced his face and trundled off to help set up the tent.

An hour later we had achieved some little comfort. The rain pattered on the canvas roof. We four set in a circle about a small fire that Chancey had built to warm our skins. The Organics formed an inner circle at the center of the greater one. The Beatifics didn't need a fire's warmth. At that moment I envied their durable bodies, so immune to fatigue, cold, and hunger. It wasn't the first time I envied them so. Harmona shivered, so I pulled her closer.

Brix stirred a pot of stew over the flames. Our four bellies growled. The Beatifics spoke among themselves, deciding on the details of future performances, while the Organics ate quietly in their midst. We drank rainwater caught in tin cups. It was cold but satisfying, perfect compliment to the hot stew. I felt the food warm my guts in a pleasant way, and that warmth spread into my arms and legs. I would miss the sensation when it was no longer possible or necessary to eat.

"Are you looking forward to it?" Harmona whispered after the meal. Her head lay against my left shoulder.

"You mean Beatification?" I asked.

"What else?"

"Of course," I said. "Every child of the Urbille dreams of his Conversion Day."

"True enough," she said. Her hot breath warmed my neck. "But most children do not get to see the things we've seen or go to the places we have been."

"It doesn't matter," I said. *Only you matter to me*, I thought, but didn't say it.

"It does!" she said, pulling gently away. She stared into my opticals. Hers were full of dancing flamelight and sparkling wetness. I had grown addicted to staring at those lovely opticals. They would change—we would change—as all things must.

But we would change together.

"I know," I told her. "I know." I squeezed her hands in mine.

She smiled at me. I saw sorrow in the smile.

"You say the kindest things." She would have kissed me then, I sensed it, but we were surrounded by the Beatifics. It would have been too brazen, too insulting to merge our flesh when they could see us doing it. The rain fell from the upper dark, and we had no idea what lay beyond our ring of firelight. There was no chance of sneaking off to cuddle and conjoin tonight.

"Are you frightened?" I asked.

"Yes," she said. "But also excited. We'll be Rude Mechanicals."

"We already are," I said.

"No, we're apprentices. As long as we wear this flesh that is all we can be."

She was right. "That is the custom. Who are we to deny it?"

She nuzzled her cheek against my arm. "Will you still love me when we no longer share this wonderful weakness?"

"Yes," I said. I meant it.

We lay down on one side of the fire, Brix and Chancey on the other. About us the Rude Mechanicals sang and whispered and chattered all night, keeping their opticals on the dark swamp that engulfed us. Some practiced soliloquies or traded lines at the edge of camp. I fell asleep with Harmona in my arms.

The whirring shuffle of mechanical bodies awoke us in the dead of night. The Beatifics were standing about the rim of the tent. Those with weapons held them tightly in jointed fists. Sala's green flamed danced at the top of her staff.

"What is it?" Harmona said. We rubbed sleep from our soft opticals, stood and wrapped wet cloaks about ourselves. The fire was still alive, but it had burned low. The rain had stopped. A strange silence lay across the swampland. A trio of yellow moons dominated the sky, perfectly placed among swirling constellations of stars. The marsh pools were mirrors of moonlight.

"What is it?" I repeated Harmona's question. Brix and Chancey were too frightened to speak.

Hangdog turned his opticals toward us for a moment. He wore a face of gray metal with painted crimson lips. "Phantoms," he said. "Wild ones. Stay in the tent."

We peered beyond the shoulders of the Beatifics as they stood like sentinels about the tent. Spectral shapes flickered between the willows. They glided slowly through the trees without leaving so much as a ripple in the pools. Harmona pressed herself against my back, clutched my shoulders. I wrapped my fingers around the hilt of my poniard, knowing it would be useless against these ghosts. Brix and Chancey came close to us. I heard Chancey's teeth chattering.

"These are no moaning fizzleshades," said Hangdog. "They're dangerous."

The luminous spirits of dead men surrounded our camp. Each one resembled the body that had once carried it through the living world. They had shed those fleshy skins long ago—as Harmona, Brix, Chancey and myself would soon shed our own. Yet our brains and spirits would find homes in finely sculpted mechanical bodies. The brains of these men had decayed long ago with the rest of their forgotten flesh. I imagined their rotted remains lying under the swamp, fodder for legions of worms and insects. Nothing left of them but moldy bones and creeping phantoms.

Some of the ghosts wore antique armor, split and dented in the battles that had killed them. Some wore great bronze helms decorated with winged dragons or devilish horns. Their skinless skull-faces were like those of unmasked Beatifics, but these were pitted bone hung with shards of dessicated flesh. Beatific skulls were smooth, silver, creations of perfect beauty. There was no beauty in the faces of these restless dead.

"What do you want?" Sala North asked. She raised her bright staff high, bathing the phantoms in her green light.

The ghosts only stared at us. They encircled the camp as the Beatifics had encircled the tent. The fire suddenly died, as if someone had poured water on it.

"Leave us!" Sala shouted. The phantoms ignored her. I could not tell if they meant us harm. They might fly forward at any moment to drain our living souls, feast on our essence as the vampires of the Organic Age used to feast on blood. But they only stared.

"They'll fade when the sun rises," said Albertus, settling the butt of his rifle in the mud between his feet. "No bodiless spirit can withstand the daylight."

"How long until dawn?" Hangdog asked.

Albertus shrugged. "No idea."

"We just *had* to take the *Lesser Thoroughfare*," Specious complained again.

Sala called for quiet. The voices stopped. In the silence a rumbling sound grew closer. A pattern of repeating thunder. Hooves beating against the muddy road. It grew louder as we listened.

Harmona held her breath. Her body trembled against mine. I felt the heat of her skin even through our damp clothing. In that moment of cold terror I cherished her perfect warmth.

"It's the highwayman," she whispered. "*The Surgeon*." I thought she might weep, but she was too scared even for tears. So was I.

"But how?" said Chancey. "He doesn't haunt this road."

"Apparently now he does," said Brix. I almost laughed at his flippancy in the face of doom. A whimper-like sound was all I could manage. My stomach tightened with fright. I wondered if the Beatifics felt any fear at all. Did fear manifest from the brain or from the body? If the former were true, then the Rude Mechanicals could certainly know terror. They stood tall and dauntless all around us, staring at the black road ahead. If they were as frightened as we Organics, none of them showed it.

A rider on a dark steed rode out of the shadows. The horse was a construct of black metal, gleaming sharply in the humid air. Its opticals were slits of crimson, the light of twin flames. Steam billowed from its snout, and its jointed legs beat steel hooves against the earth, slamming the road with violent speed. Its pace decreased as the rider approached our camp.

In the saddle the Surgeon sat tall and grim. A wide-brimmed hat kept his face in shadow, but his opticals gleamed silver through that patch of darkness. His cloak flapped like a pair of gargoyle wings, settling slowly about his shoulders as the horse slowed. The phantoms parted before him, and the steaming horse walked closer to us.

"We know who you are," Sala North said. She held the flaming staff between herself and the rider.

"Then you know what I want," said the highwayman. His voice was cold, slicing through the air like a blade.

"We are an acting troupe, not a merchant caravan," said Sala. "We have no wealth to give you. Go and rob someone else."

The highwayman laughed, but there was no joy in it.

"I know who you are too, Sala North," he said. "And *what* you are." His steed stepped closer, and Sala's light turned the black leather of his garb to glimmering shades of green.

His gloved hand reached up to remove the scarf that hid his lower face. A naked silver skull gleamed at us. "You are like me," he said. "A victim of the Potentates. A slave of the Urbille." I wondered why he wore no sculpted face. Why defy this basic custom of Beatific society? Perhaps it was part of his rebellion against the established order.

"We are nobody's slaves!" Albertus said. He aimed his rifle, but Sala reached out and forced its barrel toward the ground.

The highwayman had not yet drawn the sword that hung at his belt. I saw a long-handled pistol there too, and another holstered on his right thigh. They were not modern Urbille guns, but relics of some distant Affinity. I could not guess at their power, but we had all heard the tales of his deadly blade.

"I say again, we have no money," Sala told him. "Leave us in peace."

The highwayman slid from his horse and stood facing our leader. He was close enough now that she might reach out and smite him with her weapon, or send a flash of emerald fire to scorch him. She did neither. A strange respect existed between them. Had they known each other in some previous incarnation? What had Sala not told us about this uncanny outlaw? One hand hovered above the pommel of his sword.

"If I draw this blade, someone here will die," said the highwayman.

"I'll burn you to ash," said Sala.

The highwayman nodded. "You might. But not before I kill at least half your troupe. These hungry phantoms obey the spell of my will. Best to meet my demands. Do so and you can be on your way."

Sala's voice broke the ensuing silence.

"What do you want then? Tell us."

The Surgeon's opticals looked beyond the ring of Beatifics. He looked at us now, the pale Organics standing next to the dead fire.

"The Organics must come with me," he said.

"Never," said Sala. The green fire blazed from her staff.

Quicker than any of our opticals could follow, the highwayman swept his blade from its sheathe, a flash of silver moonlight. A high-pitched tone rang through the night. Sala's head rolled from her shoulders and fell into the mud. The long blade slid back into its scabbard with a hiss. Sala's body fell forward, and the flame of her staff extinguished itself.

Albertus raised his rifle but a swarm of phantoms fell upon him, tearing him apart with ectoplasmic claws and teeth. In seconds he was nothing more than a pile of broken gears, torn wires, and silver bones. One of the ghosts carried Sala's severed head to the highwayman, who tore off its gold-and-ivory mask. He fitted her face over his naked skull, staring at us through Sala's stolen visage. Her skull glistened like a silver orb, balanced on his open palm. There was no blood, only a few drops of oil. He dropped the skull into the ashes of the cookfire.

Harmona leaped forward, but I grabbed her arms and pulled her back. It had all happened so fast. Nobody knew quite what to do about it. We all stood there, Beatific and Organic alike. Except Harmona. Tears burned on her scarlet cheeks.

"Do something!" she cried.

"There's nothing we can do," I said. It was true.

The highwayman walked into the midst of our camp wearing the face of our dead founder. The Beatifics moved out of his way, each of them surrounded by a halo of spectres. We were helpless, completely at his mercy. Tears filled our soft Organic eyes.

"Come with me now," said the highwayman, "and none else will perish this night."

He reached an empty hand toward us.

We said nothing. Moved not an inch.

"*Why?*" Harmona said. "Tell us why." She glared at him with more courage than I had ever possessed. Right then I loved her more than I ever had.

"To save your lives," said the Surgeon. "If you return to the Urbille, you will die. All four of you."

"You're a liar," Harmona said. "And a murderer!"

She would have torn Sala's face from him, or at least tried to. I held her tightly.

"You must believe me," he said. His opticals swiveled toward each of our wet faces, one by one. "I'm here to *save* you."

"You killed Sala!" Harmona shouted.

The Surgeon shook his head. He removed the gold-and-ivory mask and his silver skull regarded us intently. "She was already dead," he said. His hand gestured to the helpless Beatifics. "All of us are…"

"It doesn't make sense," said Chancey. He sobbed as he met the Surgeon's stare.

"It will," said the highwayman. "Return to the Urbille and you will be destroyed. Replaced by an automaton with your lifeless brain inside its silver skull. Oh, you will believe you are still alive, but you will not be. Your brainless bodies will be given secretly to the Potentates of Urbille. They will devour your flesh, as they devour all flesh that grows in the city. A machine will replace you, but it will not be you. It will only be a prison for your immortal soul. One from which you will never escape."

"How…" I said. "How can you know all of this?" He was telling us the truth. Somehow I sensed it. He had no reason to lie. He could have killed us right then, or have his phantoms drag us away. But he wanted us to come willingly. He wanted us to see the truth.

"I know it," he said. "Because I used to create those machines. I robbed the living of their bodies to provide sustenance for the Potentates. I transplanted thousands of brains into hollow shells, never suspecting what I was really doing. Not until…" He decided not to finish the last sentence. A great sorrow hung about him like an unseen fog. I felt it as surely as I felt Harmona's warm body in my arms.

"You…you really are a Surgeon?" Harmona asked. She relaxed in my arms, and I let her go. She too sensed the truth of the highwayman's words. She felt his aura of mingled sadness and revelation. I saw it in her face. She believed him too. Perhaps it was his subtle magic that bewitched us, as it had charmed the wild phantoms.

"My name is Wail," said the highwayman. "I used to be called Doctor Wail." He lifted Sala's gold-and-ivory face again, stared at it. "Sala North was one of my finest creations. Or so I believed. Now I understand the reality of things. I did not create her. I destroyed her, as I have destroyed so many."

If his glassy opticals could shed tears, he would have been weeping then. Waves of raw emotion radiated from his slim body. Suddenly I knew why his words rang with truth. He was an empath, a sender and receiver of emotions. Brix and Chancey knew it as surely as Harmona and myself. Our fear had given way to sorrow while he spoke.

The Beatifics stared at us now, awaiting our decision. They could not feel these broadcast emotions. Emotions were wholly Organic things, like body heat and salty tears, and the sharing of bodily fluids. I examined their well-designed faces, imagined each naked silver skull just beneath their masks. Skiptrain stood closest to me. It seemed impossible that he and the rest of the Rude Mechanicals weren't truly alive—that the entire population of the Urbille were merely machines who believed themselves to be living beings. Yet I knew it was true. The Surgeon's words, and the rush of his honest emotions, had convinced me. Convinced us.

I touched Harmona's shoulder, turned her to look at me.

There were no words. We wrapped our arms about each other, our lips pressed together in desperate hunger. We no longer cared if the Beatifics witnessed our merging.

Brix and Chancey embraced beside us. The Surgeon said nothing.

"Where will you take us?" I asked.

"A safe place," said the highwayman. "Where the Potentates and their gendarmes cannot reach you. Others are already there. Hundreds like you. An Organic army."

"Why are you building an army?" Harmona said.

"Why does anyone build an army?" said the highwayman. "There will come a day when we storm the Urbille and take it from the Potentates. On that day the living will reclaim the world. A new Organic Age will begin. You will help to build it."

The irony struck me like a physical blow. A dead man with the semblance of life would lead an army of the living to reclaim a dead city that believed itself alive.

"What *are* the Potentates?" I said.

"Carnivores," said the highwayman.

I took Harmona by the hand. "We will come, if you keep your promise not to harm any more of the Rude Mechanicals."

The Surgeon bowed from his waist and restored Sala's face to the front of his skull.

I turned to Brix and Chancey. They looked at one another, then at Harmona and me. "We've got to stick together," Brix said. "We frail Organics."

Harmona picked up Sala's fallen staff. The green flame re-ignited at its head. She looked at Skiptrain, who nodded. The staff would be our memento of Sala's generosity, her kindness, and her towering talent. It carried her stubborn power inside its metal.

We followed the highwayman away from the tent, to where his black and steaming steed awaited. He sang a brief incantation and the wild phantoms dispersed, gliding into the shadows of the swamp.

"Can you teach me that song?" Chancey asked.

"That and many more," said the highwayman. "All in good time."

The first rays of a golden morning broke over the tops of the willows. The Rude Mechanicals gathered about their silent steam carriage. Their opticals were still fixed on us. I could not guess what they thought of us now. Did they understand? Did they admire our sacrificing ourselves to save them? Did they believe that was all we were doing?

Skiptrain raised his arm and waved goodbye. I waved back at him.

The black horse blew a fresh cloud of steam from its nostrils as the Surgeon climbed into its saddle. It carried him from the road onto a narrow causeway running between the pools of marshwater. Harmona and I walked on his right side, Brix and Chancey on his left.

He led us deep into the green beauty of the marshland, and we followed him across several Affinities, taking routes unknown to travelers from the Urbille.

We decided to form a new acting troupe once we reached our destination. Our hard-won skills would not go to waste. We were Sala North's legacy. We would never become Beatifics, but we were still actors. We would never be Rude Mechanicals, but we were free to be ourselves. We would entertain our fellow Organics in the noble tradition to which we had pledged our lives.

Sala North had taught us how to act.

The Surgeon would teach us how to live.

SHADES OF LOVECRAFT

Anno Domini Azathoth

Late in the Year of Our Lord 1781 word reached the King of Spain that an uprising of Quechan Indians had destroyed two respected missions in the Arizona territory. Many priests and colonists were slaughtered. The loss of these missions closed the Anza Trail where it crossed the Colorado River, isolating the region from New Spain for years. Yet in truth it was not the wholesome Quechan Indians who assaulted the people of these missions—who marched their captives into the scorching desert toward torture and death.

To King Charles III, lost in the treacherous maze of his European ambitions, this tiny sliver of the New World was no great loss. The Crown of Spain had lost its interest in Spanish territories north of the Rio Grande, despite the numbers of settlements, soldiers, and missions that lay scattered across those untamed lands. Another power was rising in the Arizona territory, one far more ancient and vast than any earthly monarch. It came like a raging tide of blood and fire to drown both the Mission Puerto de Purísima Concepción and the Mission San Pedro y San Pablo de Bicuñer.

I, Father Francisco Gonzalez y Rivera, know the truth behind those three terrible days of slaughter. It haunts me like the ghosts who wail in the night outside my little cave. In order to pacify the restless spirits of my missionary brothers, and to rid myself of the awful secrets I have kept across lonely years, I will set down on these pages the truth of what occurred in the sweltering month of July in the Year of Our Lord 1781.

Having done this, I will carry this manuscript to the nearest mission and place it in the hands of a Holy Father who yet retains his faith in the Jesu Christi. It was this all-consuming faith that drew me across the world to spread its light in the dark places. Yet the darkness itself—and the dreadful reality which lies at the heart of it—has stolen that faith from me, as it has stolen my health, and the greater part of my mind.

I will not die a hermit confined in this squalid cave, beholden to the crippling terror of my revelations. Instead I must do as the Revelator of old: I will inscribe the truth in black ink on yellow parchment. And when I have entrusted this knowledge to one who carries the strength of the Nazarene in his heart—for he will need such strength to endure these revelations—I will free myself from this frail body with blade, or pistol, or the swift tug of a hempen rope about my neck.

I do not expect that my words will reach Charles III, or that he would deign to read them if they should be carried across the great sea to his throne. No, I need only one living mind, one soul, one fellow human being to share this terrible truth with me. I cannot die until someone else knows what I have discovered.

I am aware that this makes me a selfish man. Perhaps a wicked man.

Nevertheless, I must write as John the Apostle did before me.

I know that I am damned by what I reveal, as you who read this account must also be.

Read on then, if you fear not damnation. Or pass these pages to someone more brave—or more foolhardy—than yourself.

··········

The first time I saw Walking Ghost, I thought he was about to kill me.

It was early evening and a purple twilight crept out of the desert with an army of night-colored clouds behind it. Walking across the courtyard between blossoming cacti, I fancied that the World of Man stood on the threshold of a great and abiding darkness. The deep night and its unseen terrors have always made me uneasy.

I was kindling the tall candles in the chapel of the Mission Puerto de Purísima Concepción when the heavy wooden door banged open. Walking Ghost stood in the doorway, dark against the dying sunlight. He looked so very different from the humble Quechan folk who lived in the vicinity of the mission and attended its daily services, that I did not recognize him as one of their own.

Taller than most men he stood, a tuft of white feathers dangling from his braids of black hair. His skin was brown as the desert, his face painted in striped crimson with coal-dark pigments about the eyes and lips. I had never seen such a display as this among the Quechan, but I later learned that these were the colors of war.

Beneath its war paint the face of Walking Ghost was grim, his eyes tightened by a strange mixture of anger and remorse.

About his neck hung several bead necklaces, and his only garb was a traditional loincloth of woven bark fibers. His muscled chest, legs, and arms were bare, streaked here and there with more paint in obscure sigils. A long metal knife hung at his waist, and his right fist clutched an axe with a head of sharpened stone. The sight of this ready weapon made me clutch the crucifix at my throat and prepare for a death that might be either swift or lingering. I whispered a quick prayer that it be the former.

Beyond Walking Ghost a band of anxious braves stood in the courtyard, painted and armed as he was. At once I knew they were waiting for him, their chosen war chief.

I greeted Walking Ghost with my open palms raised and trembling.

"Welcome, friend, to the Mission Puerto de Purísima Concepción." My throat was dry, my words unsteady. "I am Father Rivera. Have you come to learn the Word of Christ?"

Walking Ghost entered the chapel. When he shook his head, I saw that he understood my words. To my surprise he sank to one knee before me and reached to take my hand. Afraid to deny him, I let him do so.

"I am called Walking Ghost," he said. "I speak your Spanish. Father Gonzalez taught me when I was a boy."

Father Octavio Gonzalez had died two years ago, victim of a nameless disease caught among the northern villages. He had gone forth to spread the Word and returned with the spite of the Devil in his blood. He had run the mission for many years before I was summoned to replace him, arriving just in time to witness his death. Several of his followers had abandoned the mission when he passed. Now there was only myself and five lesser priests, all of whom were absent from the place on this day. We had enjoyed great success in converting the Quechan people along the river valley.

"Father Gonzalez was a good man," I said, making the sign of the cross.

"I learned of your Jesus in this place," said Walking Ghost. "I learned the stories of his great wisdom and strong magic. This is why I have returned."

"I do not understand," I said. "Do you wish to make a confession?"

Walking Ghost shook his head, white feathers and black braids bobbing. I sensed a great urgency about him, something I had not noticed until now. My fear had subsided, allowing my perception to increase. He was troubled. Grieving. And his grief had turned to rage.

"Three nights ago a Maricopa war party raided my village," said Walking Ghost. "Many men were killed, and two women." He paused, drawing a deep breath. His eyes turned from my own to regard the tomahawk in his clenching fist. "Several children were stolen. One of them was my daughter Laughing Rain. Another was Bright Star, the son of my brother."

The anger seethed from his dusky skin like invisible heat. It was difficult for Walking Ghost to put these memories into words and relive the pain of them. There are those among the Spanish who believe the native peoples of this land do not share the same emotions as Europeans, but I have seen that they are every bit as human as the whites who steal their land and make them slaves. They feel as we feel, they know love and pain, joy and sorrow. They love their children no less than any Spanish mother or father does, and they know too often the horrible agony of losing them. I have counseled many Quechan whose children died of fever or acts of violence.

"I am sorry for your loss, my son." The words seemed hollow, even in my own ears.

Walking Ghost looked into my face again. "War is our tradition," he said, without a trace of pride. "We raid the villages of our enemies as they raid ours, and we steal their women and children when we can. Since the time of my father's fathers it has been so. When I was younger, Father Gonzalez told me this was an evil practice, and I believed him. Yet how does one stop the waters of a river that has been flowing for ages?"

I had no answer to this wise query.

"Often a ransom is paid, and the children are returned to their own tribe," said Walking Ghost.

"And when there is no ransom?"

"The children are adopted by the new tribe. The one that stole them. Yet such children are little more than slaves until they grow old enough to fight as men or give birth as women. It is not a good life for those raised in this way. Some choose death for themselves. Sometimes they earn death through defiance."

I began to understand the presence of the eager braves outside the chapel.

"We have no ransom to pay," said Walking Ghost. "So we walk the war path to take back our stolen children. We have fasted for two days, eaten the sacred herbs, and prepared ourselves for the spilling of blood."

"And you come now to ask the church's blessing?" I frowned at Walking Ghost's hopeful face. "I am sorry, my son, but I cannot—"

"*Magic,*" said Walking Ghost. "The Maricopa's numbers are great, and they would rather kill the children than let us recapture them. We need a strong magic. I ask for the magic of the Christ. Give me this magic, Father. I will use it to bring back our children. If you do this, I will dedicate myself to the service of your Jesus, and my children will also serve him. We will ... *convert.*"

This last word was difficult for him to speak. I balked at the pitiful irony of his request. What magic had I to give? I shook my head and dared to lay my hand on his brawny shoulder.

"I am sorry. I can give you no magic to help your war. The Glory of Christ is a doctrine of peace. He teaches us to turn the other cheek, to love our enemies, to spurn the ways of violence."

Walking Ghost stood up and his anger erupted. "Your Spanish soldiers have slaughtered our people for generations! Made slaves of them! Turned their minds from the Old Ways and made them tillers of the soil. Your guns and your spears have pierced our hearts and driven us away from the river. You speak of peace, but you practice war like us. You are no better."

I stood silent for a moment, wondering if he would split my skull with his hatchet. "Walking Ghost," I said, "do you see guns or spears in this place? We are not soldiers here, but simple men of Christ. All I can give you are my prayers and my blessing."

To my surprise Walking Ghost kneeled again, bowing his head.

I performed a simple blessing, speaking the appropriate phrases in Latin, which he must have taken as some kind of mystical spell. Perhaps this was what he wanted all along.

"Go with God, my son," I said.

Like a spark blown on a current of wind, Walking Ghost fled the chapel. A chorus of hooting, howling braves greeted his return to the war party. Then came the thunder of horses' hooves as the warriors raced away from the mission to seek the village of the Maricopa.

··•·•·•···

In the hot, dry days that followed I heard nothing of Walking Ghost and his war party. Yet I kept them in my prayers as I had promised, even when a new crisis arose to command my attention. Father Juan Espinoza had failed to return to the mission for eight weeks.

Ignoring the warnings of the local natives, Father Espinoza had determined to carry the Word of Christ to a distant and shunned tribe known as the Azothi. Their remote village, according to the few Quechan who would speak of it, lay deep inside a vast territory of sand dunes. No water or game was to be found in that hellish swathe of desert that resembled the great Sahara more than any of the North American territories.

The Quechan called the Azothi the "Lost Tribe," an appellation that I misunderstand as referring to their physical separation from the other tribes. From time to time bands of these dune-dwellers would venture into the more populous realms to trade silver nuggets for corn, melons, and iron implements. Such a contingent of Azothi had visited the mission a week previous to Father Espinoza's departure, although they would not set foot inside the chapel.

Each of the Azothi tribesmen bore a singular deformity of some kind. The first was a one-armed, emaciated wretch whose lank hair was greased with animal fat and heavy with mangy feathers. The bones of his ribs protruded from his chest at revolting angles, stretching his skin to the point where it seemed ready to burst at any moment. His eyes were rimmed with red as if he had been crying tears of blood, and his spear was thickly hung with dried scalps.

The second of the Azothi was a hunchback. His head was bald, a condition I had never before seen among the natives, and his face was an unwholesome ruin. There were no lips at all covering his misshapen teeth, which protruded in several directions from inflamed gums. One of his eyes had been torn out, leaving a raw wound adrip with pus. This hideous fellow carried a Spanish musket, obviously stolen from some murdered soldier.

The third strange one bore the useless stumps of three extra limbs jutting from his back, and he walked with a sideways gait akin to the locomotion of a crab. Half of his otherwise normal face was mangled, the piteous remains of a terrible burning, perhaps done intentionally to increase his fearsomeness. A necklace of ears hung about his neck, along with several talismans crafted of human bones. He carried axe and spear, both heavy with scalps.

These three pilgrims stood outside the mission gate, observing our humble adobe structure with bizarre amusement. Father Espinoza went out to welcome them inside, but still they refused to enter. Instead, the hunchback handed to Father Espinoza a curious green stone marked with an unidentified sigil. I watched from the courtyard through the open gate as the three Azothi shambled away. They seemed to be *laughing*, though I could not see any possible source for their humor.

Father Espinoza stood for a long time at the threshold, staring at the egg-sized stone and its obscure glyph. Eventually one of our brother-priests stirred him from his reverie, and he came dazedly inside to take his evening meal with us. However, the green stone continued to fascinate Father Espinoza throughout the next week. He carried it with him incessantly, even during our morning and afternoon services. One of the brothers told me that he had even taken to sleeping with the stone on his pillow. I decided to speak with him about this obsession, but

Espinoza himself distracted me from such a course with the announcement that he would seek out the Azothi in the land of dunes.

"I must convert these poor wretches," he said. "It is my duty under Heaven."

We applauded the bravery of his intentions, and I approved his request against my better judgment. I knew he would defy me if I forbade him to travel among the dunes. The Azothi had cast some kind of glamour over his soul, and he felt bound to them by a morbid fascination. He would not be able to rest until he made the effort of saving them from a heathen fate.

Father Espinoza left the mission with two mules, both heavily burdened with tin pots, casks of bright beads, and other gifts for the Azothi, as well as a good supply of water gourds and dried foods to sustain him on the journey. A single Quechan youth had agreed to guide him through the dunes, though I do not know what Father Espinoza used to bribe this fellow. Most of the Quechan would barely acknowledge the Azothi, let alone go to seek them where dusty death waited among the hot sands. Taking with them the blessings and faith of the mission, Espinoza and his guide departed at sunrise.

Two months later Father Espinoza was still missing. Yet his guide had returned two days ago on the back of a scrawny mule. Both boy and animal were half-dead from thirst, and had nearly starved to death among the dunes. The boy lay in a deep fever, raving in his native language about something that had terrified him. I tended to him myself, cooling his brow with a damp cloth and praying over his sickly body. I hoped he would not expire before telling us the fate of Father Espinoza. Missionary work was ever dangerous, and the valiant priest might be dead. I had had sent him into that forbidden waste. The responsibility of it lay upon my soul, a yoke of guilt that weighed me down.

The Quechan boy, whose name was Quick Eye, revived a bit on the third evening of his convalescence. I fed him broth with a wooden spoon. He shivered in the close air, and responded to my questions with minimal answers.

"Where is Father Espinoza?" I asked him.

"He is ... with *them*..." said Quick Eye. He would not say the name of the Azothi.

"Is he alive? Healthy or wounded? Does he suffer?"

"Alive..." said Quick Eye. His face twitched in uncomfortable spasms. "He lives..."

"Why did he not return with you?"

"He is one of them now," whispered Quick Eye.

I was confused. "What do you mean?"

"A piper at the gates of ... the night that lasts forever..."

"Do you mean he chose to remain among the Azothi?" I asked.

Quick Eye knocked the bowl of soup off its table and clutched the collar of my robe. His eyes were filled with panic, his nose and mouth dribbling across his chin.

"It lies at the Center!" he panted. "The Center of All! It eats the stars and vomits up devils to serve its madness. They will open the Gate... Not even the Jesus can save us, Father! Not even the Jesus!"

I could get no further sense from Quick Eye that night, so I left him to his sickbed.

"I must go into the Land of the Azothi and find Father Espinoza," I told my brother-priests. "It is my responsibility alone."

They prayed for me, but they did not argue.

·········

In the morning Quick Eye had regained his senses enough to draw me a crude map, yet he refused to accompany me on the journey. I could not fault him for this. The Azothi had abused him to the point of near-insanity, and the dunes had nearly killed him. Even now the heathens might be doing worse to poor Espinoza. I knelt before the great crucifix and prayed before setting out with my own pair of mules. Unlike Espinoza, I rode on the back of a sturdy pony, my two beasts of burden tied behind it.

Crossing the river valley, I entered the brown and cracked floor of the desert. My broad-brimmed hat protected me from the sun but not from the oppressive heat. I passed through scattered villages, meeting fewer and fewer friendly faces as I drove westward. At length I reached the badlands where only the lizard, wolf, and rattlesnake keep their homes. The gnawed bones of men and horses lay in the shadows of leaning boulders. I crossed a dry riverbed filled with flat, black stones. Spiny saguaros here stood taller than Spanish trees, gnarled and twisted into grotesque forms that reminded me of the three misshapen Azothi.

After several days I reached the border of the Azothi territory: A sea of rolling dunes where the wind swept eternally among swirling clouds of sand. I abandoned the pony, for the sand was too deep for its hooves. The mules fared better, though it was slow going. The blue sky mocked me with its crystalline purity, while I sweated and marched and rubbed sand from my eyes, nose, and mouth. At night the cold descended and I wrapped myself in blankets, warmed by brushfires until the wind and sand smothered them.

I lost track of days among the dunes, for each one flowed into the next, an unbroken stream of scorching torment. My faith gave me strength (for it was still mighty in those days). I navigated that sea of sand by rock formations rising like the ruins of primeval towers. These crude obelisks and Quick Eye's map led me to a great, sandy basin. There the huts of the Azothi sat like clusters of white mushrooms about a broad, black pit.

It must be a deep well, I thought. *The only source of water in this forsaken domain. That is how they can live in such a place of death.*

I stumbled from the dunes into the shallow valley at their heart. The ever-present howling of the wind was soon replaced by a strange music. Coming closer to the village I saw smoke rising from a great bonfire, burning fiercely in the middle of the day. The famished mules trailed behind as I walked into the village, as if they sensed something unnatural there.

My exhaustion was smothered by curiosity as I moved between the concentric rows of huts. I saw none of the deformed folk, but the music was clearer now, the sound of blaring wooden flutes and wild drums. It swirled and cascaded about the rising plume of black smoke. There was no discernible pattern to the sounds, only a twisting melody that rose and fell and rose again without pause or refrain.

No one had come forth to greet or accost me, and I saw now it was because the entire population of the village was gathered at the ceremony of the bonfire. At the edge of the open well the tall fire burned, and a hundred Azothi danced about the blaze in a circle of sweat and crazed activity. Many villagers held pipes to their lips, blowing discordant melodies that careened and blended into a screeching mass of noise. The drummers sat outside the circle, banging with hands and sticks against their rawhide instruments.

I saw now the true nature of the Azothi. Like the trio who had visited the mission, they were all horribly deformed. Yet the three who had shown themselves to the outside world were the *least* monstrous of them all.

An aged native capered madly, tendrils of veiny skin hanging like serpents from every part of his body, flapping and pulsing to the rush of his hot blood. Another man bore six arms instead of two, each one twisted and atrophied into little more than crooked claws. Naked backs and chests were ripe with pustulating sores. Several enraptured faces had been stripped of flesh in part or whole in ritual mutilations, noses hacked away leaving two jagged holes. Obscene cheekbones sprouted from red muscle, yellow teeth clacking wildly. Eyeballs bulged and rolled in the maimed faces of these living skulls, both males and females.

A legless and armless girl writhed like a snake upon the shoulders of a hunched and faceless youth. An impossible tongue fell like a red tentacle from her mouth, licking at the faceless one's head, which was little more than a fleshy ovoid with a central cavity that could not be called a mouth. Canine teeth gnashed inside this orifice, and a blind tongue shot out to entwine itself with that of his limbless bride.

On stunted legs they ambled and danced about the flames, some with swollen lips wrapped about the ends of curling flutes, impervious to the waves of heat rolling from the blaze. The ugliness and diversity of their mangled bodies cannot be overstated. If I had any food left in my belly, I would have expelled it immediately, but I could only wretch and heave pointlessly as the ceremony continued. I fell to my knees, clutching at my seizing stomach. Yet I could not tear my eyes away from the grotesque tribe and their hideous rites.

A wrinkled gnome who was all head, arms, and legs without any torso ambled among the dancers. A lopsided flutist with jagged bones protruding from his torn and bleeding flesh played as feverishly as the rest of them. Some crawled on hands and knees, more like dogs or malformed coyotes than men, licking and snuffling at the ankles of their fellow celebrants. Indescribable acts of carnality were also part of the lurid festivities, and the howls of ecstasy were indistinguishable from cries of pain and torment.

The number and variety of the lost tribe's deformities is beyond my capacity to set down on these pages. To describe even these few memories brings a fresh pang of the nausea and revolt that overcame me then. This was a ceremony that no white man was ever meant to see. I had invaded their forbidden land, intruded on their malign remoteness. Witnessing their depravity firsthand was the penance I paid now for this crime. Recalling the tale of Walking Ghost's stolen children, I wondered how many of these Azothi were stolen from the tribes of their true parents, adopted and mutilated in ceremonies like this one.

I noticed then a singular figure crouching on a pile of rocks before the flames. I would have seen him at once if the dancers had not commanded my attention with their noisome antics. He sat in a place of honor, Lord of the Flame, and yet he was only a boy. The oddly shaped stones of his perch, I was now certain, were human skulls. The boy watched the dancers and waved his arms frantically, tongue exposed, eyes squinted in his tiny head. He leaped and capered upon the skull-throne like a hairless simian, his expression one of sheer idiocy. He could not have been more than nine years old.

This boy-chief wore a strand of green stones about his scrawny neck. His forehead bulged above dim, unblinking eyes. His fingers were overlong and his feet were twisted inward, so that he would have to use his arms to walk in an ape-like manner. Yet he could leap and clap and howl with disturbing ease, and this he did while his people performed their grotesque ritual for him. From each of the boy-chief's shoulder blades rose a curving bone spur, as if there might one day be a set of bat-like wings sprouting there. The flesh of his back was extended by these spurs, yet like so many of his people the skin looked drawn, tight, and ready to burst.

I recognized the green stones about his neck. One such stone had captured the soul of Father Espinoza and led him to this place.

I screamed, loud enough to be heard among the wild cacophony of pipes and drums. I could not prevent it, for I had spotted Father Espinoza among the revelers, dancing naked with a crooked flute in his mouth. His flesh was newly pocked with ritual scarring, and the green stone hung about his neck on a leather thong. His beard and hair had been shaved completely, but I knew him. It was this shock of recognition that caused me to cry out. I might have invoked the holy name of Jesus, or it might have only been a wail of astonishment and pain. I do not remember this detail.

A mass of bloodshot eyes and hideous faces turned toward me now. The chaos of drumming and fluting fell apart, diminishing until the only sound was the crackling of the great bonfire. Even the idiot boy-chief was silent. He too stared in my direction, jutting chin and saurian eyes evoking a mockery of human arrogance.

The transformed Espinoza spoke my name aloud, and I fainted.

·········

I awoke some hours later to the smell of roasting meat. My mind was an empty vessel, my memories temporarily stolen by some force that I cannot name. Some might call it the Grace of God, but I no longer believe in such ideas.

I lay on a pile of dirty hides inside one of the domed teepees. The desert heat was lessened by the shade of this squalid dwelling, yet still sweat drenched my body. My first recognition was my own nakedness. The savages had removed my threadbare robe, leaving me only a loincloth not much different from the traditional Quechan garb. A second realization came to me then, as the shame of undress quickened my pulse: I was not alone in the hut.

The bald hunchback who had visited the mission sat over me, watching with his single watery eye. Uneven teeth protruded from his ruin of a mouth, and the puckered flesh of his empty eye socket had blossomed into a swollen mass. As I looked upon his nightmare visage the memories of my ordeal came flooding back. Fear stole my breath away as my empty stomach growled. I had not eaten for several days. My lips were parched and inflamed from my time among the dunes, my face chapped and red. The hunchback handed me a gourd full of water.

I took the vessel and drank its contents, sloshing the cool liquid down my throat. Never had I been so grateful for the simple gift of freshwater. I thanked Christ silently that these heathen grotesques were civilized enough to offer me this refreshment at least. Yet still I was afraid. The smell of the hunchback's unwashed body filled the hut. I recalled the horrid ceremony and the idiot-child who was the chieftain of this unholy settlement.

The hunchback spoke to me in crude Spanish. I was too hungry, scared, and exhausted to be surprised by his linguistic ability. "Why you come here?" The words were further distorted by his misshapen teeth and lack of any true lips, but somehow he formed the words.

I told him my name and station. "I came here to find Father Espinoza."

The hunchback nodded. "You find him."

"Yes." I forced myself to sit upright. "Where is he? Where is Espinoza?"

"We bring to you," said the hunchback. "At feast. Tonight."

I realized that the only light in the teepee came from a small fire of twigs and grass. Outside the entry flap gleamed a sliver of starry sky. I had lain unconscious all day and well past dusk. Suddenly I remembered the two mules. I had little doubt that the feast my caregiver spoke of would include the cooked flesh of those poor, undernourished beasts of burden. The Azothi had likely slaughtered them and taken the simple gifts that I had brought. At the moment I was so hungry I did not even mind the thought of dining on tough, greasy muleflesh. I had done so twice before this, in the season of drought when there was no other provender. The Arizona territory is a cruel and unforgiving land, and missionaries are above all else survivors. They must endure the harshest of deprivations in the name of the church and its teachings. Such suffering, they say, is good for a man's soul.

"Come," grunted the hunchback. He motioned me to follow him, then led me out of the hut into the greater village. I walked unsteadily, ashamed of my near-naked body, yet the few shambling natives who moved between the domiciles paid little attention to me. The hunchback took me to the largest of all the domed teepees, where a stream of white smoke poured from the roof-hole toward the blinking stars. Near the great well the bonfire burned low, and the scent of the roasting mules lay heavy upon the night air.

Inside the big dome—a reeking sweat lodge—some dozen male Azothi squatted in a ring about a dancing flame. Among their number were the other two who had visited the mission, the half-faced man and the one with the malformed rib cage. I will not describe in detail the various deformities of the other men in this council, for I have revealed too many of these horrors already. I trembled in the heat and stink of the lodge, afraid and repulsed, yet determined. I asked the Lord to help me endure this audience. Even such wretches were worthy of the

Word of Christ, who walked among the lepers and the damned. Perhaps these miserable oddities of existence needed salvation more than any other tribe I had yet encountered. I hoped Father Espinoza would attend the sweat council as well, and explain his part in the strange behavior I had witnessed.

They placed me in a position of honor, and the hunchback translated my words as I spoke to them of the Messiah and his message of peace for humanity. The monstrous tribesmen listened intently, silent as stone. At times their eyes turned to regard one another in unspoken agreement or mutual wonderment. They listened as if they had heard all of this before. I realized then that neither myself nor Father Espinoza was the first missionary to visit these wretches.

I told them the story of Virgin Birth, the miracles of the Christ, his death and resurrection. I invited them to visit the Mission Puerto de Purísima Concepción to discover the glory of my god, which was also their god. They only need accept him into their lives to be transformed, to be filled with the joy of Heaven and the blessings of the One True God.

When I had finished my sermon, I gave a solemn prayer for their village, while they watched in detached curiosity. I raised my head, having finished the benediction, and was shocked by their reaction. They howled and beat at the earthen floor with their malformed hands. It took a moment for me to understand that they were *laughing* at my sermon and prayer. Some of them rolled on the floor, clutching distended bellies. Others wept as they guffawed and shook.

Apparently I had greatly entertained them with my religious storytelling.

I endured the laughter with a stoic calm, but eventually found myself laughing along with them. Their mirth was an infectious disease to which I had no resistance. The hilarity ended when a hideous crone brought into the lodge a large clay bowl full of steaming meat. She placed the meal at the center of the congregation and departed. The Azothi insisted that I have the first piece. I was ravenously hungry, so I did not refuse. The bones had been removed and the meat was greasy yet tender. Not at all like the bitter, stringy meat of the mules I had eaten during the year of drought. Seeing my enjoyment the Azothi council joined me in the meal. In no time at all we had scraped the big bowl clean. The meat had been seasoned with some unidentifiable spice. Perhaps that was the reason for its succulent flavor, or perhaps it was simply my own state of extreme hunger. Even rancid fare will taste palatable to a starved man.

As my hunchbacked translator chewed a final mouthful, his one eye turned to regard me. I noticed then that the entire council was observing me in the same curious way. Perhaps they wanted another story of Jesus and his miracles. I considered telling a parable.

"Espinoza," said the hunchback. Drool and grease dripped from his malformed mouth.

"Father Espinoza?" Finally I would get to speak with the man I had come to rescue from this strange place. "Where is he?"

The hunchback gestured to his unpleasant mouth. I failed to understand. His bony finger extended then toward my own lips.

"Espinoza," he said again.

A congregation of glimmering eyes stared at me from nightmare faces.

Panic rose in my bloated belly. A sharp pain lanced my gut. I yelped and ran from the sweat lodge into the crooked lanes of the village. Three huts away I saw what I most dreaded to see in that moment: My two scrawny mules, unharmed and tethered to a post.

It was not these beasts the Azothi had roasted.

I fell into the sand howling and vomiting, writhing and cursing, having entirely lost my senses. What a great and terrible sin I had committed without even knowing it. I might have seized a knife from a passing native and ended my own life then, so great was my anguish. But the Azothi council rushed from the sweat lodge and grabbed me by the arms. Their grip was incontestable. They hauled me toward the great, black pit that I had taken for a well, and forced me to stare down into the darkness of it. I could not see the bottom, nor could I smell any scent of water rising from its depths.

Someone forced my head back, and the hunchback came forward with a smaller bowl. He lifted it over my mouth, which the others forced open, and poured a thick black potion down my throat. I tried to spit it back at them, but someone kicked me in the gut, forcing me to swallow the noxious fluid. I fell forward onto my belly, my head hanging over the very lip of the pit, and the Azothi moved away from me.

Whatever drug they had mixed in the bowl took effect immediately. The living world receded from my perception. I stared into the yawning void of the pit, and that abyss swelled to become the cosmos entire. Stars gleamed and swirled in the dark gulf. I floated among them now, my frail body forgotten. I was nothing but a simple mote of awareness suspended in the Great Nothingness that surrounds and encloses our tiny world.

I saw other worlds hanging in the depths of eternity, spinning like minute jewels about flaring alien suns. I understood the pit now. It represented that Great Nothingness that confines and sustains all of creation. The secret mysteries of the cosmos, the blasphemous truths hidden from a humanity that wraps itself in veils of ignorance and illusion. I saw the boiling depths of Eternity and the swirling night of Infinity, the awful immensity of existence itself, the Ultimate Secret of creation.

And there, at the shuddering heart of All That Is, I glimpsed the vast singularity of seething, ever-changing unflesh that churns without end at the nexus of all possible realities. The amorphous, bubbling god-thing that reigns supreme by virtue of its mindless and limitless power. The bloated and monstrous King of All Creation, the core of the rotting universe.

The blind idiot-god, the daemon sultan whose ageless name I heard whispered and echoing in the corridors of supernal night.

Azathoth.

About this centrifugal mass of celestial chaos I witnessed a writhing procession of devils and demons, piping eternally the Song of Creation and Destruction, beating madly on drums that are the husks of shattered worlds, and I knew these terrible beings were the Angels of Azathoth, who was the true and oblivious master of all conceivable worlds and times.

Now I understood the horrid ceremony of the Azothi, who worshipped this One True God, and I knew the significance of the idiot-boy who was their chieftain, a living avatar of their insane deity.

I saw yet another vision as I lay squirming at the edge of the pit: The Azothi themselves studying the patterns of stars in the desert sky, spilling the blood of women and children into the great pit, raising their hideous hands and faces toward the swollen moon. The mindless core of existence writhing and pulsing, squeezing bits of its limitless confusion into the mortal world.

Azathoth, reaching across the threshold of the void, breaking open the Gates of Eternal Night, sending colossal tendrils forth in bottomless, questing hunger to invade and consume mankind, leaving the Azothi to watch over the corruption and decay of their dying world. The daemon sultan would save its faithful ones for last, and while mankind fell to chaos and red ruin, the grotesque children of Azathoth, they who opened the Way for his infernal presence, would rule as senseless tyrants and feast on the flesh of the innocent.

They were the Pipers at the Gates of Eternal Night. They would fling open those gates when the stars were right, and Azathoth would pour forth upon the earth like the ancient Flood.

They would feed the world to their mad god, and help him devour it.

I regained my senses lying next to the pit. The thrashing of my body had turned my face from the deep darkness toward the glittering stars. I looked upon the face of the night and I *knew*. This was the terrible season the Azothi had long awaited. These now were the patterns of constellations they held necessary to bring their mindless god into the world. First they would drive the Spanish conquerors from the surrounding lands, then their conquest of the world itself would begin.

Someone pulled me to my feet. It was the imbecile child who was chief of the tribe. He smiled at me, blinking, and put a green stone into my palm. It was the very same stone Father Espinoza had carried, the one that had bewitched him, drawn him here to be slaughtered and devoured by the Azothi. And myself.

The child spoke to me then in perfect Spanish, and his deep voice was that of a man.

"Rejoice, Father," he said. *"In thirteen days the Gates will open."*

I shoved him, meaning only to push him away from me, but he tumbled backward into the black pit. He did not scream as he fell, but plummeted silent as a stone into the void.

I ran, clutching the green stone in my fist as if it were the last drop of my sanity.

I raced howling into the dunes, and the Azothi did not care to stop me.

·········

How I escaped death among the dunes a second time I do not know. Perhaps some charm of the Azothi's unholy magic led me from that place. It could be that the green stone I clutched was enchanted with some protective spell, or curse. Perhaps my survival was simple dumb luck. Yet some time later I staggered, nearly dead, from the killing sands. My singed flesh was pealing, my tongue swollen from extreme thirst, and I had not slept for days on end. I remember only running through terrible heat, as if the entire world was burning about me. I ran with mindless, moronic glee, desperate to escape the Land of the Azothi.

I collapsed somewhere along the trail to the mission. Walking Ghost and his Quechan brothers found me there, though I do not remember it. They carried me back to the mission, where I awakened a day later, still half-starved, my face obscure behind a madman's tangled beard. Yet my body had been washed and dressed in a clean robe. For a moment I thought the entire ordeal had been only a dream, and I had awakened from it into the comfort of my own sleeping cell in the Mission Puerto de Purísima Concepción.

Walking Ghost sat patiently at the side of my bed, and for a moment I saw the face of the hunchbacked Azothi. I started away from him, but he grabbed my arm and spoke gentle words.

"Be calm, Father," he said. "You know me. Look at my face. You know me."

Then I recognized him. I raised a hand and found that my fist was still clenched. I opened it painfully to see the green stone lying in my dirty palm. The strange glyphs carved into its substance pained my eyes.

"It is true," I said.

"What is true, Father?" Walking Ghost asked. His war paint was gone. His face was young and handsome. He wore the simple shirt of a Quechan farmer with breaches of soft leather. I stared at him, but could not explain myself. So I listened, trembling, as Walking Ghost told me his story.

"The magic of the Christ is strong," said the warrior, smiling. "Stronger than the magic of the Maricopa. Thanks to your medicine, Father, we took back our stolen children. We killed many Maricopa warriors, yet we lost no men of our own. My daughter is safe now with my wife, and my brother's son with his true father. So I must keep my promise. I will walk the war path no more. I will lay down my knife and axe to plant the corn and squash. I will accept the Word of Christ, as will my children. We will live in peace here in the river valley."

"No," I said. "No, you must not." Walking Ghost looked at me with disbelief. "The Gates will open soon! The Azothi are coming—they need sacrifices! Go and tell the Fathers! We must fight! We must *kill* them, keep their god behind the stars! Thirteen days! Only thirteen days!"

I must have been screaming, for the sound of my voice brought my brother priests running into the room. Waking Ghost regarded me with awe and horror. I strove to resist the hands of my brothers on my body—I remembered the grasping claws of the Azothi—yet I was too weak and famished. They overpowered me easily, and persuaded Walking Ghost to leave me in peace.

Then the Fathers tied me to the bed, so insistent was I that they listen to me. I told them all that I had seen, but they did not understand. I warned them that the Azothi would come for them soon. How many days had passed since the idiot-boy placed the green stone in my hand? I told them that the people of the river valley would be slaughtered, that everyone here would be sacrificed, yet they only shook their heads and told me I was "sick." They prayed for me, but they would not heed my words.

I understand now why they considered me insane. How could anyone believe what I had seen? Father Espinoza could not verify my story. Even if he had not been cooked and devoured, it appeared that he had actually converted to the faith of the Azothi. Perhaps, he too, had only been a misguided madman. I screamed and wailed and insisted that my brothers listen to me.

"You are all going to die!" I bellowed.

They locked me in my cell. Eventually I ceased raving and fell asleep.

I dreamed of the ultimate chaos boiling at the heart of Eternity and woke up screaming the name of Azathoth.

·········

So it began: First the news came that savages had attacked the Mission San Pedro y San Pablo de Bicuñer. The chapel was burned to the ground, the surrounding field set aflame, and all the priests slaughtered. The women and children of the nearby pueblo were taken as captives. This came as no surprise to those who knew the ways of the warring tribes.

When Father Ramirez whispered to me of these terrible events, I knew that the Azothi would neither adopt nor ransom their captives. They would torture them, spill their blood and bones into the great pit in the name of Azathoth. Only blood and pain could open the Gates of Eternal Night. I had seen it in my vision.

Father Ramirez indulged me by listening patiently. Yet he would not untie my restraints, and he did not believe me. He prayed once more for my lost sanity, asked Christ to bestow me his infinite mercy. This only enraged me more, and I spouted blasphemies.

"We are next!" I told him. "They will come for us!"

Two days after the slaughter of the Mission San Pedro y San Pablo de Bicuñer, the Azothi descended upon our own mission. They came in the night, setting fires and slitting throats. The black coyotes of the desert came with them, tearing out the throats of men and lapping at their blood. I lay helpless in my cell, weeping while the slaughter proceeded outside the adobe walls. I smelled burning wood, then burning flesh.

The cries of women and children drifted to my ears, and Father Ramirez came rushing into my cell. He locked the door after him but it splintered open. An Azothi rushed in with a flint-headed spear and impaled him through the belly. Ramirez fell across my bed and his blood stained my new robe.

I thought the Azothi spearman would kill me too, but instead the one-eyed hunchback entered my cell. He laughed upon seeing my helpless state, then raised his bloodstained knife and cut my bonds.

"Come," he said through broken teeth. His companion grabbed my wrists and dragged me out of the cell into the courtyard. There I was forced to my knees among a crowd of wailing women and children. The Azothi strolled about the burning mission grounds like gruesome warlords, cherishing their victory.

They mutilated the bodies of my brother priests, hanging them from the walls with strands of their own entrails. Yet they refused to kill me, even when I begged for death. They tied rawhide thongs about my wrists, as if I were one of the women. They led me away from the burning mission as if I were no more important than any of their captives. The crying of the women echoed the despair in my own soul. I knew what awaited us at the heart of the unholy wasteland.

Once again I endured the hellish crossing of the dunes, this time with my wrists bound and in the company of thirty-six women and forty-eight children taken from the peaceful Quechan river valley. I would have prayed for death then, yet I no longer possessed the faith to do even that. I had seen the reality behind the myth of a Supreme Being, and it was not my god. It was the god of these monstrous freaks. They had stolen my faith, my sanity, and my mission.

All I had left was my life, and they would take that too in good time.

The stars were ripe for the great bloodletting.

For three grueling days the deformed ones led us through the waste, allowing us barely enough water to stay alive. The cries of hungry children filled the hours. When the sun went down we were allowed to rest, after marching all day beneath the burning sun. Every one of the captives, including myself, fell immediately to sleep. Yet often one of us would awaken from terrible nightmares, only to fall unconscious once again. I remember waking several times to the low chanting of the Azothi, who stood about us in a circle with their bulging eyes turned to the stars. Even this cruel trek of deprivation and misery was part of the coming sacrifice. The greatest of their ceremonies had already begun.

On the fourth day we reached their village, where the great pit yawned open to receive us. They fed us well then on dried strips of meat. I chose to continue my starvation, yet I did not have the heart to tell the ravenous women or their little ones the nature of the flesh upon which they were fed. I kept the dreadful truth to myself, and emptied my mind of what was to come.

The Azothi arranged their captives about the lip of the pit, forming a circle. They waited for sundown. When the first shadows of night crawled from the desert, they would begin the torture and slaughter of their victims, one by one until the great circle of blood was complete, and all our bodies had been cast into the void of the pit.

I watched the sun sinking behind the dunes, glad that I would not live to see the shape of the world that was to come. A world where the Children of Azathoth would reign supreme over seas of blood and empires of bleached bone. The women and children, their bellies stuffed full of unwholesome meat, fell to sleep about the pit, while the Azothi sharpened the stone blades of their knives. I saw the hunchback mark me with his evil eye. He would take my life himself, but not before he had squeezed enough pain and anguish from me to satisfy the great ritual.

As the last rays of sunlight died between the dunes, and the first stars of evening awoke in the sky, the Azothi began their chanting. The most hideous and blood-eager among them stalked toward the captives with naked knives displayed.

A black-feathered shaft appeared in the throat of the hunchback. A second arrow fell out of the twilight and caught him full in the breast. The knife fell from his gnarled fingers. A rain of arrows fell now among the Azothi, raising cries of pain and alarm. The chanting was broken by howling war cries. Shadowy forms darted from behind the huts to pounce on the grotesque worshippers. Axes bit deep into malformed flesh, shattering brittle bones.

The sounds of battle aroused the women and children about the pit. A great band of painted Quechan braves descended upon the village. I heard the thunder of a Spanish musket, followed by several more. Bare-breasted warriors came running toward the pit, cutting through the Azothi with knife, spear, and hatchet. They offered no mercy to their deformed foes.

I watched with little excitement as the Quechan slaughtered the lost tribe. The moon rose full and red as blood above the horizon. Several Azothi corpses were tossed into the pit, and the Quechan began to free the captives of their bonds.

A plumed and painted warrior crept to my side and sliced the thongs that bound my wrists. Only when I looked into his pigment-smeared face did I recognize Walking Ghost. The naked stars glimmered in his black eyes.

"You are free, Father," he said. I must have grunted, or said nothing at all. He picked me up and tossed me over his broad shoulder. In this way Walking Ghost carried me away from the black pit and out of the burning village, while his war-brothers set fire to every last teepee.

We fled the heat of rising flames into the cool embrace of the desert night. The joyous cries of families reunited came to my ears, but beneath them I heard still the sonorous chanting of the Azothi. I feared that I would hear that chant forever after in the low sighing of the winds, in the babble of rushing waters, in the voices of men and women and children who had never seen beyond the Gates of Eternal Night.

I recall very little of what followed. I must have slept for the entire journey out of the dunes. Yet when I awoke, I lay in the camp of Walking Ghost, who had returned with the rescued captives to the river valley. He sat next to me, along with several of his loyal braves. They had not yet removed the war paint from their bodies, and their faces looked strange and monstrous.

"Here, Father," said Walking Ghost. "Drink this."

"No!" I knocked the bowl of river water from his hands as if it were poison. "No! Get away from me! Stay away!"

"Father!" Walking Ghost came after me as I shuffled away from his campfire. "I broke my vow of peace to save these people. To save *you*. What should I do now? Will the Christ forgive me?"

I had no answer for him. I ran from Walking Ghost as if he were the Devil himself. Perhaps my dead brother-priests were right all along—I had been driven mad and would never be sane again. I ran into the land of the brush and cactus, where my only company was the mute serpents and quiet lizards. There I found a shallow cave to shield me from the bite of the sun. I lay there for days, rising only to seek a stream for water and to break open a cactus with a piece flint. I pulled the spines out and ate the vegetable flesh. Never again would I suffer the touch of meat on my tongue. I have no idea what became of the green stone and its disturbing sigils.

Several years I have lived alone in this cave. My nightmares have all but faded, yet my memory remains. Sometimes the peaceful Quechan bring me corn and beans to eat. They consider me a holy man, but I never give them blessings. I have come to understand that, to them, simply being in my presence is blessing enough.

They cannot know that I am cursed.

Doomed to know the truth of the horror that lies at the Center of Creation.

·· · · · · · · · ··

Now comes the time that I must leave my little cave. I will carry this testament to the nearest mission, where the truth has some small chance of being acknowledged, and perhaps preserved. In this way I hope for some small measure of redemption before I cast aside the burden of mortality.

I can only hope that my eternal spirit, set free of its confining flesh, does not plummet into that great void where the ultimate chaos waits to devour all that exists.

I pray to the god whom I no longer serve that death is, after all, an *escape*.

Yet I fear that it is only a *doorway*, a passage to some new and more hideous realm.

THE THING IN THE POND

They say Old Man Carter started digging the pond back in 1931. His wife and two little boys had died from tuberculosis. Folks said he'd lost his mind. He never even shed a tear at the funeral, but as soon as his family was laid to rest he went on home and started digging. Most folks thought he was digging a well at first. Others claimed he was digging the pond that his poor wife had always wanted. I remember my granddaddy's take on it:

"Jeb Carter is plum crazy."

Some men deal with grief in unexpected ways. Old Man Carter turned his grief into a sadness that would mar the earth itself. He dug, and he dug, and he dug. Folks brought him sandwiches from the General Store and farmers' wives brought him chicken dinners. After a week the hole was forty feet deep, and they lowered his meals into the hole with a bucket-and-rope. Carter had rigged up a pulley system to haul up buckets of dislocated earth all day long, and a few local boys helped moved the dirt piles aside to make room for more. Everybody figured he'd give it up eventually.

Carter stayed in that damp hole, sleeping only when he'd exhausted himself, then getting right back up and digging again. All day every day—dig, dig, dig. He sent up the loose dirt in five-gallon buckets one at a time. People even came from other counties to stand at the top of the hole and watch Jeb Carter digging his way to nowhere.

"He's bound to hit China someday if'n he don't quit," some said.

"Shee-it, he'll die before he digs that far," said others.

"I read a book says they's fires deep in the earth," said a boy. "Fire and magma. He keeps on digging he'll open up Hell itself. Burn 'im alive."

"He's lost his mind," they all agreed, but nobody could blame him.

After all, he'd lost everything else.

So after a while most folks forgot all about Carter and his hole. That is until the hole filled up with water that spewed out to drown the whole pasture overnight. Nobody saw Carter come out of that hole, and the county men said he'd struck some underground reservoir or river that had proceeded to drown him. In less than a day there was no more sign of the crazy old man or his hole. There was just a big pond of deep green water, sparkling in the sunlight.

Nobody went near the Carter place for months. Down at the barber shop folks would mention Old Carter and imagine his bones lying at the bottom of the pond, or maybe stuck deep down in the hole that had birthed it. At night the pond was a black mirror reflecting the stars, and the smell of the deep earth hung in the air about it.

Wild things don't fear what men fear, so it wasn't long before the pond was lousy with fat, burping frogs. A forest of tall reeds grew about its edges. A few years later, a group of young boys snuck out to the Carter pond to hunt bullfrogs. Seven boys went down there after midnight, but only six came home. I was one of those boys, so I can tell you what happened.

Johnny Haxton, always the wildest of our bunch, decided to go for a moonlight swim. The other boys stalked the reed forest, stabbing their three-pointed gigs into every frog they could find. Johnny yelled at us to jump in. "The water's fine, boys!" he said. I remember him doing the backstroke, and I almost took off my muddy shirt and joined him.

Then I heard a gulping sound and Johnny was gone. In the center of the pond a ring of quiet ripples marked the place where he had been. I dropped an impaled frog into the burlap sack I was carrying and watched the ripples, waiting for Johnny to come back up. After about thirty seconds I started calling his name. I saw his hand come up once, the water splashing, and something dark as a shadow emerged for a half-second. Johnny's hand went back under, and there was only the sound of bullfrogs croaking between the reeds.

"Johnny!" We all screamed his name. We stood in the mud on the edge of the dark water, screaming his name over and over. Looking at the pond was like looking into the night sky. Constellations glowed like scattered diamonds. Even the ripples disappeared. We hollered for Johnny as tears fell down our faces, but not a single one of us dared to dive in there and help him. Not a single one.

We ran from that pond like the devil himself was at our heels. Next day the county sheriff sent a diver in there to comb the pond, looking for Johnny's body. It made the headlines of all the local newspapers, but they never found so much as a little finger. Johnny was gone, just like Old Man Carter was gone. Carried deep into the earth by the thing in the pond.

Nobody went down there to hunt frogs again.

The old Carter house stood half-submerged at the pond's western edge. If you walked the dirt road that wound past it, you'd hear them frogs croaking and burping from the shattered windows of the house. Only frogs and toads lived in that old house now, and every kid in Ellot County knew it was haunted. My pa whupped me good for my part in Johnny's disappearance. He warned me I'd get worse if I ever went near that pond again. So I didn't. But I did see Johnny again a few months later.

It was April and a big storm blew in, thunder and lightning and sheets of rain thick enough to drown a man in the street. I was in my bedroom reading *Tarzan and the Jewels of Opar*. Johnny had loaned me his dog-eared copy the week before he died, but I hadn't got around to reading it until now. I was so involved in the ape-man's adventures I forgot about all the storm. Ma and Pa were huddled by the fireplace in the livin' room with my little sister Sara. I was in another world altogether, a world of lost cities and deadly jungles, lost in the pages of my book.

Somebody knocked on my window. I looked up from the book, but the window was a gray mirror slick with raindrops. A pale shadow stood out there in the rain, something I could barely see. The knock wasn't loud, and I thought maybe I'd imagined it. But then it came again, low and insistent. Johnny Haxton used to knock on my window like that when he wanted me to sneak outside after dark. My first thought was "Johnny! He's still alive! He didn't die in that pond—he ran off. And now he's come back to tell me he's okay."

I went to the window and opened it. It was cold, and the air stank of fish scales and worm flesh. A dark figure stood in the rain, about Johnny's height. He'd moved back from the window a ways, and the rain obscured his face. But I could tell it was Johnny Haxton. Same skinny arms, same wild hair, and the same knock on my window.

"Johnny?" I stuck my head halfway outside.

"It's me," he said. His voice was hoarse, like he had a mouthful of mud caught in his throat.

"You're alive?" I said. The rain splattered my face.

Johnny didn't say anything, just stood there in the cold rain. A different smell reached my nostrils, and it reminded me of a dead dog's carcass I had once seen rotting on the side of the road.

"I found him," Johnny said. I still couldn't see his face well.

Thunder broke the sky above us.

"Found who?" I said, but I already knew.

"Old Man Carter," he said. I noticed he wasn't shivering at all.

"Come inside," I said. "Come sit by the fire."

Johnny raised a hand. "No," he said. "I gotta get back soon. I...I wanted to let you know."

"Let me know what?" I asked. "Where did you run off to?"

"Down there," he said. One of his bony fingers pointed to the sopping ground. "He's down there. Been down there all along."

"Down where?" I asked. My hair was soaked, and the rain wetted down my nightshirt. I shivered the way Johnny should have been shivering. The cold air was seeping into my room, along with that rotten smell. Something had died out there in the mud, a drowned rat, a dog, maybe a stray cat.

"It's wonderful, Teddy," Johnny said. "You have to see it. It's better than Opar. Better than Atlantis. Better than Camelot. Come with me...you'll see."

I shook my head. "Come inside, Johnny. I don't know what you're talkin' about."

"*Tsath*," Johnny said. "City of the Sleeping God. It's been there forever...longer than the United States...longer than Egypt...ever since the Great Cataclysm. The Children of Tsathoggua built it from sapphire and quartz. It's magnificent, Ted. And now they worship even stranger gods..."

"Tsathoggua?" I remembered the name from an issue of *Weird Tales*. "The frog-god? That ain't real, Johnny. It's just a story. Come inside and get warm now."

Johnny laughed, and his teeth chattered.

"Now why would I lie to my best buddy?" Johnny said. "I just want you to see it with your own eyes. To see *them*. Come with me now, and you'll never be cold again. This is your only chance..." Johnny reached out his hand and stepped closer to the window.

The lightning flashed and I saw his face. The skin was loose and pale about his skull, bloated and crisscrossed with blue veins. Black weeds hung tangled in his hair, and his clothing was nothing more than muddy rags. His eyeballs had fallen too far back in their sockets, and it was clear now that the rotting smell was him.

Johnny was dead after all, but somehow still walking and talking.

"Old Man Carter struck an underground river," Johnny said. Dark foam streamed from his shriveled lips as his lower jaw clacked. "The deep water pulled him right down and the current washed him all the way to K'n-yan. That's where they found his body—on the shore of the sunless sea."

I told Johnny to shut up. Tears streamed from my eyes even as the rain washed them away. His dead mouth kept on moving, and his words burned into my memories.

"They raised him up," Johnny said. "Now he serves them. There is no greater honor."

"I don't want to hear any more—"

"He came for me," Johnny said. "So they could raise me up too. Oh, you should see it. The towers of blue crystal, the domes bright as gold, alive with atomic fires. They move like angels in globes of light, drifting and flying and making love…they made us their slaves and now we'll never have to fear death again. What's there to be afraid of when you've already died? They raised us up, Ted! Come with me before it's too late! Let them raise you up!"

Johnny's hand came closer and I slammed the window shut. I must have screamed because Ma and Pa came rushing into my room. Ma told me later they found me crying and drenched on the floor by the window, but I don't remember that. They put me to bed and I lay in a fever for the next three days. I never told them about Johnny, or the things he said to me. I guess I figured nobody would believe me.

I never finished Johnny's *Opar* book. I couldn't touch it anymore. Every time I tried, I'd see his swollen, rotting face on the page. *"They raised him up!"* He say it again in my dreams, or during moments of quiet contemplation. I started sneaking whiskey from my old man's stash to dull my dreams and still my racing thoughts. I think Ma knew I was drinking, but she didn't say a thing about it. The booze kept me calm.

A month later I dug through the attic and found that old copy of *Weird Tales*. I found the story that mentioned Tsathoggua. Supposedly it was a massive, toad-like entity who dwelled in a deep cavern beneath the earth during prehistoric ages. There was no description in that story of a fantastic underground city known as Tsath, but it did mention various pre-human races who worshipped the toad-god with sacrifices of living flesh. But this was just a story in a pulp magazine—the kind of publication my parents called "ungodly trash," and would throw into the fireplace if they got half a chance.

By winter I had convinced myself that Johnny's visit had been only a nightmare. I walked by the pond and it was frozen over, as it always was during the cold months. It seemed harmless under all that ice. I tried again but still couldn't finish the Tarzan book Johnny had given me. Eventually I dropped it into the fireplace, along with that copy of *Weird Tales*. I thought maybe burning them both would end my nightmares, and it worked for a while.

On the day I turned eighteen the local draft board let me know I was going to fight Nazis in Europe. The States had joined the war two years previous, and things weren't going too well over there. Sixteen young men from Ellot County entered the service that month, although some had volunteered for duty. It didn't matter—willingly or unwillingly—we shipped off to basic training, then to the battlefields of France.

The endless fear and trauma that comes with fighting a war kept me from thinking about Old Man Carter, his pond, or Johnny. At times I completely forgot about them. Sometimes, though, we'd march by a quiet little pond in the French countryside, and it all came back like a case of mental indigestion. Unlike the other fellas in my unit, I wouldn't swim in or drink from any ponds. I had no problem with honest, free-flowing rivers, but I kept away from standing bodies of water as much as possible.

I remember sitting in camp one night, eating stew out of my helmet, imagining that every pond in the world was linked by a network of subterranean rivers, and that all of these rivers led to a sunless ocean that carried bones, jewels, and the bodies of dead men to the shore of K'n-yan. There, on sands bright as crushed sapphires, busy skeletons and restless mummies roamed about picking up useful and fascinating refuse for the Masters of Tsath. In the back of my mind, I saw the walking dead march from the sunless sea to the glittering spires of the toad-god's city. Among those diligent corpses I recognized the faces of Johnny Haxton and Old Man Carter, although how I recognized them in such a decayed state, I couldn't begin to say.

A buddy woke me up. I'd fallen asleep near the campfire while the rest of the unit bathed and splashed in a pond next to a burned-out French farmhouse. They teased me for a while about my fear of ponds, a terror so great it gave me mumbling nightmares. But I wasn't so sure my vision of Tsath had been a nightmare at all. It seemed as real as the war itself: A manifestation of impossible horrors made real. I didn't say anything like that out loud. I didn't want to get kicked out of the army as a nut-case.

One morning near Toulon a division of German forces ambushed us and killed half the unit. I took a bullet in the leg that left me lame, so I'd get out of the service honorably, not by virtue of insanity. I didn't want to go home. I didn't want to go back to Ellot County and Old Man Carter's pond. Still the power of that dark water pulled on me like a magnet. There was no escaping it.

"I know you want to stay here and see this out with your buddies," Captain Ross told me. "But it's time for you to go home. You're no good to us with a busted leg. Count your blessings, Ted. You did your part. Now go home and rest." I thought about the men who had died next to me. I thought about the men I'd killed, either long-range or face-to-face. There were so many of them, I had lost count. I heard their screams again, the boom of the artillery. I cried in that hospital bed like I'd cried the night dead Johnny came to my window. The captain held onto my shoulders like a father would. He was a good man. The next day I began a series of flights that would take me back to the States. On that same day, Captain Ross went back to the front, where he took a German bullet in the head and died instantly. I found out about it when I opened a letter that had passed me on the way home.

Ma was sick with the cancer and wouldn't last much longer. Pa was taking it hard, hitting the bottle. My little sister was just old enough to care for them both. They were happy for a little while to have me home again, but they could tell I wasn't the same. I didn't talk much anymore, and when I did they cringed at the things I shared. Nobody wanted to hear about the war—not the bloody details, the spilled brains, the slaughtered children, the constant staring into the face of death until you were numb and half-dead yourself.

I'd been back for three days when I found myself limping by the old Carter place. It was high summer, hot and humid. The pond was still the same size, but its waters were darker now. The sunlight couldn't penetrate its surface at all. The old Carter house had fallen to rubble, half of it lying underwater. The cries of bullfrogs and toads filled the air, and I sat there until dark.

The moon rose full and round. I remembered looking at it from a battlefield five thousand miles away. Stand anywhere in the world and you'll see the same moon as everyone else. The moon is a constant, like Carter's pond. Now I saw the moon's reflection gleaming on the surface of the pond, and a sudden understanding washed over me. It all made sense. Before me lay the gateway to an eternal world where change was a myth and death a distant memory. I bent down to drink the cool water, and my tears added a pinch of salt to its sweetness. I waded in and floated on my back atop the water, the moon fixed in my vision like the answer to an unasked question.

I waited for Johnny to come back. Waited to be pulled low so I could be raised up.

I was ready now. Sometimes the waters rippled and bubbled around me, releasing odd vapors into the air. Sometimes I called Johnny's name, but it didn't do me any good.

Maybe I'd waited too long and the gate to K'n-yan was closed forever. Maybe I would never walk the glimmering streets of Tsath, where statues of the toad-god stood like stone behemoths above luminous ramparts.

Now they worship even stranger gods...

When the sun came up, I swam to the pond's edge and fell asleep. I woke up and walked back to my folks' house to write all of this down on paper. People were bound to wonder about me like they wondered about Old Man Carter, and I wanted to explain things myself. I didn't show what I wrote to anyone yet. I knew better. They'd use it as evidence to lock me in a crazy-house.

Two nights later Ma died in her sleep. We buried her on the hill behind the house, and my father stopped talking to me. We drank together, but we didn't talk. My sister moved out of the house to live with a young man she'd been courting for a while. There was nothing else she could do for Pa and me.

Pa was still snoring when I got up this morning. I spent the last of my army pay on a case of good whiskey and left it for him on the dining room table. Then I hobbled over to the old Carter place and took a swim in the pond. Now and then deep rumblings came from below the water. I imagined scaly things swimming up from the sunless ocean with tongues extended like octopus tentacles, pulling me down, deep into the world below the world, where glorious Tsath awaited my service. Where Johnny's bones rambled along golden beaches gathering the detritus of mystery and carrying it back to enrich the treasure vaults of the Masters.

I floated on the black water, reflected constellations swimming about me.

Still Johnny hasn't come for me. Neither has Old Man Carter. I should have taken Johnny's invitation on that cold rainy night so many years ago.

Now I have to do things the hard way. I found a big rock in the pasture, as heavy a stone as I could carry. It didn't take long to weave some reeds into a sturdy rope. I tied one end to the rock and the other about my waist.

As soon as I finish writing this, I'll wade through the mud to the center and let the stone carry me down...down into the swirling depths of Carter's well...down into the rushing chaos of that nameless river...beyond that into the currents of the sunless ocean...and ultimately to the glittering shore of the toad-god's kingdom. When I close my eyes, I see the crystalline towers of Tsath rising toward a stalactite sky, where flocks of serpent-bats glide like sparrows. I see myself marching along the jeweled strand, once again part of a unit with a purpose. Fleshless and deathless beings with no more blood or tears to spill.

One of them is my best friend.

Whoever finds this notebook has a choice. You can believe everything I've written, if you have a mind to. Or you can toss it into the fireplace like a worthless old pulp and watch it burn. Some folks just can't abide the truth. Especially when it's ugly. But for others the truth is all they have, no matter how bitter, strange, or unbelievable it might be.

The black toads gather around me, croaking their ancient songs.

They know what's coming next.

See you soon, Johnny.

THE LORD OF ENDINGS

I FOUND THE OLD hermit sitting like a stone in the desert. His skin was gray as granite , pitted by the timeless winds. His ramshackle hut stood between two boulders deep into the great, dry plain where the pale-skinned invaders never go. I drank the last of my water the day before, and I was thirsty. The old man gave me wellwater and dried lizard flesh. He seemed to know why I had come.

As I rested in the shadow of the boulders, he brought me a small vial carved of black stone, perhaps basalt. A curiously shaped pebble served as a cork, and the symbols of a language I had never seen wound across the container's smooth surface. I gave thanks to the Great God, but the old man did not seem to like that. He covered my mouth with his gnarled, dusty hand and whispered a single word in my ear. A word that I had never heard before, yet one whose meaning I understood. It was the secret name of that which I sought.

Weariness overcame me, and I fell asleep in the lee of the big rock. When I awoke the moon had risen, and the old man was gone, his hut abandoned. I think he wondered deeper into the desert. But he had left a canteen of water for me, and it sustained me until I made it back to the outskirts of town.

The pale devils in their green-and-brown uniforms stared suspiciously at me as I passed, shifting the weight of their machine guns on their shoulders. How I hated them. They were from a land far away, where green things grew everywhere and water flowed so freely that they wasted it. They were the conquerors of my land, the unworthy inheritors of our empire of sand and sun. How ironic that they could never survive more than a few days in the desert, never understand the rules of life here among the people born to this harsh and beautiful land. Yet they came years ago with their bombs and their guns and their bone-crushing machines.

With their shackles of steel on our wrists, they call themselves *liberators*. Pale devils.

When I reached the small, filthy room that I called my own, I ate sparingly and washed the desert from my skin. Then I opened the stone vial that the hermit had given me. I sniffed at its open mouth, smelling strange, faraway odors. A sweet decay filled my nostrils like the thick smoke that pours from a bombed-out apartment building. Then, without another thought, I drank the tasteless fluid within, pouring the last of its oily drops down my throat. A great wave of fatigue swept across me, and I lay down on the worn cot that served as my bed. The room began to spin, and I smelled the distant odors again. I fell deep into slumber.

I opened my eyes in a flame-lit cavern, surrounded by walls of gleaming subterranean rock. Figures of gods and monsters spilled across the cavern, visions of an ancient world carved by ancient hands. Twin braziers of dancing flame hung from golden chains, and at my feet lay the moldering skeletons of two men, their beards and hair still growing from desiccated flesh. Their robes had once been rich, the color of silver and gold, now faded to the shade of dust. One of the dead men held a jeweled scimitar in his bony fingers. I would need it more than he, so I pried it free and took his leathern scabbard as well.

The old man's potion had worked exactly as I had been told it would. I stood at the threshold of a strange and wonderful place. Beyond a broken set of sphinx-carved doors, a stairway wound downward into darkness. Without a torch, I followed the stairs deeper into the dreaming realm, aware that it was not my physical body that descended, but a living manifestation of my very soul. My skin tingled with excitement in the dream, and perhaps it tingled as well where my body lay on that cot in the distant waking world. If this much were true, perhaps the rest of it would be. Perhaps the one I needed to find lay somewhere at the bottom of these winding steps.

Passing through another shattered gate, I emerged in a twilight realm of waste and shadows. The husks of trees lay about me like the bones of fallen giants. A sweet-smelling wind blew across the remains of a once-mighty forest. Something had crushed this wilderness, and a sea of rotting leaves spread across the devastation like a brown blanket. Here was the source of the strange odors I had smelled from the stone vial: the decaying remnants of a land ripe with death-colored fungi. The full moon floated above like a golden sphere, obscured by vapors of green and violet and scarlet, the shifting auroras of an unearthly sky. Alien constellations glittered, and a stray comet passed across the inky vault, a streak of burning sapphire.

I walked through the remnants of the dead forest, where not a tree remained standing. Shadows swirled from the rotting leaves, watching me with luminescent eyes. Perhaps they were the ghosts of the creatures who once lived among the colossal trees. Eventually I came to a great hill, and I climbed through drifts of gray dust until I stood at its summit. I stared across the vast lands beyond.

What I saw reminded me of my homeland so impossibly far away. A sweeping landscape of dunes. Yet these sands were pale as powdered bone. A black river wound like a snake through the withered field, and I could tell that this land had once been green and fertile, perhaps not so long ago. Like the shattered forest behind me, it had once been a paradise to rival the ancient realm between the Tigris and Euphrates. Now a cold wind filled the air, and the stars quivered as if touched by a nameless fear. I saw a great bat glide across the moon, or something similar to a bat whose body was distorted and swollen beyond all proportion.

I walked into the rolling fields of white sand and saw the skeletons of men and women lying half-buried in the drifts. I headed for the black river and the sand-choked ruins of a small town. Two more sets of ruins sat further along the river's course, so I made my way toward the nearest.

A thing like a crippled spider rose out of the sand, staring at me with the head of small child, eyes swollen like boiled eggs gone rotten. Mandibles clacked in its distorted mouth, and it drooled a dark fluid. The tips of its eight spindly legs were the hands of infants. I raised the stolen scimitar as it scuttled toward me with a cry of desperate hunger. I slashed it with the weapon, and it fled across the bone-colored waste, a trail of steaming blood in its wake. I was glad it had feared me, for I was not sure I could have killed it. Yet still I heard its horrible, whining cries ringing through the waste as I approached the ruined town.

Cottages and warehouses had crumbled inward or fallen to splinters, and sand filled the basins of dry fountains. Gardens floundered beneath thriving curls of thorn and bristly weeds, and fruit shriveled into black husks along bony vines. Human skulls littered the streets, alongside the smaller bones of delicate four-legged creatures. A black shape leapt from the shadows to perch on a block of crumbled masonry. Immediately, I knew what the smaller skeletons were. A lithe, black cat stared at me with piercing eyes of green. It hissed at me. I could see that it was starved, for its skin stretched tightly across its protruding ribs. I don't know why I pitied the poor creature, but I did. I discovered that I carried a pouch of dried fruits, so I gave it half a fig and poured a little water from my canteen for it to drink. I noticed the canteen in my hands was the same one that the old hermit had left for me in the desert of the waking world. As I moved through the dead village, the cat followed me like a shadow in the pallid moonlight.

I reached the river, where the sluggish current barely moved. The dock was splintered, and a riverboat lay shattered on the bank. Three emaciated villagers in rags rushed toward me from the shade of the broken vessel. One carried a twisted staff, one was an elderly woman, and one was a boy barely old enough to shave. The stink of death hung about them. I thought of the refugees who fled across the deserts of my homeland to escape the wrath of the pale devils.

"Hail, Man of the Waking World," said the staff-bearer. By his curious beard I could tell he was a priest. "Long has it been since your kind have walked this way."

"What happened here?" I asked. I hoped they would not ask me for food or water, for I did not have much to give. The black cat leapt onto my shoulder, as if it had belonged to me for years.

The bearded priest lowered his head as if reluctant to speak. The boy hid behind his mother. I knew then that the youth's mind was not intact, for his actions were those of a frightened child.

"Once, in a kinder age, this was the sweetest of towns," said the priest. "Peace, prosperity, and wisdom ruled here until..."

I stepped closer to him. "Tell me," I asked. My eyes commanded him.

He turned toward the river, which reeked of dead fish. "See now the River Skai, once a font of crystal clear waters. See how it carries the black blood of the Dreamlands along its length. See the distant, frozen slopes of Mount Lerion, from whence the river flows. Once the mountain was green and fertile as were all the lands here: Bold Hatheg and Solemn Nir. Those who survive say even bright Celephais has fallen to ruin. Along the southern river route, the towers of mystic Dylath-Leen have crumbled, and that city's far-ranging galleons sail no more. Now only the spirits of roaming dead live in these lands. So it has been...since *he* came."

"Of whom do you speak?" I asked.

"His names are many," said the priest. His voice was a rasping whisper. "But should not be uttered. He is the Lord of Endings."

I remembered the single word the old hermit had whispered in my ear.

The woman and her dim-witted son wept softly now. I took pity on them, and gave them each a fig from my pouch. With such kindness I pried more information from the bearded priest. He told me that the Lord of Endings came bearing the wrath of the Outer Gods, those ultimate beings that dwell beyond space and time.

First, the Lord of Endings came to the monolithic palace in distant Kadath where the Gods of Dream lay in decadent splendor. For their arrogance, or perhaps on a cosmic whim, the Lord shattered the castle of the dream-gods, and strangled each of them. One by one, the Lord broke their bodies against the stones of their fallen palace, and he scattered their bones to the wind: Karakal the Fire-god, Nasht the Wise, Tamash the Trickster, even Zo-Kalar the Master of Life and Death. Lobon, the God of Peace, died on the Lord's flaming spear. And there were many more whose names I do not remember.

Without the power of the gods to sustain their green and fertile domains, the Dreamlands began to wither and decay. The bones of the slain gods turned to dust and fell from the clouds to bury the land. This was the source of the white sand. The rivers all ran black with the blood of dead gods, deadly poison to drink.

"What of the Lord of Endings?" I asked. "Where did he go when his destruction was complete?"

"Men say he raised a palace for himself in the West, among the Gardens of Nightmare. There a legion of spirits and fiends flocks about his eminence. They say he awaits the coming of something, or someone. Perhaps he waits for this land to be reborn, that he may one day destroy it again." The priest looked at me with a glimmer of hope in his sad eyes. "But I see a strange fire burning in you, Dreamer. Do you seek the Lord of Endings?"

I nodded, and the bearded priest smiled.

"Cross then the black river," he said. He grabbed my shoulders, stared deeply into my eyes. Then he saw the scimitar I had stolen from the dead man whose beard was similar to his own. "You bear the power of the Waking World within you," he said. "Avenge us, Dreamer. Be our champion, Man of the Waking World! It is *you* the Lord waits for, I know it. He waits for his own ending. Go now, seek the Gardens of Nightmare. There you must slay the Bitter Lord with this holy blade that you bear, the Sword of Kaman-Thah, whose bones now rest in the Cavern of Flame. Go and avenge us!"

The old woman kissed me and the mindless boy hugged at my waist. The three pitiful survivors wept as I walked down to the black water's edge. The cat screeched and leapt from my shoulder as I waded into the River Skai. I was careful not to drink any of the black water. There was almost no current, and I could see dimly the gray waste of the far shore. The swimming was easy, but I felt massive, slimy forms brushing against me under the waters. Once a tentacle wrapped about my leg and threatened to drag me under, but I pierced its spongy flesh with the scimitar, and it let me go. I reached the western shore exhausted and lay down on the bone-colored sand to sleep.

I thought of the Lord of Endings as I lay there, and of the single word the old man had whispered in my ear. I wondered if, when I slept here in the dream-world, I would awaken in my squalid room and have to start my journey all over again. But the potion I had drank was powerful. I awoke from a dull oblivion to find myself hot and dry on the western shore of the River Skai.

The sun had emerged from roiling clouds of blood and soot. The heat shimmered across the blistered bone-sands. Accustomed as I was to the stifling heat of my homeland, this did not bother me. I drank a bit from my canteen, ate a tidbit from my pouch, and began my walk into the West.

I passed armies of skeletons fallen across the sand, both human and demonic of aspect. Carrion birds the size of men picked at beasts whose blood had dried to crimson powder. I walked among the husks of broken cities, pillars of graven gold smothered in the dust of godly bones. In empty lakebeds I saw the skeletons of fantastic serpents and fish-bodied men. Trees stood here and there, petrified into obelisks of black stone, hanging thick with dried skulls like over-ripened fruit. I wondered who had left such grisly totems, for there was no sign of anything living about me.

Mine was a timeless journey through a land of murdered beauty. Had the old hermit traveled here years ago, when these barren wastes were luxuriant forests and plains of golden wheat? Had he drank the alien wines of these broken cities and frolicked with veiled dancing girls between columns of veined marble? The ghosts of dead dreams flickered in the air, lost and abandoned on the hot winds. Whole families lay fleshless and scattered across the dunes. Bones rattled and tumbled. I wept often during this journey, cursing myself for wasting bodily fluids. How long would this endless day last?

Finally, when my food and water were long gone, the sun completed its trek across the gray sky, and a bloated moon rose to replace it. I stared into the depths of its vast craters, where shadowy beasts moved and flourished among cities of lunar fungi. So far away seemed the golden moon, and beyond it the swimming stars of the dream realm.

The strain of an eerie music roused me from my moon-reverie. I stood, staring across the dunes, and saw a mass of dark shapes moving through the night. Hunched, twisted, and clawed, these marchers plucked bones from the sand like a maiden might pick the brightest flowers from a meadow. The procession sang a mournful song of low pitch and deep timbre, a dirge that chilled me to the bone. It called me toward the grotesque marchers. I walked toward the singers on numb feet as the chill of night sank deep beneath my skin.

Beneath the murky melody of their song I heard again the words of the bearded priest: "Avenge us! Avenge us!" I heard, too, the forbidden word the old hermit had whispered into my ear back in the waking world.

The marchers stared at me with phosphorescent eyes. Many wore tattered robes like shrouds robbed from graves. Their faces were the heads of great worms, eyeless and dominated by mewling, dripping mouths lined with yellow fangs. Others stood taller than a man, yet bent and terribly malformed. Their apish arms and giant hands plucked skulls from the sand and stuffed them into ragged sacks. Still others in the procession were lovely skeletons wearing the crowns of ancient empires. The flames of forgotten sorceries burned in sockets that living eyes had long abandoned.

At their midst, borne on a palanquin of dried skin hoisted by hulking, headless demons, sat a bloated entity wrapped in silvery silks. From the deep shadows of its hood, crimson tendrils snaked and waved like the feelers of an insect. These appendages seemed to conduct the procession in its somber song. When the hooded face, thankfully hidden from my sight, turned toward me, silence replaced the weird melody.

My hand went to the hilt of the scimitar. It seemed the spell of the music was broken. I expected the bone-gatherers to leap upon me, to tear me limb from limb and throw my bloodied pieces into their bulging harvest bags. Yet the thing on the palanquin merely quivered its scarlet tendrils at me in some curious pattern, and the lesser creatures motioned me to follow them across the cold sands. As they picked up their low song again, I found myself trailing behind them. Phantoms swirled about us as we walked, moaning in accompaniment with sad harmonies.

The procession topped a high dune, and the moonlight showed an expanse of dark vegetation. Stooping willows waved in the absence of wind. Enormous blossoms lifted their stamens to the light of the winking stars. Winged clusters of barbed flesh flitted through the air like desert bats. The great oasis did not smell of leaf and petal, but reeked of musty tombs. In the center of the valley stood a fantastic palace carved from massive blocks of ruby, emerald, opal, and beryl. It gleamed like a castle of Heaven, surrounded by the waving stalks of the nightmare gardens, and it sparkled with the refracted light of moon and stars. I followed the singing bone-gatherers toward its gates.

As they walked, the singers fed the hungry, grasping blossoms with treats from their bags of bones. Great petals closed to crunch skulls into powder. Claw-like appendages reached forth from behind black leaves to grasp eagerly at tossed bones. The sweating trees quivered, their trunks gleaming like mottled serpent-skin, branches waving like the tentacles of sea-creatures. The severed and living heads of beautiful women hung by their hair from the branches of twisted willows, gasping like fish to draw air into lungs that no longer existed. Their bulging eyes stared at me as I passed, accusing me of crimes not yet committed. They wept tears of blood which fell to the ground and fed the roots of the sighing trees.

Finally the singing procession led me to the threshold of the jewel-palace, a great portico surrounded by a mass of grinning skulls. The palanquin-borne creature gestured at me, and the singers divided about my person. Each of the fiends motioned me to enter. Could it really be this easy to find and enter the domain of the Lord of Endings? Perhaps the slayer of gods expected me, as the bearded priest had thought. Perhaps he had guided me all this way.

I drew the Sword of Kaman-Thah and walked through the skull gate.

A vast, domed hall opened above me, where the light of stars pierced the diamond-carved roof. Splendid women danced within, their naked skins all the colors of the rainbow, their veils translucent, their bodies virginal and pure despite the lewdness of their dancing. They swirled about a central dais where sat a throne of black metal. Chained to the throne's base were several dying men, their flesh ripped and flayed, filling the chamber like the stink of rotting flesh and feces. The dancers moved not to the dictates of any ethereal music, but to the invisible melodies of the prisoners' suffering, which hung thick in the starlit air. A great weariness fell upon me, and I shivered with the scimitar clenched tightly in my fist.

On the throne, draped in robes of spilled blood, sat the Lord of Endings. A giant he was, his skin pale as that of a maggot. He wore a crown of bleached skulls with living eyes that glanced nervously about the hall. The Lord himself had neither eyes, nose, or mouth. His mighty head was faceless, featureless, smooth as a pearl. His great, claw-tipped hands gripped the arms of his throne. The faceless head turned almost imperceptibly toward me. I felt his gaze despite his lack of eyes, for it fell upon me like a great heat or a freezing wind.

Again I heard the voice of the bearded priest in the back of my mind: "Avenge us! Avenge us!" I ignored it.

I spoke the word that the hermit had whispered to me in the waking world.

I spoke the secret name of the Lord of Endings.

"*Nyarlathotep...*" I laid my sword at his feet and bent to kiss the bloody floor.

He spoke to me then, in words that no living ears could ever hear.

At last, the gateway opens, said the Lord.

"Give me the strength I need to do what must be done," I begged, weeping before him. The dancers swirled about me like a flock of restless spirits. They were so beautiful, their feet stained in the blood of the chained and dying men.

You shall have it, said the Lord.

I bowed low, offering my life to him.

·········

I awoke back in my tiny room, a terrible taste in my mouth. The stone vial lay empty beside my cot and sweat drenched my body. I stood, filled with a dizzying strength. I wretched violently, spewing sickness from the pit of my stomach.

I vomited forth a black puddle of viscous liquid. It spread across the unclean floor of my room. Again I puked, unleashing more of the noxious stuff. And again, as if I were going to spill my guts across the floor. Eventually the wretching subsided. The pool of black slime bubbled and swirled before me. It rose, taking the shape of a dark-skinned man. He smiled at me, no longer eyeless, and I praised him once more with his secret name.

His caress sent electricity running across my skin.

I found for him a fresh robe and a white turban. As he dressed I sent word to my brothers. When it got dark, they came and took him away, showing him a deep respect that came unbidden into their hearts. They took him into the desert, where he could begin his duties as their new leader.

Early the next morning I carefully strapped to my body the explosives my brothers had left for me. Then I prayed, not to the Great God, but to the Lord of Endings, using his secret name. I asked him to provide my brothers with the great strength he had given to me.

I put on a long coat to hide the explosives upon my chest. I walked down the street to the hospital where the pale devils, the invaders, constantly stand guard. I saw one of their large, green trucks there, so I knew there would be many of them inside at this hour.

I walked into the waiting room and took my place among the wounded and ill. In the corners, pale faces stared at me from beneath desert-brown helmets. Piercing blue eyes that should never have looked upon our sands. I noticed a live newscast playing on the television.

A man wearing my own white turban spoke loudly on the screen. He spoke of striking against the invaders, of liberating our homeland from the pale devils. Of our Holy Crusade against the infidels.

Through the glare of the television screen, his glittering eyes stared directly at me. He was the Lord of Endings, and he announced his presence to the world. He had come to lead our struggle. Now the waking world would know his power as the dream-world already had.

I watched his entire speech, sitting alone in a crowded hospital.

Now it is time.

I stand and pull the pin on the device strapped to my chest. As the hospital turns to flame around me and the screams of the dying fill the air, I whisper his name one last time.

Nyarlathotep.

THIS IS HOW THE WORLD ENDS

They always said the world would end in fire.

Mushroom clouds, atomic holocaust, the pits of Hell opening up and vomiting flame across a world of sin, corruption, and greed. The world would be a cinder, and Christ would come down from the clouds to lift the faithful skyward.

I used to believe those things. My daddy taught me the Bible, and Revelations was his favorite chapter. He believed in the wrath of God, and he feared the fires of Hell.

But the world wasn't burned away by righteous fires. There was no great conflagration.

The world didn't burn.

It drowned.

One thing the Bible did get right: the sea did turn to blood.

The coastal cities were the first to go. Two years ago the first of the Big Waves hit. The newscasters called them "mega-tsunamis." Los Angeles, San Diego, Seattle, San Francisco...so many sandcastles flattened and drowned. Watery graves for millions. New York, Miami, even Chicago when the Great Lakes leapt out of their holes like mad giants. A single day and all the major cities...gone.

After the tsunamis came the *real* terror. The waves washed terrible things onto the land...things that had never seen the light of day. Fanged, biting, *hungry* things. They fed on the bodies of the drowned, laid their eggs in the gnawed bodies. Billions of them...the seas ran red along the new coastlines. Survivors from Frisco fled inland, carrying tales of something even *worse* than the vicious Biters. Something colossal...some called it the Devil himself. It took the fallen skyscrapers as its nesting ground, ruling a kingdom of red waters.

I heard similar tales from western and eastern refugees. They fled inland, away from the stench of brine and blood, and the drifting islands of bloated bodies.

The military tried fighting back, but there were too many of those things claiming the coast. That's when the plague started. It floated across the land in great, black clouds, like dust storms during the Depression. Those who breathed the stuff didn't die...they *changed*. They grew gills, and fangs, and writhed like snakes, spitting venom. Feeding on each other. Soon there weren't any more soldiers.

I heard they tried nuking Manhattan, where something big as the moon crawled out of the ocean . The missiles didn't fire. Something shorted out all the technology, every computer on the continent...probably the planet...every piece of electronic equipment...all dead. Air Force jets fell out of the sky like dead birds. Somebody called it an electromagnetic pulse. As if the rules of the universe had shifted. In a flash, the modern world was done.

There was nothing to do but run. Hide.

Hordes of the Biters took to roaming the plains, the hills, the valleys and mountains. Those poor souls that didn't get taken by the rolling clouds eventually got rooted out by the Biters, or the worm-things that followed them around. Big, saw-toothed bastards, like leeches the size of semi-truck trailers. I saw one of the Biter hordes hit Bakersfield, saw a school bus full of refugees swallowed whole by one of those worms. Still see that in my nightmares sometimes...the faces of those kids...sound of their screams.

Whiskey helps, when I can get it.

About fifty of us from farms in the San Joaquin Valley had banded together, loaded up with guns, ammo, and canned food from Lloyd Talbert's bomb shelter, and headed east in a convoy of old pick-ups and decommissioned Army jeeps. We figured out that the black clouds usually preceded the Biters, so we stayed one step ahead of them. We tried to pick up some relatives in Bakersfield, or we would have avoided it altogether. Barely made it out of there, and we lost twelve good men in the process. Nobody got rescued.

It had rained for two months straight in California, nonstop ever since the Big Waves. Farther inland we went, the less rain we got. We figured out that the Biters liked the wet...they hated the dry lands, so we went on into Nevada. Thought we'd find kindred souls in Vegas.

That was a mistake.

Sin City had been smashed flat by something terrible that came out of Yucca Mountain, where they buried all that nuclear waste. We couldn't tell what it was, but we saw it slithering through hills of rubble, rooting up corpses like a hog sniffing for truffles. We watched it for awhile from a high ridge, until it raised itself up and howled at the moon. Its head was larger than a stadium, and it split open like a purple orchid lined with bloody fangs. What grew along the bulk of its shapeless body I can only call…tentacles. Looked like something from a B-movie filmed in Hell. It was the Beast That Ate Vegas.

Then it belched out one of those black clouds, and slammed itself back into a sea of debris that used to be a sparkling dream of a city. This cloud wasn't like the others. There were things inside it…flying things…maybe they were miniature versions of the Vegas-eater. We thought our vehicles could outrun the cloud, so we headed back west, until the Flyers came down on us.

I was riding in a jeep driven by Adam Ortega, a man I'd known since Iraq. We were two lone wolves who had gone through a lot of shit together and somehow came out alive. One of those Flyers swooped out of the dark and landed on his face. It smelled like fish guts. He screamed, and the beast pointed its orchid-face at me. A cluster of pinkish tongues quivered between the rows of fangs, and I raised my shotgun just in time to blow that thing to Hell. My shot also took Ortega's head off. God knows I didn't mean to do that. I was scared.

The jeep veered off the road, hit an embankment, and sent me flying. I blacked out, and when I woke up the entire convoy was in flames, every man lost beneath a mess of black-winged monsters. But they had forgotten me, at least for a few minutes.

They were good men, all of them, but there was no helping them now. Some had brought families with them. I heard women screaming. And children. Me, I'd always been alone, ever since my divorce. Farm life was lonely life, but it was good. My daddy passed away three years previous. Now that I think about it, I'm glad he went before all this happened. And that I never had kids of my own to see all this evil shit coming down. But some of my friends had loved ones they weren't about to leave behind, so there they were…deep in the middle of the shitstorm with the rest of us. I hid in a ditch and watched a few stragglers try to escape, but the Flyers tore away from carcasses like flocks of ravens and flapped after them.

I still had my .45 Desert Eagle and knew I was probably dead anyway. I could run, maybe live awhile longer. But one of the women trying to outrun those things was pregnant. So I started picking off the Flyers chasing her, one by one. A man ran behind her, and the things took him down. He screamed her name and I knew who she was.

"Evelyn!"

That was Johnny Colton and his wife. They hadn't been married more than a year.

Johnny's blood spouted as the damned things tore his heart out, then set to work on his face.

I ran toward Evelyn, shooting two more Flyers out of the air. I'm a pretty good shot. Got a lot of practice in the Mideast. Kept up my skills at the shooting range over the years.

One of them landed on her back and she fell, not twenty feet from me. I was afraid of shooting her, so I came at it with the hunting knife from my boot. Sliced it clean in half, but its blood was some kind of acid, splashed across my left cheek...burned like the Devil's piss. Still have one helluva scar from that.

I helped Evelyn to her feet, and we ran together. She cried out for Johnny, but I wouldn't let her look back. The black cloud was bearing down on us, blotting out the stars and moon. I smelled the stink of the ocean rolling over the desert...the smell of dead and rotted marine life.

I grabbed a satchel of gear from the overturned jeep, and we took off into the desert. The Flyers must have forgot us after awhile. They had a big enough feast back on the highway.

As the sun came up, red and bloated in the purple sky...it had never looked right since the Big Waves...we came into Pahrump. The tiny town was deserted, and corpses littered the streets. We saw they had been gnawed up pretty good, probably by the Flyers...or something just as bad. There wasn't a single living soul there. But we did find a good supply of canned food, bottled water, a gun shop full of ammo and a few rifles, and some other odds-and-ends.

It was Evelyn who told me about the old silver mine on the edge of town. She was a Nevada girl before she married Johnny.

"Maybe we can hide there...in the mine tunnels," she said. "Maybe they won't go underground. Those mines are pretty deep. We'll be safe down there, Joe."

I didn't believe we would, but I looked into her big, blue eyes, crystalline with tears shed for her dead husband, for her dead relatives in San Joaquin... for the whole damn world gone to Hell.

"Yeah." I lied to her. "We'll be safe down there. Good idea."

We loaded wheelbarrows with provisions, water, guns, blankets, and I picked up an old ham radio from the gun store. I didn't expect it to work, but it was something. Something to pin our hopes on. When the world is ending, you'll take anything you can get.

Evelyn was five months along when we moved into the mine. We weren't exactly *comfortable* down there in the belly of the cool earth, but it was as close as we were going to get. Even a blanket laid over hard stones feels good when you're half dead from exhaustion and worry. She tended the wound on my face, and I told her hopeful lies to settle her nerves. I said this would all blow over and things would be back to normal in a few months. I didn't believe a word of it. Maybe she did, or at least she wanted to.

I started playing with the radio, hooking it up to a portable battery and listening to the static. I scanned every frequency, every day for weeks, but there was nothing out there. Nothing at all. I imagined all those ham radio geeks lying dead in their basements, or their bones in the bellies of nameless beasts, their radios crushed to splinters or lying in forgotten barns covered with dust.

Slowly, the months crept by. It turned out Evelyn was right. We were safe underground. Her belly grew bigger, and she stopped moving around so much. I started mentally preparing myself to deliver the baby, something I had never done before. But I'd seen so much blood and suffering, first in the war, now at the end of the world, that I knew it wouldn't matter. How hard could it be to pull this little bugger out of his momma's belly? *She* would do most of the work.

"I'm gonna name him Johnny," she said. "Like his father."

I smiled as if it mattered. The kid had no future in a world like this. I cleaned my .45 and contemplated putting us both out of our misery. Why go on living? What was the point? We'd both be better off dead. I loaded a clip into the chamber and tucked the gun behind my belt buckle. I went over to sit by her on the makeshift bed we'd been sharing. I had never touched her sexually, but we'd hold hands in the dead of night. It brought some measure of comfort...more for her than for me, I told myself.

The baby was kicking today, and she was excited. I lowered the flame in our lantern and told her to get some sleep. I might sneak out later and hunt a hare for dinner, I told her. I always said that, but I'd never found any living game outside in the three months we'd been there. Still, sometimes I'd sneak out between the rolling black clouds and scavenge, or look for signs of life. I knew I was kidding myself, and I was tired of it.

She would nod off soon and I would end her life painlessly, one clean shot through her skull and another to finish off the unborn child.

Then one last round through the roof of my mouth and right into my brain pan.

All this suffering would be over for us. The baby would never know a world of crawling Biters and hungry Flyers. It was the right thing to do, I told myself, my mind made up.

But Evelyn...she stopped me without ever knowing my plan.

She looked up at me with those big, blue eyes, her dark lids heavy, and she raised her head a bit.

She kissed me, damn her.

She kissed me like she loved me, and I took her into my arms. We lay there for awhile, then fell to sleep. After that I knew I could never kill her. Not even to spare her the pain of living in this dying world.

Two weeks later she went into labor. I had the towels and the boiling water, and even some painkillers I'd looted from a burned-out drug store in Pahrump. She started screaming, and I could see the baby pressing outward from inside her belly.

She screamed, and I coached her to breathe, breathe, breathe. She pushed, and she screamed. A gout of blood and placenta flowed out of her, and I knew something was wrong. Her screams reached a higher pitch, and she called out for Jesus, for her mommy and daddy, for poor old Johnny.

I fell back when her stomach burst like a ripe melon, a gnarled claw protruding like a dead tree branch. She writhed like a snake, and her wailing was a white noise in my ears as the thing inside her ripped its way out. It slithered across her splayed abdomen, and she fainted. I couldn't move...I stared at Johnny Colton's baby, my mouth hanging open, my heart a hunk of lead in my chest. The stench of the deep ocean filled the cavern, overpowering the human odors of blood and afterbirth.

Its head was a bulbous thing...emerald and coated with bloody slime. Two lidless eyes bulged like black stones, but it had no other face to speak of. A mass of quivering tendrils writhed below the eyes, headless snake-things dripping with gore and mucous. It crawled out of Evelyn's body, and I knew she was dead. Nobody could lose that much blood and still be alive. She was a hollow shell. Her vacant eyes stared at the tunnel's rough ceiling. I remember thinking it was a good thing she didn't live to see this thing that had grown inside her.

It hopped from her corpse in a splash of dark fluids, walking on its clawed arms and feet. Two more appendages grew from its hunched little back, and as they spread I heard a crackling sound like stretching leather. They looked like the wings of a big bat, though far too small to carry this thing with its melon-like head and bloated stomach. It had to weigh at least twenty-five, thirty pounds, I was sure.

It looked at me for a timeless moment, then turned to explore its dead mother's body with those twitching facial tentacles. I heard a horrible sucking sound as it lapped up Evelyn's blood like mother's milk, and then the cracking of bones as its tendrils encircled and squeezed her body into pulp. Already it looked somehow larger.

The sound of her bones snapping broke my trance, and I leapt for a sawed-off shotgun I kept near the blankets. It turned to face me again, as if it knew I was about to put an end to it. The big, black eyes narrowed in their sockets, and the remnants of its own afterbirth sluiced from its hidden squid-mouth. It stared down the twin barrels of my gun, and I swear it spoke.

Even though it was only minutes old, it hissed at me, a single word I had never heard before, but somehow sounded familiar. Maybe I'd heard it in a nightmare.

Cthulhu, it whispered before I blew its head off.

I've heard that word for months now. Every time I close my eyes.

Sometimes I dream of New York, or Los Angeles, or even London. I see the great landmarks of the world that was...the towers that once conquered the sky...I see them tilted and crumbling and fallen into the sea, and a mass of cold-blooded amphibian things swirling about them like maggots on a decaying corpse.

I see Evelyn Colton's baby, too, or something like it. It stands above those ruined cities, wings spread like thunderheads, singing a wild song of triumph and murder. It squats like a colossal ape on the skeleton of the Empire State Building as if it were no more than a fallen log in some world-sized swamp.

I see its *children*, spreading across the globe, filling the low places with brackish seawater, turning the high places into wastelands. A billion-billion monsters spew from the angry seas, screaming its name beneath the bloody moon.

Cthulhu.

Flocks of Colton-babies fly down from the cold stars, soaring around their god like masses of buzzing flies.

That's what it is, I come to understand...it's their god.

It's the god of this new world.

It's been a year now since I buried Evelyn. Her grave sits in one of the mine's westernmost tunnels, marked with a cross I took from the husk of an old church.

I listen to the endless static on the ham radio every day. Found a little generator in the ruined town, and I've been siphoning gasoline from an abandoned filling station to power it. The static fills my ears, and sometimes it even drowns out the echoes of Evelyn's wailing as that thing tore itself out of her. Sometimes I broadcast, not giving away my location, but hoping someone—anyone—will answer. I feel like those SETI scientists who used to beam radio messages out into space, into the darkness of infinity, on the off chance that someone out there is listening.

But there's only static.

It rains all the time now, up there. I can't even go topside anymore because strange things move through the rain clouds, and the puddles breed miniature terrors.

The world is still drowning.

The stink of oceanic brine rolls down into the tunnels of the mine.

I tune the dials of the ham radio, call out a few more S.O.S. messages.

The .45 sits on the blanket before me. I stare at it, gleaming with silver promise.

Evelyn isn't here to stop me this time. One quick, clean shot, and I won't smell the ocean stench any more, won't have the dreams anymore, won't hear the static. The unbroken, white static.

My bottled water is running out. I can't drink the rain, but I know sooner or later I'll have to. I don't want to think what it will do to me. But thirst is a demon no man can outrun for long. I sit staring at the gun, listening to the radio static, making my decision.

I pick up the .45 and slide the barrel into my mouth. It tastes cold and bitter. Static fills my ears. I fix my thumb so that it's resting on the trigger. I say a silent prayer, and think of my daddy's face.

Something breaks the static.

A momentary glitch in the wall of white noise. I blink, my lips wrapped around the gun. I pull it from my mouth and fiddle with the nobs. There it is again! A one-second break in the static...a voice!

I turn the volume up, wait a few moments, then pick up the mic, dropping the pistol.

"Hello!" I say, my voice hoarse like sand on stone. "Hello! Is anybody there?"

White noise static...then a pause, followed by a single word, ringing clear as day from the dusty speaker, thick as mud.

Cthulhu.

I drop the mic. Something twists in my gut, and I step back from the radio like it's another monstrosity burst from Evelyn Colton's belly.

Again it speaks to me, a voice oozing out of the cold ocean depths.

Cthulhu.

The word sinks into me like a knife, a smooth incision...a length of cold metal between the eyes would be no less effective. The pain is a spike of understanding. I bend over, my hand hovering between the silver-plated pistol and the radio mic. I grab the mic, not the gun, and raise it to my lips.

I stare into the darkness at the back of the cavern and sigh out my reply.

"Cthulhu..."

I drop it to the floor and kick over the little table where the radio sits. It crashes against the stone, spilling the lantern. Flaming oil ignites the blankets, and the cavern fills with noxious smoke. I turn my back on it and walk toward the smell of briny rain, my throat dry as bone.

As I come up out of the silver mine for the last time, the storm rages, winged things soar between the clouds, and I hear a chorus of howling and screeching punctuated by thunder. Thirst consumes me.

I open my mouth to the black skies and drink the oily rain. It flows down my throat like nectar, quenching my terrible thirst in the most satisfying way. It sits cool and comforting in my belly, and I drink down more of it.

I'll never again be thirsty, I realize.

This isn't the end of the world.

It's the beginning.

My body trembles with hidden promise. I know I've got a place in this new world.

Towering things with shadow-bright wings descend to squat about me, staring with clusters of glazed eyes as I crumple...shiver...evolve.

I raise my blossoming face to the storm and screech my joy across the face of the world.

His world.

Cthuuuuulhuuuuu...

Spreading black wings, I take to the sky.

THE EMBRACE OF ELDER THINGS

MOMMA ALWAYS SAID THEY'D come for me one day. She did everything she could to make me seem like a normal kid. It wasn't her fault what happened. She used to tell me "Take responsibility for your actions." So I'll take all the responsibility for what happened to her.

The Lunar Police came to our pod at four in the morning. Someone had heard Momma screaming and reported it. Officers pounded on our door until I opened it, then they poured through the doorway with plasma rifles pointed at my head. The first one who found Momma threw up all over the carpet. The next one came at me like he wanted to stomp my head in. He grabbed me by the throat, which he should not have done. So he got what Momma got.

When the officers saw what I could do to one of their own, they had no more questions about what happened to Momma. I cried about losing her, but I was too angry to cry for the officer. I hadn't meant to kill either one of them. It was the ants running around in my brain. Momma always said they were only emotions, but they were a lot more than that.

I had an ant-farm once, and I used to watch them crawling through their tunnels and running errands that I couldn't understand. When she asked me about my tantrums, I told her there were ants running through tunnels inside my head. "My brain is an ant-farm," I said more than once. She used to hold me close and tell me it was all in my imagination. "They're just runaway emotions," she said. She told me not to tell anybody else about the ants, or the accidents they caused. Whenever they began to squirm and dance inside my head, things usually got out of control. I had shattered plates, broken windows, and destroyed video screens without meaning to.

A new squad officers came to the pod wearing shielded helmets. I couldn't read their thoughts through the headgear. They surrounded me like I was some kind of wild animal, and they escorted me across the city to the Institute. I walked between them, two in front, two behind, while the city-dome sparkled with stars above our heads. The ants in my brain were sleeping by that time.

As we walked through the city, I watched Earth sparkling above the dome: A huge blue sphere with swirls of white clouds. "It used to be green and blue," Momma would tell me as we watched it together. "It used to be so beautiful before the floods." I couldn't imagine Earth looking any other way. I knew there was not much land down there anymore, but to me it was still beautiful.

At the Institute they stripped my bloodstained clothes off, made me take a shower, and gave me a tiny room to sleep in. It felt like a prison cell, but I had never seen a real prison. Everyone who attended me wore the same kind of helmets, so I couldn't find any of their surface thoughts. The ants in my brain were still sleeping when the guards brought me to Dr. Silo's lab.

Dr. Silo was older than anyone I'd ever seen. Momma told me once that he was an original founder of the Luna Colony, which means he was over a hundred years old. I asked her how he lived for so long, and she said it was his clever science. "You will be a great scientist one day too," she told me. I didn't bother to tell her that I had no interest in science.

"Hello, Jarden," Dr. Silo greeted me with a big smile. "How are you feeling today?" His teeth were impossibly white, and his bald head was covered in brown spots and wrinkles. He did not wear a helmet, but I couldn't sense his surface thoughts either. I had no idea why.

"You're not wearing a helmet," I said.

He smiled at me again. "I am not afraid of you," he said. "And I want us to be friends."

I looked across his cluttered laboratory and out the big window. I could only see the western hemisphere of Earth from this vantage point, and there were no island chains in view—just the endless blue of Earth's single ocean. "There used to be seven oceans," Momma had told me. "But one day they all flowed together and drowned the cities of man. Now there's only one ocean."

"Why do you want to be my friend?" I asked the doctor. Most kids and adults hated to be around me. A side effect of knowing what everyone was thinking. People didn't like me for that reason. So eventually I learned to stay in the pod with Momma. I'd see other kids playing outside, running through the hydroponic gardens or playing tag near the dome's edge.

Dr. Silo chuckled. "Well, because you're a very unique person. Are you aware of that?"

"I'm different," I said. "I know that. Can I have something to drink?"

He ordered a fruit juice for me, tapping on a holographic display linked to his office pantry. It came in a cup of black plastic, but tasted cool and sweet.

"Jarden," he spoke my name again, "Can you tell me what happened to your mother?"

I was glad he asked. I needed to talk about what had happened. To explain it.

"We had an argument," I said. "I wanted to go outside. Just for a while. She kept telling me that it wasn't a good idea. 'Wait until you're seventeen' she always said. That's still three years away..."

"So, you hurt her...because she wouldn't let you leave the pod?"

"No, it wasn't like that," I said. "I heard what she was thinking. I read her thoughts, like I read everybody's thoughts. I can't help it most of the time. And the ants in my head started buzzing. They were angry. It was their fault, not mine." I didn't know if that was true, but I wanted to believe it. I started to cry, wiped my cheeks with the back of my hand. "Only babies cry," she used to say.

"You read thoughts?" Dr. Silo asked. "We call that Advanced Psychic Ability."

I nodded and sipped the juice.

"What did you see in your mother's mind?" he asked. "What made your ants so angry?"

"Hate," I said. "She hated me. She wished that I had never been born. Can you imagine that? Your own mother wishing you'd never been born?"

"Then what happened?"

"I accused her, but she denied it. I saw the raw hate in her mind, and how she lied even to herself about it. The ants stomped around in my head, and then they started screaming. Before I knew it, I was screaming too. Then.... Then..."

Dr. Silo gave me a moment. A wall of digital displays blinked and flashed behind his head, and I scooted my chair to stare out the window again. The blue waters of Earth looked calm and warm against the cold stars.

"What happened, Jarden?" Silo asked.

"She died," I said. "The screaming ants in my brain killed her."

Dr. Silo sat quiet for a while, letting me weep in peace.

"I understand," he said eventually. "It was only an accident. You didn't mean to hurt her, did you?"

I said nothing. I couldn't stop the tears. I drank the juice until it was empty. Wiped the snot running from my nose on the sleeve of my shirt.

"No," I said. "Yes. I don't know..."

"It was an accident," Dr. Silo said again. He smiled at me like he had when he first saw me. "The same thing that happened to Officer Skeller. You didn't mean to do that either."

"Is he dead too?" I asked.

Dr. Silo nodded. "I'm afraid so. Neural disruption resulting in terminal brain hemorrhage. Like an overloaded processing unit."

I remembered the blood spurting from Momma's ears, mouth, and nose. Silo was right. I didn't want to hurt her. I loved her. It was the ants. The screaming ants. They had built a series of tunnels in my brain and there was no way to get them out.

"What are you going to do with me?" I asked.

I tried harder to read his surface thoughts, but I got nothing. I had never met anyone whose naked thoughts didn't swirl about my head like bothersome insects. It was another reason I stayed inside most of the time. "We have to keep this a secret until you turn seventeen," Momma always said. "Then you'll be old enough to apply for Mars Colony. There are too many people on Luna, and they'll be afraid of you. Mars has less than a hundred miners, and they always need more labor. You'll have your own pod there, and the pay is good."

We argued about this plan frequently. "I don't want to be a miner," I told her. "I don't want to live on Mars either."

"You don't have any choice," she would say. "If they find out what you are—what you can do—they'll dissect you or kill you. Or both. So we have to keep your secret."

Dr. Silo gave me another glass of juice.

"Well, we're going to run some tests," he told me. "Take a look at your very special brain with magnetic imaging and some non-invasive neural mapping. Nothing to be worried about. It won't hurt a bit. You'll stay here in the lab with me for a few days."

"Why?" I asked.

Dr. Silo took off his spectacles and rubbed his chin. "We've been waiting for someone like you," he said. "The first evidence of APA in a lunar colonist. You could be the key to our future."

"Why can't I read your thoughts?" I asked. "You don't have a helmet on, but I can't see anything. Are you a robot?"

Dr. Silo laughed. "Have you ever seen a robot this lifelike? Human technology isn't that advanced yet." I had to admit that he was right.

"Then why can't I read you?" I said.

"Perhaps you're not trying hard enough," he said. "Go ahead. Take a look. Give it all you've got." The smile disappeared from his face. I stared into his green eyes and listened for his thoughts. The ants buzzed in my skull again. Annoyed, but not enraged. Not yet. Some kind of invisible barrier protected the doctor's mind, like Luna City sitting under its protective dome of super-glass.

"Perhaps this will help," said the doctor. He reached out slowly and took my hand.

All at once his thoughts came flooding out. Images, memories, formulae, concepts without name or explanation. I was a tiny thing caught in the flood, and it threatened to wash me away completely. My hands gripped the edge of the table.

Visions of the Earth below flowed into my mind, not the images from old movies and documentaries that showed the planet's past. No, these were recent memories from Earth's surface as it existed now, a century after the great floods. I saw a single continent rising from the world-ocean, a range of black mountains rising at its middle like the spined ridge of some gigantic monster. In the shadow of these mountains stood a city I recognized from historical studies. Built of ancient stone devoid of color, it grew like a fungus on the side of the black mountain range. Its walls were the size of lesser mountains. Twisted towers defied the Earth's gravity, rising between domes and bridges of alien design. This was the Original City of the ETs, the Elder Things. The creatures who inherited the drowned Earth when they woke from their long sleep beneath the Antarctic. Everyone on Luna knew this, the most important event in recent history. But now I saw it all in Dr. Silo's mind, horrible things that most people only suspected of existing down there.

The Elder Things glided between their towers on leathery wings, thousands of them, barrel-shaped oblong bodies with star-shaped heads and a row of five arms like wormy tendrils growing radially from their middles. They resembled plants more than animals, but I saw them feed on earthbound humans harvested from distant islands. The hairy primitives howled as they were forced into huge corrals like so much livestock. They reminded me of the carefully bred sheep we kept in Luna City, and they served the same purpose for the Elder Things.

So it was true. There were humans still living on Earth, spread across those island chains.

I knew the ETs would feed on lunar citizens too, if they could.

"We're 239,000 miles from Earth," Momma used to say. "ETs don't even know we're here, so we've got nothing to fear from them. They roam the Earth, and the waters of the Earth. We're safe here, where they can't reach us." All parents told their children a version of this comforting truth. We could look down on the horror of Earth-life, maybe even understand it. But it could not touch us. The ants inside my head buzzed and whined.

Dr. Silo's visions continued flashing inside my head. I saw the deep sea bottom now, and a mountain of quivering, snapping flesh that rolled across the sea bed. A seething mass of eyes, fangs, and tentacles swept up every living thing it its path: octopi, swordfish, coral forests, and entire schools of eels. The Elder Things glided through the water like rockets, directing their formless servants across the undersea. They rumbled through through the streets of drowned human cities, toppling hollow towers and further reducing the cities of man to gray mud. Eventually there would be nothing at all left of human civilization. What the ocean didn't destroy, the servants of the ETs would annihilate.

"They're called shoggoths…"

I heard the words inside my mind, but they weren't human words.

Somehow, I understood them anyway.

The shoggoths swept out of the sea like living monsoons and poured over islands one by one. Wailing savages attacked them with flaming torch and spear. The Elder Things flew above the fray, letting their fleshy slaves do the hard work. Shoggoths grabbed up the tiny men and women, tearing them to bits, absorbing human flesh into their own pulsating masses. Hungry ETs swoop down to feed as well. Snake-like tubes with fanged mouths swelled up from their five-pointed heads, wrapping about their victims to slurp at fountains of spewing blood.

The ants in my skull danced and raged.

I blinked, pulling back from the table as I pulled my mind away from Dr. Silo. The images disappeared, and I was back in his sterile lab again. He spoke to me without moving his lips. Now I heard only the thoughts he wanted me to hear.

"Do not be afraid, Jarden," he said. "You are not like the others of your kind. You are special. We hoped that one day we would find someone like you. It was only a matter of time. It is why we allowed this colony to survive."

"I know what you are," I said. My skull buzzed and I heard the crackle of electricity. The lab room was quiet, the Earth spinning blue and silent beyond the window.

"Of course you do," he said. "And now you know why I don't need a helmet."

"You're one of them," I said. "An ET."

Dr. Silo pulled a small device from his pocket and showed it to me. It looked nothing like the other technology in his lab. More like a smooth, five-pointed amulet of green stone. "Molecular manipulation," he said inside my head. "This device allows me to assume a human form, so I can mingle with your kind. So I can monitor them."

"How long?" I asked. I remembered the tales of Silo's advanced age. He certainly looked a hundred years old, if not older. But that wasn't his true flesh. He was far older than a mere century. Nobody knew how long the ETs lived, or if they ever actually died.

"We don't," he responded to my unspoken thought. "We are immortal."

"So you've been here all along," I said. "You helped found this colony."

"Not exactly," he said. "But decades ago I replaced the original Dr. Silo."

"What do you want with me?" I asked. My head hurt now, the ants stomping and wailing, filling my skull with a dull pain. Usually if I stayed calm, they would go away. I tried, but my pulse was racing. For the first time since coming to the lab, I was afraid.

"I told you before that we wish to study you," he said. "I was not lying."

"I could tell the police your secret," I said. "Everyone will know."

My eyes glanced at the comm button on the nearby wall. I wondered if I could reach it before Dr. Silo could stop me.

"You might do that," he said. His lips still hadn't moved. "But your Lunar Police are not likely to believe a child who murdered his own mother. You have no proof."

"I'll tell them anyway," I said.

"If you do so, I will destroy this colony and every last human life in it."

"What do you want from me?"

My heart beat faster inside my chest. Pressure in my head continued to build.

"You will come with me," Dr. Silo said. He stood up and began speaking with his mouth again. He stared out the window at the watery Earth. "There will be a special place for you in the Original City. A place of honor. We will study your brain and see how we can reproduce it in our lesser servitors. The shoggoths are much too dimwitted for interplanetary application. Once we have remade them with the ability to think and reason, to communicate via telepathy, and taught them the arts of telekinesis, we will be ready for the next Great Migration. As I said, you are the key to our future."

"You want my brain," I said.

"Correction," said the doctor. "We already have it."

The ants screamed then, louder than they had ever screamed.

Their screams poured out my eyes like invisible flames. Dr. Silo screamed too. His fingers fumbled with the device he was holding, and he dropped it to the floor where it shattered into pieces. His skin bubbled and bulged. Blood poured from his ears, mouth, and nose, just like Momma's had done. But unlike Momma he didn't die. He *changed*...

His bald head exploded, and a pink, star-shaped organ burst like a bloody flower from his neck. His arms withered and folded into the main substance of his body, which bloated and swelled until his clothing was torn to shreds. At last I stopped screaming, and I backed away from the gore-splattered table. The ants fell to silence in my mind again, but Silo's transformation was not yet finished.

His body swelled into a barrel-like shape, and five segmented appendages burst from his lower portions, the meat of his legs dividing themselves and lengthening with the sound of cracking bones. Five major tentacles emerged in a ring about his midsection, each one topped by a mass of lesser tendrils. Five bloodshot eyeballs stared at me from his starfish-shaped head, and his fanged feeding tubes quivered in the air. There was nothing left of his false human shape, except for a single layer of shredded skin on the lab floor.

Silo stood more than twice my height now, and five fan-like wings raised from the vertical ridges of his bloated torso. I huddled in the corner of the lab, weeping and shivering. The ants in my head weren't angry anymore. They were spent. I wondered if they would let this thing devour me now. I had no more anger left. Only paralyzing terror.

"Your power is impressive," said the ET, speaking inside my head again. "You are a true prize." He shambled closer on his five lower extremities, two upper tendrils reaching out to caress my face and body. In some horrible way the creature attempted to hug me like a human.

"Leave me alone," I said. "Leave Luna City alone. You don't belong here."

"That depends on you," he said. "Come with me willingly, Jarden. No more resistance. If you do this, I will spare your colony."

I sensed the thought-forms streaming from his mind. They were louder than ever now. There was much I could not identify there, but I could tell he was telling the truth. Making me an honest offer. I stood up from my sanctuary in the corner of the lab. The tendrils waved expectantly. If he wanted to kill me, I would already be dead. I was too valuable to kill.

"If I go with you," I said. "Will you keep your word?"

"Of course."

"But how?" I said. "There are no more Earth shuttles. How can we get...down there?" I pointed to the blue Earth outside the window.

"My kind are nearly indestructible. We can pass through the void without need of metal shells or external technology. We engage in deep hibernation and soar like meteors toward our destination. It will take me less than three days to glide from Luna to the Earth."

"What about me?" I asked. "I can't survive a trip like that."

"It doesn't matter," said the Silo-thing. His five sets of tendrils quivered. "All I require is your brain, which I will store and carry safely within my carapace."

The meaning behind these words made me tremble.

"So you are going to kill me," I said. The ants began to dance and buzz again. I touched my face and discovered that my eyes had been bleeding. I blinked and my vision blurred.

"No," said the ET. "You misunderstand. I will preserve your prime organ inside a jar of specially treated nutrients. When we reach Earth I will transplant it into a fresh human body acquired from one of our island preserves. None will dare to eat your flesh, or to harm you in any way. You will be studied, honored, and revered. I will give you a new body, an older body, stronger and more fit. Haven't you always wanted to visit Earth and see its glorious waters for yourself?"

So he had been reading my mind too. Every child of Luna dreamed of escaping into the past where the Earth was green and fertile and free of flesh-eating monsters. Every child of Earth wanted to go home. Even those of us who were born on the Moon.

I stepped closer to the waving tendrils.

"We have a deal," I said. "Leave Luna City in peace. I will go with you."

There was nothing left for me on Luna anyway. I had no parents, no family, no friends.

"Excellent," said the ET. The creature's tentacles reached across the room for a cylindrical jar with a pressurized lid. A clear fluid sloshed inside, but there was plenty of room there for a human brain. The ET asked me to lie on an operating table, and it dosed me with anesthetic. As the lab and the monster began to fade, I remembered my mother's face.

"I don't want to be a Martian," I whispered. Sleep came fast and deep.

I did not think there would be any dreams then, but somehow there were. I saw my father, walking me through the public parks of Luna years before he died in a shuttle accident. He and my mother looked so happy together. They held my hands in each of their own. Together we looked up at the Earth, so blue and gorgeous against a backdrop of stars. The dream was also a memory.

"Someday we'll get back home," my father said. "Someday…"

I dreamed about many other things during the time my brain was separated from my body. Some were only memories, some were pure inventions, and others were indescribable visions that I would never be able to put into words. After some unknown interval of time, I opened my new eyes.

A council of Elder Things stood about me, wings fluttering, eyeballs and tendrils aquiver.

I looked down at my new body: A muscled brute, shaggy and naked except for a dirty loincloth. I flexed my new hands, which were calloused with the marks of spear, harpoon, and axe. I looked up, past the alien towers, and for the first time I saw what the Moon looked like from the surface of Earth. From this distance Luna City was only a small dot of light, sitting alone on a barren moonscape.

The Elder Things bleated and whistled and croaked in their excitement, wrapping curious tendrils about my stitched skull and bearded face. Strange machines rose behind them, and they conducted me into a maze of tubes and circuitry and alien contraptions. Here they would study my unique brain and learn how to recreate it in their cloning vats. For a while they tinkered and fussed over me, running tests with glowing rods, casting lights through my skull and out the other side, and indulging many other processes that I did not begin to understand.

Later they flew me up to my own private chamber atop a strangely shaped tower. They even brought in a captive island girl to accompany me in my high prison. She spoke no language that I could understand, but I read her simple thoughts easily. At first she feared me, but then seemed to recognize me. She cuddled close and slept beside me on a carpet of seal fur.

As I slept that night, the ants inside my brain returned. They moved like shadows in my dreams, scuttling and chirruping and growing larger. I had never heard them speak before now. But they spoke in some kind of dream-language that I understood only because they willed me to.

"You have served us well, Little Host," they hissed. "Now our invasion begins."

Ancient enemies of the Elder Things, they had found access to this world through the tunnels of my brain. Now the fleshy ant-farm in my skull broke open, and its occupants flooded the Earth. I saw that they were not truly ants at all, but giants made of living darkness. Their eyes were orbs of solar flame. I woke shivering in the darkness next to my new mate, and the nameless ant-giants came pouring from my brain. They flowed like black blood from my new eyes, ears, and mouth, slinking across the floor and rising into massive insectoid shapes, one after the other filling the room with their massive bulk. They flowed from my high tower cell as the oceans had once overflowed the continents.

In the streets of the Original City they demolished towers and trampled domes into dust, catching Elder Things like flies in their hungry jaws. A war of monstrosities raged below my high prison, and the Earth itself rumbled with the strain of it. The island girl leaped screaming through a star-shaped window and fell into the chaos below.

Dr. Silo's words echoed inside my hollow mind.

"You are not like the others of your kind. You are special."

My new body lay dying, smiling, listening to the howls of shoggoths and shadows.

I was home.

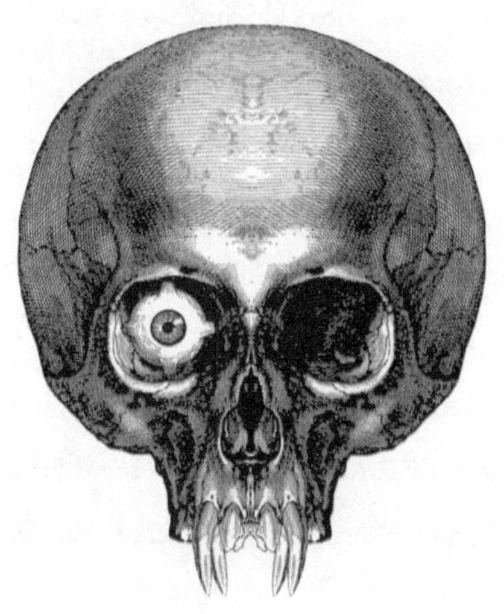

Publication History

"The River Flows to Nowhere" first published in *Weirdbook* #33 (2016)

"Behind the Eyes" first published in *Space & Time* #105 (2009)

"The Man Who Murders Happiness" first published in *Weirdbook* #35 (2017)

"Love in the Time of Dracula" first published in *The Audient Void* No. 5 (2018)

"I Do the Work of the Bone Queen" first published in *Whispers from the Abyss* (2013)

"The Taste of Starlight" first published in *Lightspeed: Year One* (2011)

"The Key to Your Heart is Made of Brass" first published in *Fungi* #21 (2013)

"Flesh of the City, Bones of the World" first published in *Fungi* #21 (2013)

"The Rude Mechanicals and the Highwayman" first published in *Fungi* #22 (2015)

"Anno Domini Azathoth" first published in *That is Not Dead* (2015)

"The Thing in the Pond" first published in *Weirdbook* Fall Annual #2 (2018)

"Lord of Endings" first published in *Lovecraft eZine* (2011)

"This is How the World Ends" first published in *Cthulhu's Reign* (2010)

"The Embrace of Elder Things" first published in *Mountains of Madness Revealed* (2019)

About the Contributors

JOHN R. FULTZ is a California writer originally from Kentucky. His published novels include *Seven Princes* (2012), *Seven Kings* (2013), and *Seven Sorcerers* (2013), as well as *The Testament of Tall Eagle* (2015) and *Son of Tall Eagle* (2017). His short stories have appeared in *Year's Best Weird Fiction*, *Weird Tales*, *Black Gate*, *Weirdbook*, *That is Not Dead*, *Shattered Shields*, *Lightspeed*, *Way of the Wizard*, *Cthulhu's Reign*, and plenty of other strange places. His latest collection of dark fantasy tales is *Worlds Beyond Worlds* (2021).

fultzauthor.com

DON WEBB has written 25 books on subjects ranging from the Greek Magical Papyri to computer security. A former cult leader, he has placed over 11,000 images of cats on Facebook and written Lovecraftian fiction for fifty years (over twice as long as Lovecraft). His most recent book is *Building Strange Temples* (2020).

DAN SAUER is a graphic designer and artist living in Oregon. In 2016, he co-founded (with editor/publisher Obadiah Baird) *The Audient Void: A Journal of Weird Fiction and Dark Fantasy*, which features his design and illustration work. Since 2017, he has worked extensively on book covers, interior art and custom typography for Hippocampus Press and other publishers. His art often takes the form of surreal collage and photomontage, as pioneered by artists such as Max Ernst, Wilfried Sätty, Harry O. Morris and J. K. Potter.

GOT WEIRD?
DON'T FORGET YOUR SHOGGOTH

From horror / sci-fi / cyberpunk legend JOHN SHIRLEY, author of *Demons*, *Wetbones* and *Lovecraft Alive!*—a unique collection of stories, organized into four sections. The first section is *Really Weird Stories*. The second is *Really, Really Weird Stories*. The third is *Really, Really, Really Weird Stories*. The fourth is—oh yes—*Really, Really, Really, Really Weird Stories*. Each section is weirder than the last, doubling its strangeness a section at a time. The collection starts out disquieting; it becomes disturbing, then it gets outrageously weird—then *mind-bending*.

The updated edition of *RRRRWS* is one of the most impressive feats of sustained and varied weirdness since Harlan Ellison's landmark *Dangerous Visions* anthologies. This edition contains four new stories, including the Lovecraftian Antarctic adventure "A Boy and His Shoggoth," and, published here for the first time, "The Whisperer Made Visible"—a tale of secret treaties with horrors eldritch and invisible.

> "A landmark collection from one of speculative fiction's wildest and greatest talents. What a joy to see it back in print!"
> —PETER ATKINS, writer of *Hellraiser 2-4* & *Wishmaster*

AVAILABLE NOW FROM

www.JackanapesPress.com
www.facebook.com/Jackanapes-Press